THE WITCH IN THE CAVE

The Witch in the Cave

MARTIN H. BRICE

London
ALLEN & UNWIN
Boston   Sydney

First published in Great Britain 1986

Allen & Unwin (Publishers) Ltd,
40 Museum Street, London WC1A 1LU, UK

Allen & Unwin (Publishers) Ltd,
Park Lane, Hemel Hempstead, Herts HP2 4TE, UK

Allen & Unwin Australia Pty Ltd,
8 Napier Street, North Sydney, NSW 2060, Australia

Allen & Unwin with the Port Nicholson Press
PO Box 11–838 Wellington, New Zealand

© Martin H. Brice

British Library Cataloguing in Publication Data

Brice, Martin H.
The witch in the cave.
I. Title
823'.914 [J]   PZ7
ISBN 0–04–823326–9

Set in 10 on 11 point Sabon by Columns of Reading
and printed in Great Britain by
Billing & Sons Ltd, London and Worcester

For L. C. Hayward
and the Tudor rebellions that started it all

THE WITCH IN THE CAVE

1

Red as the autumn leaves, the red stag stood, reading the wind from the sea. In front, the oaks and hazel gave way to a shallow depression of limp grasses, clumps of bramble and fern.

The stag was uneasy. He looked into his memory of scents and sounds and colours. He knew that open ground of old. He knew that the younger saplings and shoots at the forest's edge, the soft-leaved ground-plants beneath them, made succulent grazing. But he also knew that those scattered thickets screened enemies, while affording no cover for deer. He knew, too, that this shallow moorland would deepen, become a valley, a gorge, a ravine. He knew that although this open ground was dangerous, that distant cleft was full of worse terrors.

In his first winter – a rare hard winter that – the young stag had scrambled up an impossible ledge to escape a bloodthirsty wolf-pack. Twice more, coming late in the season, his herds had been pursued through the gorge. In the narrows, only a couple of deer at a time could squeeze past rocks and fallen trees. Laggard hinds had been hamstrung by sharp canines and pulled down.

And last fall, right at the end of his herd's passage through the chasm, they had been panicked by a small bear blundering out of one of the caves beside the tumbling stream. Leaping among moss-covered boulders, one of the hinds had slipped on a sodden log and snapped a leg. The stag had defended her, one of his tines catching the bear's eye. The brown beast had retreated snarling and the satisfied buck had followed his disappearing herd out towards the marshes. The injured deer had been left behind, frantically trying to rise and escape her lonely doom.

The stag's memory told him all this, but his instinct told him that through that meadow and gorge he must go, he and his herd. Only that way could they reach the big waters within swimming distance of forest-clad islands safe from winter's marauding predators.

For a moment the scent of the bear stirred strongest in his memory. Then it was gone. Had it come from upwind? Or had it been borne on a back-eddy, a tricky current of air? The wind was so light, so faint, so mist-laden. All nostrils, ears and eyes, the stag swept the depression again.

Just back in the shelter of the dripping forest the hinds waited, ears watching their master. One of them moved restlessly. The stag's mind noted the slight rustle. He too was impatient. This year his herd had been one of the first to start their journey from the tangled woodlands and across the limestone ridge. He knew that they were the first of the season along this particular trail. But other herds, other stags were not far behind, and after them the reindeer – and slinking along with them would come the wolves. The herd must move on. Yet again the stag read the ground and the air. Then he stepped forward and walked down into the depression.

The hinds followed. For the first time since they had begun their migration they were not confined to a hoof-wide track or narrow glade. They began to spread out and find appetising herbage. Occasionally a hind paused, erect, ears spread, alert, anxious. Then her neck snaked downwards again and the deer resumed her grazing.

The stag did not eat. He circled his herd, shouldering into them, nudging them along, trying to keep them together. As soon as he had got a couple moving in the right direction, two or three others spotted something delicious somewhere else and wandered round to the far side of a bramble thicket.

The depression in which the herd was grazing was bounded by tongues of woodland running out from the virgin forest which flanked the ridge. These thick belts of trees were dark and still, silent save for the clatter of a falling leaf, the first mist of autumn proving too heavy for its weakened stalk. The moisture bloomed acorns, nuts and crab-apples, spangled webs and plopped heavily upon branch and root below.

In the distant treetops on the left a jay screeched. Somewhere else a squirrel chattered. A tree-creeper probed elm bark, flew to the base of another tree and started climbing again. A redbreast trilled on a hazel, its twigs already promising next spring's catkins. Below, two eyes watched the deer through a curtain of ferns. The eyes moved from side to side. The eyes narrowed with satisfaction.

Their owner backed on hands and knees, his toes feeling stealthily for the quietest path, guiding his body over the roots of a big oak. A bow and a leather quiver of arrows lay there. The man swung himself onto his haunches and squatted, thinking. Never before had he known the deer to be on the move so early. It was too good an opportunity to miss. This time they would have to listen to him.

2

He was up in one movement and jogtrotting along a faint trail. As he got farther away, his progress became less stealthy. He came out of the trees at a run, hair and beard flying in the breeze of his passage, his feet stumbling over parched stubble.

Far behind him, out of sight and sound, yet unaccountably nervous, the stag circled his hinds.

2

The encampment was surrounded by a hedge on top of a rough bank of earth thrown up from a ditch outside the circle. In some places, the hawthorn bushes had not taken root, or had been broken down. Here stakes had been rammed into the soil and interlaced with pliable branches. The entrance could be blocked by an impenetrable thorn tree, which had been chopped down near the cornfields. It was pulled into position when dusk fell, but had been partially dragged aside at dawn, thus allowing the returning hunter to pass through. A bear's skull glared at him from a post at the side.

The tribe was getting ready to move. Hide coverings were being stripped from tent poles and rolled up. The bare framework was broken down, the sticks laid side by side and then lashed together with lengths of leather thong or cow-hair rope. Bundles were being balanced on the backs of cows and then tied on. Other cattle were being loaded with straw baskets and leather bags, or were being secured to rough sledges piled with bundles of skins, pots of grain, and stone tools.

One optimistic farmer was trying to get his pig to carry a burden, with encouraging suggestions from his neighbours. A child strained to lift a stone quern heavy beyond his strength, and dropped it on a set of rough black pots. His efforts were rewarded with a wallop and a screech. A little girl chasing a large terrier tripped over a leather bottle of beer and got her fingers trodden on by a man who jumped to right it.

An old woman's fingers struggled with a knot until younger hands reached for the thong, unpicked and retied it deftly. 'Your help is good, Mother, but we have a long journey this day. You will be tired. Put on your winter cloak. I know it is thick and the sun will be hot, but it will be easier to wear it than carry it. Then hold the child and stand there, away from the cattle.'

Following her own advice, the young woman picked up a thick sheepskin, swung it around her shoulders, and tied the neck fastening. Twitching the garment straight, she looked at it, took it off again and shook it vigorously. Clouds of dust erupted from the pelt.

There was dust everywhere, from beaten clothes, dropped tentpoles, and the shuffling or stamping feet of some forty men, women and children, plus several score of animals. They were mostly small brown sheep and goats, coarse-haired and horned, but there were also numbers of skinny yellowish pigs and hairy longhorned cattle.

Over the past few months their brute minds had come to accept a simple rhythm. As soon as milking had been done, they had been driven out to graze. They were tethered or hobbled to make sure that they did not wander too far into the woodland or trample through the uprooted thornbushes that marked the small fields of wheat and barley.

They had been watched over by children, already skilful with bow and arrow, and able to deal with most four-footed and winged predators. If something more threatening appeared, a shout of alarm brought help from the encampment or from one of the fields. There was always somebody there scraping away with an antler hoe – except in the heat of the afternoon sun.

Then no living thing displayed much energy. Untamed nature was still, while the domestic beasts rested in the moist shade of the forest's edge chewing young elm shoots, or stood in one of the few boggy ponds that retained water for any length of time after an infrequent heavy rainstorm. An occasional snatch of sultry song from a blackbird or the notes of a child's pipe framed the lazy silence.

Then at last it was time for the evening milking. The animals were herded back to the enclosure, one or two hunters returned, and finally the entrance was blocked against the marauders of the night.

That had been the animals' daily routine, but this morning that customary pattern had been disturbed. The beasts had not been let out after morning milking. Instead they were being chivvied this way and that, from one corner into somebody else's path, while some were having uncomfortable things put on their backs or tied behind them. They were confused, thirsty, hungry and very irritable. They lowed, squealed, and bleated. They trampled, stamped, shoved forward, backed up, and shouldered sideways, dust from their pummelled hides adding to the powdery miasma within the teeming circle.

There was only one quiet corner in the whole encampment, and that was at the far side opposite the entrance. It was not marked off by stakes or hurdles, yet it had a peculiar separateness. It began just beyond the communal firepit, which served as a natural meeting-place and a continuing source of fire for the whole of the tribe. Every tent had its own little hearth, but big fires could be kindled in the pit, while glowing embers could be preserved inside a substantial hollow trunk, blackened and smouldering in the grey ash. A pile of firewood was off to one side, while a little further away in the other direction, peg marks and postholes showed where two tents had recently stood.

These two sites had now been cleared and everything packed onto five cows and sledges, all being tended by an elderly-looking man. Another man with his arm at an awkward angle, was holding the bridle of a heavy-headed, short-legged grey pony peppered with brown spots. Beside him stood a greying woman with heavy cold-weather robes in her arms. All three persons were wearing sheepskin cloaks and had leather bags slung across their backs. Similar packs, polished greenstone axes, bows and arrows, were lying at the woman's feet. The three stood deferentially, in the manner of servants, watching three figures in front of them.

The man in the centre was powerfully built, taller than the rest of the tribe. He wore a bear's paw on a leather thong around his neck and was grasping a pointed staff twice his height with a bear's head carved on the top. To his right stood a boy, to his left a girl – both young adults rather than children. A darkening down shaded the boy's cheeks and chin; the girl's breasts were forming. Like his father, the boy was tall and wore a necklace of bear's teeth, a similar circlet framing the girl's throat. Otherwise they wore the same as everyone else in the compound, a short kilt made by cutting a waist-sized hole in a single ragged skin of fur or hide.

There the similarity ended, for while the rest of the tribe – and the tall boy – had black, wavy hair, the big man and his daughter had cascading locks of flaming red. The girl was even more remarkable, for her skin was incredibly pale, almost as white as the ivory teeth about her neck.

All three held themselves proudly erect as they surveyed the activity before them. The boy was looking from one incident to another, trying not to miss anything that was going on. The girl had a faint smile of contempt, as though gazing down on an amusing scene from some lofty plane. The man was shaking his massive head sadly and slowly from side to side.

It was towards these three that the early morning hunter pushed his way, answering cheery greetings with an excited wave and a frenzied shout, 'The deer are running! The deer are running!'

He broke clear of a jumble of sheep and opened his mouth to

cry out his news again, this time addressing the big man with the bear totem.

'Kheila-hidd!' The red-haired girl's tone was sharp; her question innocent. 'Kheila-hidd, how thick is your skin?'

Kheila-hidd, the hunter, looked at her and back to her father. 'The deer are running, Htorr-mhirr,' he said.

'Kheila-hidd! Answer me! How thick is your skin?' There was sarcasm in the girl's voice. 'Does it bleed when pricked, Kheila-hidd?'

'Yes, yes. Of course my skin bleeds when I prick it.'

'Then why is there no blood on your body, Kheila-hidd, your arms, your legs?'

The puzzled reply: 'Why should there be blood on me, Mhirr-cuin?'

'Because the hawthorn bush has not moved from the entrance during the whole of the night when you left the enclosure. So the thorns must have pricked you as you pushed through the branches. Or did you pass through the impassable thorns without harm?' The girl was all sweetness. 'Come, Kheila-hidd, tell us of your magick art.'

Kheila-hidd sensed that the tribe had paused in their tasks, awaiting his reply. He hesitated. 'There was no magick. I clambered over one of the hurdles.'

'You clambered over one of the hurdles.' She was still a child compared with the hunter, smaller and slighter than he, but her voice made him wince. 'During the night. Even though you knew that thus you were opening a door to the Ghosts of Darkness. Have I not warned you often of the danger? Did not Vhi-vhang remind you of the danger from the Ghosts of Darkness?'

A woman had appeared beside Kheila-hidd. She was not very old, but her hair was grey and brittle, and she moved with a tired stiffness. In spite of the growing warmth of the morning, she had wrapped and fastened her winter cloak of beaver skin tightly about her. From time to time she coughed harshly.

'The Ghosts of Darkness live only in caves,' she began. 'I have always said this. We left them behind when we left the caves behind. If there are ghosts here, they do not harm our hunters when they go abroad at night. Only the wild beasts can do that.' Vhi-vhang coughed again and went on: 'The hedge is to keep out wild beasts. If the Ghosts of Darkness have followed us here from the caves — if they are so clever — why do they wait to be shown the way over our hedge, Mhirr-cuin?'

The redhead looked at Vhi-vhang with surprise. 'These are

7

strange words from the Tribe's Witch, Vhi-vhang. You chant secret words to the Ghosts of Beasts when summoning them to the hunt. You chant secret words to the Ghosts of Flowers when curing sickness. Why do you do these things if you say there are no ghosts, Vhi-vhang?'

The people had abandoned their work and were listening attentively to this dialogue. Vhi-vhang finished coughing again. 'I have never said that there are no ghosts, only that the Ghosts of Darkness cannot harm us now that we have left the caves. It is well known that the wild beasts have ghosts. The hunter and the witch must together summon their ghosts. But when the summoning is done and the wild beasts are coming, then the hunter must depend upon his own skill. Plants too have their ghosts, and we should apologise to them when cutting them down or pulling them up. But when that has been done, the secret of curing lies, as you all know, in the potion. The chant tells me the time needed for preparation and the ingredients that should be put in. But why do these things concern you, Mhirr-cuin? You are not the Tribe's Witch.' There was mild rebuke in the woman's voice.

Mhirr-cuin's eyebrows tightened. Her pallid face grew whiter. 'No, I am not the Tribe's Witch, Vhi-vhang, but I deserve to be. I feel the power within me. Alone, I commune with the Ghosts – and I tell you . . .' The red-headed girl reminded them with quiet menace. '. . . as I have told you before, – that the Ghosts of Plants and of Animals and of Every Thing, are all ruled by the Four Great Horned Ones: the Ruler of Air; the Ruler of Fire; the Ruler of Water; and the Ruler of Earth. Vhi-vhang never told you that, did she? Why? Because she . . . did . . . not . . . know.' Mhirr-cuin emphasised each word and paused for some sign of contradiction from the old witch, but none came. The child continued: 'But *I* tell you, the Four Great Horned Ones not only rule all things, they made all things, and they know all things. All the other Ghosts are subject to them. The Four Great Horned Ones have terrible appetites. They punish with fearful torture those Ghosts who do not bring them meat. Therefore the Ghosts themselves prowl around everywhere, searching out the unwary and taking them as bloody offerings to the Four Great Horned Ones.'

Mhirr-cuin's voice dropped to a sneering whine, her clawing hands twisting, dragging words out of the air. 'Neither the Ghosts nor the Four Great Horned Ones want your apologies, Vhi-vhang. They lust after sacrifice. And if they do not receive it, they will inflict terrible retribution upon any transgressor – no matter how

8

unintending – and upon his family and upon his tribe. All of you . . .' Her left forefinger arced around the crowd. '. . . and all your animals and everything that is yours, have been put at risk by this one man.'

The finger pointed straight at Kheila-hidd. They all looked at him. He swallowed. 'How did you know? Your tent was laced. Everyone was asleep. Vhi-vhang was asleep: that is why she said nothing. Even the gatekeeper was asleep.'

'I was not,' a voice from the crowd.

Mhirr-cuin's finger instantly changed direction. 'You were asleep. My Ghost saw you. My Ghost saw you too.' The finger had flashed back to Kheila-hidd. 'My Ghost saw you and my Ghost told me. While I commune with the Ghosts and with the Four Great Horned Ones, my Ghost walks abroad.' Her voice fell to a faint whisper, which every man and woman and child heard as though inside his or her own head. 'My Ghost sees everything. My Ghost tells me everything.'

The girl's left arm was rigid. She had closed her right eye and bent her right knee slightly, so that her toes were just clear of the dirt. The silence was total. Even the livestock were quiet and motionless. The air itself was still. A wispy puff of ash dust rose from the firepit, danced a few feet and fell.

3

The big man – Htorr-mhirr – broke the spell. 'My daughter, you do indeed have great gifts, and you have told us many things, but while she lives, Vhi-vhang is the Witch of the People of the Bear. She is well-named The Life-giver, for she has healed many.' Htorr-mhirr noticed his daughter's eyebrows rise slightly. 'And she has eased the last days of those who could not be cured. Now, Kheila-hidd, tell us your news.'

'A handful of days ago,' began Kheila-hidd, 'you – Htorr-mhirr – told me to scout the path for this day's journey to the encampment for the winter and our meeting with the Marsh People. The night before last, I awoke in the dark and remembered your words. I did not want to say that I had not scouted the path, so I left then at that very time. I did not want the gatekeeper to know that I had not yet done as you had asked, so I climbed over a hurdle to get out.'

He glanced at Mhirr-cuin, expecting at least some comment about everybody knowing now, but she was staring fixedly at a woman whose belly was swollen huge with child. Sensing something, the woman looked up, stared back at the redheaded girl, then dropped her eyes again.

Kheila-hidd went on: 'It was an easy path to scout. It will be an easy path to travel. I saw no sign of wolf or bear. I saw no sign of the Marsh People, neither on the path nor out on the Great Marsh.' Kheila-hidd was happier now. 'The enclosure is in good order. Some parts of the hedge are torn and a fresh hawthorn bush will have to be cut for the entrance.' He wished he had not mentioned that, but Mhirr-cuin was studying a growing patch of blue in the morning's grey clouds and took no notice.

Kheila-hidd hurried on with his tale: 'I went down to the edge of the Great Marsh. The duck are flying in early and so I knew that the deer would be coming early too. So I went straight over the top of the hill until I reached the rim of the Great Gorge, for I know that the biggest herds always pass through it. Then I tracked along its edge looking for any movement below. There was none.' Kheila-hidd was enjoying himself. 'I crossed the path to our old spring enclosure and went towards the Great Forest. Just before

10

dark, I entered the woodland yonder which sticks out from the Great Forest, so that I could watch the open ground beyond. Just before sunrise, I saw the deer – three handfuls and a big stag.'

'Are you sure they were not roebuck? Roebuck live always in the Great Forest. They do not move with the seasons. They come out and eat our corn. They become invisible when we hunt them. They step over the traps that we dig for them. They are impossible to hunt. We can only kill them when they are eating in the cornfields.'

Kheila-hidd was offended. 'Htorr-mhirr, I am a hunter. I have always been a hunter. I have never scraped the earth with antler or stick. Roebuck are impossible for other hunters to kill, but I can do it easily. I know roebuck – and I know red deer. And the deer I saw this morning were red deer. The stag was the biggest I have ever seen.'

There was a stir of conversation from the crowd.

'What do you suggest we do?' The tall young man with the necklace of bear's teeth made his first contribution to the discussion.

Kheila-hidd was flattered. 'When I saw them, they were grazing beyond the trees.' He waved an arm in the appropriate direction. 'They were hungry and they will stay there some time. They are always frightened of the Great Gorge, so they will not go there quickly.' He began explaining his plan. 'All the men will take their bows and reach the first cliffs of the Great Gorge by the time the sun is halfway through his climb. I know the place. The pony riders will go from the encampment across the old cornfields through the woodland yonder to the pasture where I saw the deer. Then they can drive the deer down the valley and across our bows. If we are lucky, the pony riders can chase the herd up the slope behind us hunters and over one of the cliffs of the Great Gorge. Then we can kill them all.' Kheila-hidd finished with a little nod. He considered saying that the deer were as good as dead already, but perhaps that was too big a statement even for him.

Htorr-mhirr contemplated this plan. 'We cannot be sure that the deer would allow themselves to be driven over the cliff. We do not have time to prepare such a hunt. Perhaps we can shoot some of them at the entrance to the Great Gorge. But that place is a long way off. The deer can pass by before you get there.' He shook his head. 'No, we have agreed that we will move to our winter encampment this day, so that we are ready to meet the Marsh People before they come. That is what we will do. It is no good to do otherwise just for three handfuls of deer. Indeed, most

11

of you are not even ready to move yet. How can you go hunting this day as well? If you want to hunt alone, Kheila-hidd, you can go, but no other man goes with you.'

There was a murmur of men's voices in the crowd; a couple of wordless shouts.

Kheila-hidd looked round at them and then back to Htorr-mhirr. 'It is good of you to give me permission to go hunting, but I choose when I hunt, and I choose to hunt this day. Why should they not hunt this day also if they so choose? Always they do what you say, Htorr-mhirr. They have worked in the fields all the summer, now they want to go on a great hunt. And it will be a great hunt. For by the time the pony riders reach the pasture, more deer will have come. If we wait until we have arrived at our winter enclosure, all the deer will have reached the islands in the waters. Then only the Marsh People will catch them. They will demand corn for antlers and deer bones as well as for the polished greenstone axes and the flint tools they bring.' Kheila-hidd took a deep breath and plunged on belligerently. 'You told the Tribe to work hard in the fields. You said we would have corn to feed ourselves and our animals in the winter. I did not believe you, but the rest of the Tribe did. They have laboured hard in the fields, but there is no corn. We may even have to eat the seed corn that you say must be kept and not eaten. We shall have to kill our animals early this winter for lack of food. But, if the Tribe hunts the deer now, we shall have antlers for hoes, meat for food, bones for tools and skins for trade – all before we meet the Marsh People.'

A delighted chorus acknowledged the logic of this argument.

Htorr-mhirr regarded the people calmly; he would not lose patience with them. 'Let me remind you of your very own customs. Unlike other tribes, the People of the Bear are not ruled by a King or Chief who owns his subjects as an ordinary man or woman owns stone-axe or cooking-pot. The People of the Bear are ruled by an Artzan – a Shepherd – who goes in front of the People. The People talk, and when he has listened, the Artzan decides, and the People follow.

'When I came to you, you were a hunting people, living in caves. Sometimes the hunters returned with much meat; usually they returned with a few nuts and berries and crawling things. You heard stories from the Marsh People about tribes who lived in the open air, grew corn in the summer, grew fat in the winter, and were never laid waste by the Ghosts of Darkness. But you did not know how to do these things. Nor could you decide who among you should decide these things. And because I was a stranger, you asked me to stay with you and become your Artzan – which I did. You talked, I listened. I decided, you followed. As is your custom.

'That is why I say when we hunt and when we move and where we go and when we plant and when we reap. And you know that we have had good harvests here. But this harvest and the last harvest have been bad ones, even though you worked hard. And you know why.' He emphasised each remark with a gesture. 'The rain did not come all the summer. Then so much rain came with fire and noise that it trod down the plants that had not been withered. The roedeer ate the rest. We cannot control the skies and we cannot control the roebuck.' He shrugged. 'But I can say there is some truth in what you speak.' He raised his head. 'We will move this day, but we will also hunt the deer.' There was a cheer. 'A hunt will provide a few more things for food and for trade.' There were more cheers. 'But do not expect the Marsh People to rejoice at what you bring them. Their way of life provides all their wants except corn, meat fattened on corn, and beer made from corn – and corn is what we do not have.'

Only a few of the tribe took note of his last words; most were making excited plans. The tall young man was talking to Kheila-hidd.

'Father,' Mhirr-cuin looked up at Htorr-mhirr. 'You told the Tribe to plant, but the rains did not come and the corn did not grow. That was not your fault. Now you tell the Tribe to hunt deer. Suppose the deer go a different path and are not killed. The Tribe will say that was your fault just as they are now saying the bad harvest was your fault.'

'How can it be my fault?' retorted her father. 'I cannot make the corn grow. I cannot make the deer do this or that.'

'No, but someone here can,' pointed out his daughter. 'Have I not heard that Vhi-vhang used to magick the deer and perform magick for other hunts when the Tribe lived in the caves? You are Artzan of the Tribe. Command her to cast a spell binding the deer to the path Kheila-hidd says they will take. Then you will have the Ghosts on your side and the Tribe will be sure of a good hunt.'

Vhi-vhang had been listening to this exchange. She shook her head slightly. 'That was all many years past. Those powers have since deserted me. Now I can only accomplish small spells, perform small cures. I cannot make the corn grow, nor make the rains come, nor bind the deer to one path only.'

Mhirr-cuin pursued the subject in reasoned tones. 'But if my

13

father were sick and asked you to heal him, would you not at least try to do so? Or is it that you do not want the hunt to be successful? Do not forget, Vhi-vhang, that my Ghost sees everything. Would you like me to tell the Tribe what other spells you cast when you think you are alone?'

A little earlier there had been movement in the crowd, but now all was still again.

'I do not . . .' Vhi-vhang shook with coughing. '. . . cast evil spells.' The last two words were whispered so hoarsely that they were barely audible.

'Did I speak of *evil* spells?' The red-haired girl was wide-eyed with astonished innocence.

Vhi-vhang made no attempt to allay the suspicions which were growing in people's minds. Instead, she suddenly capitulated to Htorr-mhirr's demand. 'Yes, I will magick the deer for you, but it will not work, because we cannot do the Horn Dance that goes with it. Only Kheila-hidd has kept his deer antlers. All the others were used as hoes in the fields – on your instructions.'

Htorr-mhirr frowned at the obvious rebuke. Angrily he declared: 'So, Kheila-hidd must dance on his own.'

Now it was Kheila-hidd's turn to protest. 'We are wasting time. I am a skilful hunter. I do not need magick to guide my arrow. The deer are already running, so we do not need magick to summon them. And *I know* which path they will take, so we do not need magick to bind them to it. We hunters must set off now. Vhi-vhang can perform the deer-magicking without any dancing.'

Htorr-mhirr sighed. Sometimes it seemed as though he had been carrying the burden of this people for ever. There was no one in the Tribe to whom he could turn for help or advice, not even Vhi-vhang, although as Witch she should have given him more assistance instead of always being so obstructive. Mhirr-ling, his own son, was a good enough lad, but he had not shown the imagination and intelligence that Mhirr-cuin displayed. There was no doubt about her talent. As soon as she could hold a flint-knife, she had carved the Bear's Head Totem as a symbol of his authority as Artzan. She was still young, but she was shrewd, and – without openly asking her advice – Htorr-mhirr realised that lately he had got into the habit of considering her stated – or even implied – opinion, when contemplating any decision he had to make.

In fact, the only recent thing he had done in the face of his daughter's disapproval, had concerned Hpe-gnorr and the ponies. Under Htorr-mhirr's direction, the People of the Bear had begun to acquire domestic animals, some from other tribes through barter with the Marsh People, and some captured, tamed and bred from wild stock. The spotted ponies which occasionally traversed the hills had been ignored in this programme – except as targets for Kheila-hidd's arrows.

The coming of Hpe-gnorr had changed that. A squat, snub-nosed man with a stringy moustache, he had been born in some far-distant tribe which had apparently learned to tame horses. While still a very young child, Hpe-gnorr had become one of the Marsh People, long-ranging travellers who had no interest in horses except as food. When he had seen the wild ponies on the hills above the wetlands, Hpe-gnorr recalled the sights of his youth and resolved to try his hand at horse-taming. Overcoming the difficulties of language, he had asked to live with the People of the Bear. Htorr-mhirr had agreed, seeing advantages to be gained from this new skill. Horses would make more useful pack and sledge-hauling beasts than the cattle they had hitherto employed. And if they could be ridden – as Hpe-gnorr said they could – then they would greatly increase mobility when hunting and when herding stock, especially in association with dogs.

The only person against the idea had been Mhirr-cuin. Htorr-mhirr had suspected that for once his daughter was frightened of something: it was very definitely man's work catching and taming these bucking creatures of the wind with their lashing hooves. But she had simply said no good would come of it.

And so far she had been proved correct. After all the energy the men of the tribe had expended, they had only succeeded in catching, taming and retaining four horses. One was so old and decrepit that it pulled Htorr-mhirr's own sledge even more slowly than a cow. The other three were much livelier; too much so, in fact. It was no easy task staying on a horse. There was a simple halter round its head to hold on to, but it was hard to grip its flanks with thighs and knees. So far, nobody had actually broken a limb when thrown, but what seemed almost as bad was the terrible jolting inflicted by the pony's backbone. Those men who managed to stay on for any length of time were so sore when they dismounted, that they could not move for days afterwards. Some people even whispered that pony-riders were henceforth incapable of siring children, although this rumour had been disproved by the fact that Tschi-tschan's woman was now expecting his baby.

Perhaps this time, thought Htorr-mhirr, they would at last be able to make profitable use of the three ponies they had learned to ride. He hoped his daughter would not be difficult about his employment of the horses in this hunt. She was bound to invoke the Four Great Horned Ones as support for her objections. He knew that he would not want to look her in the eye if she did that. Mhirr-cuin was so intense about her Ghosts and especially about the Four Great Horned Ones. He wondered where she had got these ideas from. Nobody had heard of them before Mhirr-cuin had started talking about them. So she could only have learned about them by communing with them in her tent!

For the first time, Htorr-mhirr accepted the idea as fact; everything suddenly made sense. Men were ruled by Artzans, Chiefs and Kings; so Ghosts must also have their own rulers. And it explained the recent crop failures. Mhirr-cuin must be right when she spoke of satisfying the appetites of the Four Great Horned Ones before doing something important. Perhaps then you could persuade Air, Fire, Water and Earth to cooperate with you and not work against you. Perhaps then they would make the rain come and the corn grow. Mhirr-cuin said they were powerful enough to control these things; all the strongest beasts had horns and that was why the Four Great Rulers also had horns – as proof of their power.

Htorr-mhirr had always found that skilful preparation and hard work usually brought success. Well, taking measures to placate the Four Great Horned Ones was only another aspect of preparing for some venture. But, what sort of sacrifice would satisfy them? For a moment his mind envisaged only too clearly what sort of food such bloodthirsty appetites might demand. He shied away from such dark horrors; he would not make such a decision as that. There must be an easier way. Perhaps the Four Great Horned Ones could be entertained? By Kheila-hidd and his dance? Yes, that was it. There would be no more discussion, no more thought. He had made up his mind.

Htorr-mhirr addressed the Tribe, taking a formal grasp of the Bear Totem in his hand. 'People of the Bear, I am Htorr-mhirr, He-Who-Stands-Like-the-Mountain-in-the-Sea, Artzan of the People of the Bear. This morning the Tribe's Witch, Vhi-vhang, will magick the deer. Kheila-hidd, the Tribe's Hunter, will perform the Horn Dance. When it is finished, the men of the Tribe will take their bows and go to the first cliffs of the Great Gorge. Kheila-hidd will lead them. The rest of the Tribe will move from the enclosure before the sun is halfway on his climb this morning. My son, Mhirr-ling, will lead them along the path to the encampment where the Tribe will meet the Marsh People. I will take the three ponies and the dogs to drive the deer onto the hunters. I have decided. I have spoken.'

Immediately, he was answering his son's plea. 'You cannot go on the hunt. I want you to look after the Tribe on their journey.' Htorr-mhirr lowered his voice. 'They need to be looked after. When they have plenty of warning, they are never ready. Yet when something happens that needs much preparation, they want to start on it at once.'

Htorr-mhirr also thought, but did not add that Mhirr-ling was far too dull to dream up any hare-brained adventure away from Kheila-hidd's influence, while his stable presence might contain whatever trouble Mhirr-cuin was smelling out − or fomenting. The former was too unkind, and the latter too vague an idea to voice.

4

The older People of the Bear had not seen the Horn Dance performed since planting their first fields of corn over two handfuls of springs ago. Many of the younger ones had never seen it done at all. Most of the men spent their energies clearing and tending the fields. Enough birds, deer and wild cattle had been killed when raiding the crops to provide a continuing source of meat throughout the summer. In the winter the Tribe lived near the marshes with their wildfowl and fish. Some of the men went off hunting with Kheila-hidd, who always knew exactly where to find game. If things became really bad the Tribe had a reserve of food in its domestic animals, killing and eating them as necessary.

But last year there had been a summer-long drought: the crops had been parched and the ponds had dried up. The cattle had ceased giving milk and had become so thin that there was hardly any meat on them. The Tribe had nearly starved last winter. This summer the drought had been repeated. The coming winter looked bleak indeed, and there was the matter of trading with the Marsh People.

So everybody wanted this unexpected deer hunt to be a success. Some of the men were keen to get away, but the rest of the Tribe were pleased about the deer-magicking ceremony. It would be something to look at and it might bring good luck. It was about time that happened. The older people said that things had gone wrong because they had neglected the ancient rituals of late; but they had been so very busy hoeing the ground, herding the cattle, and scraping skins. Besides, there had been nothing to fear once they had left the caves behind. However, the younger ones argued that out here in the open air there were different things to fear, different ceremonies to perform. That was exactly what Mhirr-cuin had been saying.

If this were true, then the Tribe's Witch ought to have known about it. She ought to have been performing these new ceremonies instead of casting secret spells that no one knew anything about. Yes, Vhi-vhang was a kindly soul and you could not imagine her hurting anyone, but she had become very irritable recently. Nor had her cures been very successful; she could not even cure herself.

18

Perhaps she was saving her power for secret arts. They would still have been secret if Mhirr-cuin's Ghost had not seen Vhi-vhang at work.

Mhirr-cuin certainly seemed to know more about these things than Vhi-vhang did. The Ghosts of Darkness and the Four Great Horned Ones were definitely more powerful than anything Vhi-vhang invoked; and a lot more frightening. Mhirr-cuin seemed to know how to get on with them. She had never been a friendly child, but now that she was getting older, it might be a good idea to keep on the right side of her.

So the People of the Bear tossed their gossip back and forth as they settled themselves into a semi-circle ready for the deer-magicking to begin.

The crowd parted to let through Vhi-vhang and her daughter Ochy, a sullen-looking child just leaving childhood behind her. Vhi-vhang was carrying a lengthy bundle which she unrolled to reveal three sticks stretching a decorated rectangle of hide. She pushed the tripod into the earth, lifting and ramming it down, coughing each time, until satisfied that it was firm. The hide pattern now resolved itself into pictures of animals: bulls, cows, stags, things that looked like dogs or wolves, birds, more stags, and even a few fishes. They were painted black and brown and red. They were standing, running, leaping and lying down. Some were dotted with red, or had red arrows pointing to them.

Vhi-vhang rested for a moment, then motioned to her daughter, who brought forward a log of wood. Its top surface had been levelled off and several rounded pits had been hollowed out in it. These were filled with various coloured pigments, greasy mixtures of earth and fat.

By now, Kheila-hidd had returned, his bearded face framed within a set of antlers sprouting from a stag's skull which he held before him. His bow and quiver were slung across his shoulders. He raised the antlers aloft.

'Are the hunters here? Are you ready to hunt?' Excited shouts came back. He rested the weight of the antlers on his shoulders and spoke to Vhi-vhang. 'Be quick woman and watch me. The deer have come so we do not need the Summoning Dance. I shall only do the Killing Dance. We want to be gone.' He immediately launched into a series of steps, turning and twisting as if trying to escape some invisible enemy.

Vhi-vhang dipped her right index finger into the brown colour, found an empty patch of hide and sketched in a pair of legs. She was muttering 'Deerkilldeerkilldeerdeerkillkilldeerkillkilldeer . . .'

in a continuous monotone. She dipped her finger into the paint again and began on the body outline. Her wrist seemed to grind in mid air. With a quiet groan she massaged the locked joint with her left hand. She opened the cramped fingers, shook them and tried again. The paint had dried. Again she dipped her fingertip in the brown and resumed her monotonous chant.

Kheila-hidd was moving faster, feet moving in complicated steps. Vhi-vhang's stag was nowhere near completion. The body appeared vertical. She traced forelegs and head, so that it looked as though the animal were leaping.

Kheila-hidd was staggering, his head bowed under the antler weight. Vhi-vhang drew antlers and reached for the red with her middle finger. The swollen joint would not straighten.

Kheila-hidd was down on one knee.

Vhi-vhang dipped her left forefinger into the red paint and swept a single scarlet stroke into the body of the painted stag.

Kheila-hidd dropped to the other knee, was on the ground, rolling over. Instantly he was up, pushing aside the antlers.

'Come on,' he beckoned. 'We hunt.'

A channel appeared in the crowd of watchers. Kheila-hidd ran down it, through the gateway and out. Over a handful of men followed with yells of excitement. Bows were flourished; the onlookers clapped the hunters on the back and wished them good luck. One or two children ran through the gateway with them and then halted just outside, waving and shouting. A dog, tail up and barking furiously, scampered to and fro under the hunters' feet until sent back. The men settled down to a steady jogtrot in silent single file, passed behind a patch of thick scrub, reappeared for an instant, and were lost to sight.

The women and children and old folk watched for a few moments more, then turned back within the encampment with resigned disappointment. They only had a few more jobs to do before they also moved off; the men would only have got in the way. Yet somehow it seemed unfair that the men should be enjoying the excitement of a hunt instead of the wearisome business of tying up baggage and looking after small children. The men would also avoid the burden of heavy packs during the heat of the day. These would now have to be divided amongst the rest of the family.

Besides, some of the younger women and most of the older children considered themselves just as skilful, if not better, archers than a number of the men who had not been hunting for a couple of seasons or more. Frustrated and cross, the women cuffed toddlers that got in the way, and walloped cattle that would not stand still.

Vhi-vhang and Ochy were facing even more labour than most other families. Because Kheila-hidd had never helped with the farming, they had no cattle, so they had to pull their sledge themselves. Now that Kheila-hidd was absent, they had the extra burden of his possessions to deal with. The little sledge was already piled so high they could hardly move it without dislodging something. Vhi-vhang managed to tie on the ceremonial antlers and wedged a bundle between them. Anything else would have to be carried on their own shoulders, and that included the magick painting. Vhi-vhang turned back to dismantle and collect it.

Some of the women were still gossiping around the tripod, having already finished their packing or being reluctant to carry on with it. Mhirr-cuin was there too, now dressed in a long green cloak that brushed the ground. She usually wore it when the sun came out, fastening it at several points down the front to protect all her skin from strong daylight. It even had a large hood which shadowed her face. The garment was of nettle cloth and the only one of its kind in the Tribe – the only one any of them had ever seen. She was the only member of the Tribe to have a tent solely to herself, and the gown conferred further distinction upon Mhirr-cuin. It also gave her the mysterious appearance of floating over the ground without moving her legs.

Mhirr-cuin was talking to Tschi-tschan's pregnant woman, Ihyselt, who was very near her time. Before Vhi-vhang could take down and roll up the decorated hide, Ihyselt spoke to her. 'The Horn Dance and your painting made good magick for the hunters. Have you no magick for the pony riders?'

Vhi-vhang said nothing.

Ihyselt went on: 'Kheila-hidd said that if they were lucky, they would drive the deer over the cliff. That would be done by the pony riders. My man is a pony rider. Do you wish him to come back with empty hands?'

Vhi-vhang still said nothing. She picked up the log of paints, dipped her finger in the black pigment, and drew a horizontal line that turned through a right-angle vertically downwards. She then traced the outline of an animal, legs flying as it fought to gain foothold in the empty air.

Mhirr-cuin turned to Ihyselt. 'I told you Vhi-vhang would grant your request. The pony riders will drive their prey over the cliff.' She glanced at the hide. 'What Vhi-vhang has drawn may look like a horse, but it is meant to be a hind without antlers. She could

21

not paint another stag with antlers because there was only one in the herd and she has already drawn him.' Mhirr-cuin's finger selected one out of the jumble of animals. 'See, here he is; the stag standing on his back legs like a man.'

Mhirr-cuin was close up to the painting. The hooded figure peered intently at the hide for a moment, then a draped arm pointed to a row of short vertical green lines, overlaid with a thick black swirl. 'Vhi-vhang, what does this mean?'

Vhi-vhang sighed. 'Once upon a time, I tried to summon the corn from the ground with a magick painting, like I summon the animals with magick paintings. But the painting did not come right, so I covered it up again.'

'Ah yes, it was wise of you not to use a bad painting for magicking the crops, otherwise they would have come to more harm than did happen to them. It is good that we know your magick paintings this day are of a stag and a hind, and not of a man and a horse . . .'

Ihyselt broke in: 'I think the stag does look like a man with horns on his head and not like a stag. And the hind falling off a cliff does look more like a pony.' Her mouth dropped open. 'Suppose that is Tschi-tschan's pony falling off the cliff.' Her body was shaking; she began to sob. 'What have you done, Vhi-vhang?' she wailed. 'What have you done?'

Mhirr-cuin was soothing her, leading the pregnant woman away. Vhi-vhang had remained silent, but Ochy sprang to her mother's defence. 'You did not think that before Mhirr-cuin suggested it. Mhirr-cuin told you to say that.'

'I did not,' countered Mhirr-cuin, turning back. She sneered. 'I did not tell Ihyselt; my Ghost told her.'

'Your Ghost, your Ghost! If there are ghosts, we all have ghosts. I have a Ghost. My Ghost spits upon your Ghost. I spit upon you.'

Ochy's black hair jerked forwards and back as she pursed her lips and spat violently upon the hem of Mhirr-cuin's garment.

Mhirr-cuin's face seemed to retreat into the cowl of her cloak. She twitched the linen softly and muttered. The spittle disappeared. Her voice came from within dark shadow. 'Have care, Ochy. Yes, you do have a ghost. But you are of the common people. Your ghost is a common ghost. I am of a House of Princes. My Ghost is a Prince among Ghosts. My Ghost speaks with the Four Great Horned Ones, who have created all things and rule all things.' Her garment was quivering with her anger. 'I tell you, in the days when the Tribe lived by hunting and gathering, the Four Great Horned Ones were content to stay within their Unknowable

22

Enclosure. They let the Ghosts of Darkness and the Ghosts of Beasts and the Ghosts of Flowers run hither and thither for them. Sometimes, the hunted animal turned to rend the hunter, or the berry clawed the food-gatherer from inside the belly, or the Ghost of Darkness wasted a man's strength and locked his bones, and their bodies were taken as offerings to the Four Great Horned Ones.

'Now the Tribe no longer lives by hunting and gathering, no longer dwells in caves. Instead, it plants crops, and herds animals in the open air. The Tribe no longer gives its bodies to the Ghosts of Darkness, the Ghosts of Beasts and the Ghosts of Flowers to carry as offerings to the Four Great Horned Ones. The Four Great Horned Ones grow hungry. The Four Great Horned Ones have stepped out of their Unknowable Enclosure to claim their gifts in person. Until the Tribe makes sacrifices to the Four Great Horned Rulers of Air, of Fire, of Water and of Earth, the wind will bear poisonous vapours upon your children and your animals, the sun will parch the crops, the rains will be withheld in the growing time, and the soil will be unfruitful. The Four Great Horned Rulers of Air, Fire, Water and Earth have spoken. I, Mhirr-cuin, have spoken.'

More women had now finished packing their belongings and had joined the group, listening with tense apprehension to the gowned figure before them.

Ochy pouted. 'If the Four Great Horned Ones of whom you speak have set their face against the Tribe, why have they sent the deer to run before our bows? Answer me that Mhirr-cuin!'

'I will answer that, Ochy. The Four Great Horned Ones have sent the Deer Ghost to play a game with the People of the Bear. The Deer Ghost taunts the People of the Bear. When Vhi-vhang performed her deer-magicking, the Deer Ghost was not bound by a witch of mighty and terrible powers, nor entranced by the sinuous steps of the Horn Dance. No, Ochy; no, Vhi-vhang. No, the Deer Ghost saw only a coughing hag whose clumsy fingers could not paint silly pictures properly, and a stupid and arrogant man who scuffed circles in the dust and hurried away trusting in his own skill instead of in the favour of the Four Great Horned Ones. The Deer Ghost despises your magick, Vhi-vhang. The Four Great Horned Rulers of Air, Fire, Water and Earth despise your magick, Vhi-vhang. Just as I, Mhirr-cuin, despise your magick, Vhi-vhang.'

Mhirr-cuin faced about, bent right forward, and lifted up her long green gown, presenting her bare buttocks to the magick

23

painting. She straightened up and walked away in silence. Her dignity heightened the obscenity of the insult. For a moment, they all stood staring at her, then swung round in alarm as the decorated hide folded up and clattered to the ground in a cloud of dust.

Ochy leapt after Mhirr-cuin, but Vhi-vhang caught her wrist and swung her back, her black hair flying. 'One day perhaps, but not this day. Help me tie this up and then we are ready.'

5

Later, Vhi-vhang and Ochy squatted waiting for the last of the Tribe to complete their preparations for the move.

'I have told you this story before,' began Vhi-vhang. 'But listen well this time, for I shall not tell it again. Many years ago before I was born, our people lived in a land of warm rain, little fields, and mountains jutting into the sea. Our people built boats and journeyed across the sea. Always they chose to settle in a land like the one they had left.

'Our part of our people stayed behind in the old homeland, until one day there came a messenger from a tribe that had travelled furthest. He said that they had found a new land. Like all the others, it was a land of warm rain, little fields and mountains jutting into the sea. But the rocks of this land held the Secret of Time. He had been sent to fetch us so that we too could share in the Secret of Time. He showed us a piece of the rock which he carried with him.

'So our people set out in small boats. They had many adventures, until there arose a great storm. All the family of our Artzan and the messenger, and many of our people were lost in the waves. The handfuls that survived, crawled ashore on the end of this ridge of hills.

'The people of that part were unfriendly and killed many of our people. So the ones that survived, fled along the edge of the marsh and hid in the caves. They killed the bears that lived in the caves and called themselves the People of the Bear.

'But caves are full of the Ghosts of Darkness that grip the muscles of your legs, that swell the joints of your limbs, and bend your back, so that our people grew old while still young. But having found the caves, they did not try to look for anywhere else to live. They were always talking about it, but having no Artzan to decide for them, they never did move.

'At last all the old ones died. There were generations of our people who knew no other life but living in caves. Our people lost all the skills we had known in our homeland.

'I was born in a cave. My mother, Vheere-cuin, Daughter of Darkness, gave birth to twins: me, Vhi-vhang, and my sister, Lhy-gnesse, Wanderer-Come-Home. Vheere-cuin was a great witch. She taught me her secrets and dedicated me to the Ghosts.

'One day, when Lhy-gnesse and I were still children, we found a boy wandering on the shore. He had red hair and wore a bear's paw slung around his neck. We became friends and he came to stay with us in our cave. He seemed of our age, but he was taller than us, so we called him Htorr-mhirr, because he stood out like the Mountain-in-the-Sea. We thought he was one of the Marsh People, but when he had learned to speak our tongue, he told us he was a prince from the land towards the sunrise. When he had been a tiny baby, an enemy had killed his mother and father, and had thrown him into the wilderness to die. The Marsh People had found him on their travels and had looked after him. He hoped one day to find out where he had come from, so that he could return there and become the true king of that land.

'I laughed at him for that, because the Marsh People are full of such stories. But I did not laugh at him unkindly, for I loved him even then. But Lhy-gnesse did not laugh at him at all, and he remembered that, though he never spoke of his childhood again. He liked us, and especially Lhy-gnesse, so much so that when the Marsh People departed on their journeys, he stayed behind with us.

'He had heard much during his time with the Marsh People and he told us so many things, that when he became a man, the Tribe asked him to become our Artzan. And this he did. Htorr-mhirr led us out of the caves. He showed us how to live in tents, how to herd cattle, sheep and goats. He showed us how to plant crops in the fields and how to bury our dead with dignity in long mounds of earth instead of pushing them into holes in tiny caves. He showed us how to trade with the Marsh People for the things we needed. We did well together, he leading and we following. His decisions were good ones, and we worked hard at his bidding. We prospered and feared no ghosts, for we had left the Ghosts of Darkness behind in the caves, and no others had set their faces against us.

'Both Lhy-gnesse and I loved Htorr-mhirr, but he had never forgotten which of us had laughed at him. So he took Lhy-gnesse as his woman. She died bearing twins: Mhirr-cuin, Daughter of the Sea, opened her womb; Mhirr-ling, Son of the Sea, followed.

'Even though I had been dedicated to the Ghosts, I wanted to spite Htorr-mhirr. So I became the woman of Kheila-hidd, He-Whose-Legs-Run-Faster-Than-His-Thoughts. He was the only man who had opposed Htorr-mhirr. He refused to give up his hunting ways to work in the fields or herd cattle.

'You were born on the same day as Mhirr-cuin and Mhirr-ling. I was now the Tribe's Witch, but my powers began to fade from the moment Kheila-hidd took me. So I vowed that you should not be given to any man, but be given to the Ghosts. I have taught you all my arts, but I have not seen any power manifest in you. I fear lest Mhirr-cuin may have inherited the power of witchcraft through her mother's blood, as well as the power of kingship through her father's blood. I do not know how she will use those powers. No witch is wholly bad or wholly good. Certainly in these hard times she communes with the Ghosts and with the Four Great Horned Ones, and she speaks on behalf of the Tribe to them, so do not think too harshly of her. I know nothing of the Four Great Horned Ones and it is too late for me to learn. Perhaps one day you will be able to commune with them. You must learn of them for yourself. I believe that you will do this. I called you Ochy, the Deep, the Ancient, the Eternal One. Your powers are deep within you.

'Although you were born on the same day as Mhirr-cuin, you are not a woman as she is. You know of what I speak. When the day of your womanhood comes, your powers will be awakened.

'Now there is one last act. This day is my last day – do not ask how I know – I know. Some witches say they dream dreams, or scry in water, leaf patterns, smoke, or goats' entrails. These are merely helpers. If you know what will happen, you know it and you cannot explain how you know it. This day is my last day. That is why I did not defend myself against Mhirr-cuin. Now I have this one last task.'

Vhi-vhang fumbled under her cloak and brought out a bluestone pebble, somewhat bigger than an arrowhead, but shaped like a polished stone axe. A hole had been drilled through it to take a leather thong which Vhi-vhang tied around her daughter's neck.

Vhi-vhang went on. 'This is the stone the messenger brought to our people. It is a piece of the Stone with the Secret of Time. One day it will tell you what you have to do. When the sun rose this day, it told me to give it to you before the sun reached the top of his climb. It is the only message it has ever given me. I have obeyed it.' Vhi-vhang leaned forward and kissed her daughter on both cheeks.

Ochy felt for the little stone with her cupped palm. It seemed comfortable resting there. Yet its presence also unsettled her. Not that it was hot to touch; nor did it glow with inner light: it was

27

just a piece of stone. Surely, if it were so important, it should look more distinguished. What was the Secret of Time it was supposed to contain? How had it ordered her mother to hand it on? When would . . .? Yes, there was something special about this stone. Ochy realised that its acquisition, its very presence, made her want to ask a whole range of questions – some about the trinket itself, . . . and others which were perhaps easier to answer.

'Mother, you said that after you laughed at him, Htorr-mhirr never spoke of his lost kingdom again. Yet Mhirr-cuin says she is of a house of princes. So, Htorr-mhirr must have told her – and Mhirr-ling.'

'No, he has said nothing to either of them. Why Mhirr-cuin says that, I do not know. Perhaps her Ghosts told her. Certainly, Htorr-mhirr did not. He told me so once, when he and I were discussing the Tribe and what is to become of it. One day when the People of the Bear are strong and give birth to other men fit to be Artzan, Htorr-mhirr will go in search of his kingdom – or, if he is too old, he will send Mhirr-ling. But until that day comes, he has vowed to himself that he will say and do nothing about this, lest, without a Shepherd, the Tribe for which he promised to care fall back into their old ways again.'

'Why can he not tell Mhirr-cuin and send her on the quest? After all, she is the first-born.'

Vhi-vhang looked shocked. 'First-born or not, Mhirr-cuin cannot be sent on the quest. Nor can she be Artzan. Only a man can be Artzan or Chief or King. That is as it has always been. A woman can be the Tribe's Witch, using her magick to help the Artzan in many ways, but the two are separate – just as men and women are separate.'

'So after you, Mhirr-cuin will be the Witch of the People of the Bear?'

'I did not say that, for I do not know. Sometimes I feel that you will be the Tribe's Witch, but I am not certain of that either. What I do know, is that your destiny is linked with that of Mhirr-ling. Not as his woman, for you have been dedicated to the Ghosts and you must keep yourself for them. But perhaps you will be Witch to his Artzan, although how this will come about, I know not.'

Ochy pondered this for a moment, then her mind returned to another topic. 'Some men acquire magick skills of great power; you have told me so yourself. Suppose the Tribe gave birth to such a man and to a woman with power of leadership. Could he not be Witch to her Artzan? They would still be separate, as custom dictates.'

28

Vhi-vhang smiled sadly. 'You ask so many questions. One day you may find the answers which I cannot give. Come; the Tribe is ready to move.'

Vhi-vhang and Ochy put their bags on their backs and took hold of the leather straps attached to their sledge. Their shoulders bowed as they took the weight and began the long haul.

During her talk. Vhi-vhang had been speaking easily. Now she coughed violently. Instantly Mhirr-ling was beside her. 'You have too much to carry. I have plenty of strength. Let me.'

He took Vhi-vhang's pack from her back, unslung his own, and then balanced one over each shoulder. Somehow he still found room for his bow. He looked at Ochy and winked. She grinned back at him; if their destinies were to be linked, what harm was there in being friendly, she thought.

Mhirr-ling felt warmed by this cheery smile. It was so rare for Ochy's usual scowling face to be so transformed. Mhirr-ling liked Ochy. He wished their families got on better together. Not that they ever fought or even shouted; there was just that perpetual atmosphere of vague animosity – which his sister seemed to delight in.

Mhirr-cuin was confronting him now. 'Why did you help them? No good will come of it.'

'Oh go away,' snarled Mhirr-ling. 'You always tell me what to do and what not to do.' He stuck his tongue out at her as he pushed past, deliberately swinging his load into her.

'That is what babies do,' she hissed. 'You are a baby, not a man. If you ever become Artzan – which I doubt – I will have to tell you what to do *all* the time.'

Mhirr-ling tried to ignore her: he would not let her spoil his day. He walked to the head of the column of women, children, old people, cattle, sheep, goats, pigs and sledges. He passed his father, sitting on his pony and flanked by the two other riders, Tschi-tschan and Hpe-gnorr. Mhirr-ling raised his hand. Htorr-mhirr nodded. Mhirr-ling brought his hand down. His voice could be heard over the stamping of feet and the noise of beasts. 'People of the Bear, we move to meet the Marsh People.'

6

As soon as Htorr-mhirr had seen the last wayward sheep chased out of the enclosure, he thwacked his pony's flanks with his legs. The three riders and their dogs set off at right-angles to the Tribe's march. They rode bareback across the dusty remains of the cornfields and along the familiar path through the trees close to the encampment. They knew just when to pull up before reaching the open ground beyond.

In a stalking crouch, Htorr-mhirr and Tschi-tschan moved towards the stronger light that showed where the trees thinned out. They crawled the last few paces on hands and knees, then peered through the last fronds of the wood.

The pasture was empty; except for a magpie balanced on a twig on top one of the patches of scrub. There were no deer. That was not surprising: they had not really expected to see the herd right in front of them. They had probably moved on down the valley, grazing as they went.

Htorr-mhirr indicated with his head, and the two men crawled stealthily through a patch of long grass, keeping to the hollows between the tussocks. Screened by a thick hawthorn bush, they got slowly to their feet. The magpie flew off without a sound. Still half-bent, they used the bush as cover to scan the valley as it fell away to the left. There was no sign of deer.

Htorr-mhirr straightened up and whistled the fluting call of a curlew, summoning Hpe-gnorr with the ponies and dogs.

Tschi-tschan spoke. 'I think Kheila-hidd was wrong when he said the red deer were running. Why can we see no sign of them?'

Htorr-mhirr pointed: 'Some plants have been nibbled.'

'Roebuck could have done that,' huffed Tschi-tschan. 'I see no sign of a great herd.'

'He did not say there was a great herd, only three handfuls.' Htorr-mhirr did not want another argument today.

'He also said they were hungry,' retorted Tschi-tschan. 'So, where are the signs of their hunger? Why can we not see them down the valley, still eating?' Before Htorr-mhirr could reply, he pushed his opinion home, cocking a thumb towards the Great Forest at the head of the depression. 'He also said that they were the first ones, with other herds close behind them. So, where is their sign?' He looked thoughtful for a moment. 'I thought Vhi-vhang was supposed to have made magick to ensure that the deer took the path Kheila-hidd said they would take.'

Htorr-mhirr pointed down the valley. 'That is the way we will go. If we meet Kheila-hidd and his hunters before we see the red deer, I shall say the hunt is over and we will return to the Tribe.'

'If we meet Kheila-hidd before we see the red deer, it will also tell us that the magick of Vhi-vhang has no power over the Deer Ghost.' Tschi-tschan swung himself onto his pony.

Htorr-mhirr opened his mouth to comment on the observation, then abruptly turned his head to shout in a different direction. 'No! No! We will not gallop down the valley lest we come upon the deer suddenly and frighten them into running past Kheila-hidd's bows too quickly. We will walk the horses.'

This command had been addressed to Hpe-gnorr, who had taken no part in the discussion, but had remained straddling his pony and scanning the ground for trail sign, while the dogs cast about for scent.

Hpe-gnorr loved riding. He loved the wind against his skin, the speed of flying over hills and water, the rhythmic pounding between his legs, the smell of the beast's sweat. As soon as the other two men had done speaking, he made to urge his pony down the valley, a movement spotted by Htorr-mhirr.

Sulkily, Hpe-gnorr circled, obeying the Artzan's command to round up the dogs. They chose that moment to give tongue and rush headlong into the woodland on the far side of the valley. Hpe-gnorr called them by name, shouted and whistled: to no avail. He forced his pony into a gallop and followed them into the trees.

Htorr-mhirr watched him go. 'The dogs are useful when our quarry is in sight, but we must train them to be more obedient when tracking their prey.' He sighed. 'Hpe-gnorr can catch us up,' and the two riders set their ponies down the valley at a walk. At every bend, every patch of scrub or clump of trees, they paused, scanned the ground ahead, and moved on again.

Hpe-gnorr did not catch them up. Whatever scent the dogs were following, it took them through a grove of oaks and out into another open valley beyond. Instantly they swung to the left and raced on down the valley, barking and yelping as they went. Hpe-gnorr noted plenty of sign here, at least ten handfuls of deer. Kheila-hidd had been right after all. Perhaps he had merely got the valleys mixed up. With a hoot of excitement, Hpe-gnorr

31

set his pony at full gallop after the dogs.

The valley became narrower, dropping around the steepening shoulders of scrubby moorland. At one place another valley came in from the right. This had been chosen by a big herd of reindeer, an early beginning to their winter migration towards the sea.

Hpe-gnorr was in an ecstasy of movement. The pony leaned this way and that, leapt a small log, ducked under an overhanging branch, scraped the side of a thornbush, sped unerringly between two jagged boulders that seemed to block the path. Hpe-gnorr was hunting the running deer just ahead of him. He did not know that now there were almost a hundred animals in front, even if he had been able to count that many.

None of them were the deer that Kheila-hidd had seen. Those hinds had indeed moved towards the woodland while browsing: that had been the trail scented by the dogs. But the red stag had followed them and forced them back into the open, on down the valley. The excited dogs had overrun the change of direction, picked up a skulking roebuck, and hurtled along that trail through the woods.

Meanwhile the red stag had been able to keep his hinds moving more quickly as he valley narrowed and the path became more constricted. They had made steady progress and had already passed the spot selected by Kheila-hidd for his ambush before the hunters arrived.

The men settled themselves under boulders and fallen trees close to the trail, so that each was hidden from sight, yet had a clear view of the valley down which the deer were expected to come.

By now the deer had paused at the entrance to the narrow gorge where the fanwork of valleys converged. The red stag got behind them, shouldering, prodding, drawing blood with his tines. The hinds did not want to go through that cleft. They could smell the sea on the wind, funnelling through the Great Gorge – and they could sense the scent of bear. There were too many terrors in that dark chasm. The hinds balked, stopped. The more the stag tried to prod them, the more they refused.

Then from the narrow fork to their right came another herd of red deer, impelled by some distant fear of their own. Startled, the red stag's hinds jumped in a sideways whirl and bolted back the way they had come. They were led by their master himself, his own deep-buried fears suddenly boiling to the surface.

32

The newcomers, seeing their bobbing tails, instinctively followed the alarm signal. Behind them crowded the reindeer, frantically running from the baying dogs and the whooping pony rider.

With each pace, the valley grew wider, a little less tortuous. Now the animals were three, four abreast, splitting to pass a tree or a boulder, coalescing again, those behind pressing those in front. And at their head, like a king leading his army, raced the red stag.

Now they were passing the last cliffs at the entrance to the Great Gorge. Here were Kheila-hidd and his men. Their bodies felt the tremble of hooves through the earth. They were tense, expectant, arrows nocked to bows, bowstrings taut. They could hear the deer, yet could not see them. Were the beasts invisible? Was it a magick herd? Then the terrible realisation: the wrong way – the animals were coming the wrong way! The leaders were already passing them; the range was increasing. The bowmen must leave their cover, try for those behind, drop some of the running deer.

Kheila-hidd loosed off one arrow, stood up nocking another to his bow; snapshot at a rusty carcass flashing by. Half the herd was past him: he must try to check the rearguard. Another arrow at his bow he ran forward, right into another hunter's line of fire.

The flint arrowhead caught him in the throat and he pitched forward gurgling. Dismayed, the other men ran down the slope towards him, jumping over stones and tussocks, ignoring the last deer sweeping past them.

Dogs were yelping and leaping at the stragglers' hamstrings and bellies as the whole herd galloped up the springtime trail away from the Great Gorge. Not a single beast had been touched by the hunters' missiles.

Now the ground was even more open, but here the widening valley forked. The red stag still pacing the horned multitude behind him, wanted to bear left, taking the shortest path back to the temporary safety of the Great Forest, along the path down which he had so recently brought his few hinds.

But here came Htorr-mhirr and Tschi-tschan, urging their ponies on to head off the escaping quarry.

The red stag had one last avenue of escape – straight ahead. He took that last chance. The herd had spread out behind him, ten, twenty animals abreast, each animal fleeing from the unimaginable fiends that peopled its brute nightmares and now encompassed it with relentless pursuit. Each animal believed that it alone was the object of death from canine teeth, from two-legged malevolence, from the bears lurking in the caves of the Great Gorge. Panic surged through its sinews.

Haunch muscles straining, antlers tossing, legs thrusting across the ground, clearing grass, bushes, gravel, a hundred deer topped the rise, smashed through a coppice of scattered trees and sparse shrubs, and plunged onto the plateau beyond.

In front of them was passing a strange procession of pigs, goats, sheep, cattle and more two-legged enemies. The terrified deer were too close to stop or turn aside. They crashed through the slow-moving column without a pause.

The Tribe's domestic animals were hot, thirsty and irritable. For them, this was the last trial. After all, they were themselves only a few generations removed from the wild beasts. Wild blood still flowed strongly and nervously in their veins. Animals being driven, animals being led, animals carrying burdens, animals pulling sledges, all stampeded.

Ihyselt looked right up at the hooves and belly of a giant red stag floating over the cow that pulled her sledge. Towering above, as high as the sky, was the powerful neck, the noble head, the mighty antlers. Then she too felt herself rising into the air so smoothly and so peacefully. Now she was able to look down upon the back of the ox that had tossed her sledge. Now she was able to look down on the Tribe: the people and all their belongings looked so small and so funny. Now she felt the babe stir within her. Now she began to fall.

On another sledge, piled high with goods, an old woman was balanced precariously. To keep her seat, she had twisted one of the baggage thongs around her wrist. In her other arm nestled a child. Now her precaution killed them both, trapped underneath the upturned sledge as it careered across the rocky soil, splintered and disintegrated.

The whole lifetime of the Tribe was condensed into one second of hoof and horn, a dust-filled universe of trampling and goring, screaming and dying.

At the head of the column Mhirr-ling and Mhirr-cuin broke right and left, unshouldering their bows. Mhirr-cuin's legs flashed white and white again through the long slit of her green gown. Mhirr-ling's bow was tangled up with the packs on his back. He got it free, nocked and loosed an arrow at an oncoming hind. The arrow missed.

The deer swerved, leapt over a woman hugging a baby to the ground, landed on the far side of the column and was struck by Mhirr-cuin's arrow.

34

The deer ran a few paces and dropped. There were no more deer in sight.

7

Htorr-mhirr reined in his pony. Dust drifted like smoke across the moor. Some of the Tribe were lying motionless; others were trying to get up and moaning. One or two of the animals were floundering with broken legs. One cow had broken her neck when the sledge she had been pulling at full gallop had jammed between two trees. There were bits of wood, parts of bundles, broken containers, liquid – beer, water, blood – soaking into the ground. Vhi-vhang and Ochy were helping the injured and making comfortable the last moments of those they could not succour. And over there, slightly apart, Mhirr-cuin and Mhirr-ling were facing each other.

'I warned you no good would come of helping Vhi-vhang,' sister accused brother. 'If you had not been carrying her pack, you could have unslung your bow, dropped the leading stag and stopped or turned aside the stampede.'

Mhirr-ling retorted wordlessly, but ... oh! She was always right. He turned away to try to organise a party of old men to round up some of the stock.

The hunters who had gone out with Kheila-hidd would not be back yet, but the two pony riders had arrived with Htorr-mhirr, and a weeping Tschi-tschan was cradling Ihyselt's body.

Of the whole Tribe, Htorr-mhirr seemed the most stunned. He walked through the disaster, feeling each death, each loss, each injury, as a blow upon his own body. He had nothing left; no strength, no cheer, to give them. Now more than ever, he was the one who needed strength, needed advice; and there was no one to give it.

'It is all my fault,' he said as Mhirr-cuin approached him. 'If I had not listened to Kheila-hidd, this would not have happened. I should have forbidden the hunt. We should only have made the move to meet the Marsh People this day.' He slouched down upon a rock, his hands on his knees. 'I have been too sure of myself. When the crops were good, I believed that I was the one who had done right, that I was the one who had brought good fortune to the Tribe.'

Htorr-mhirr shook his head. 'And when the crops were bad, I

said we will do this or that, we will go here or there, plant now or another time. I still believed that we could make the crops good by our own hard work. I realise now that I should have listened to you. I should have offered proper sacrifices to the Ghosts and to the Great Horned Rulers of Air, Fire, Water and Earth. But I did not. I have offended against them. I have aroused their anger and they have inflicted a terrible punishment upon the Tribe because of me.' He gestured feebly with his wrists. 'All this is my fault.' He raised his face to Mhirr-cuin, seeking guidance in her cowled eyes. 'Tell me, daughter; how can I sacrifice myself to the Four Great Horned Ones? How can I give them my blood so that they turn their anger away from the Tribe? Tell me what to do and I will do it.' And his body began to shake with massive sobs.

Mhirr-cuin put her arms around his shoulders, holding his face to her small body. 'Father, Father. Yes, I will tell you what to do, and you must do it. Yes, you have been proud, trusting in your own efforts and not in the Four Great Horned Ones. So you feel like this: sick in your heart. This is your punishment – humiliation. So you must sacrifice your pride to the Four Great Horned Ones, and in future do only as they say – and I will tell you what they say. But the punishment of the Tribe: that is a different matter. It is Kheila-hidd and Vhi-vhang who made that happen: Kheila-hidd because he scorned my talk of the Four Great Horned Ones and because he alone ignored the path which you – The Artzan – said the Tribe should take; Vhi-vhang because she showed no respect to the Four Great Horned Ones and her feeble magick mocked their powers. It is they who must be sacrificed to the Four Great Horned Ones. Only their blood will turn that anger away from the Tribe.'

Htorr-mhirr looked up at his daughter; she seemed to have grown taller during her speech. 'We cannot sacrifice them both. Kheila-hidd is already dead.' Mhirr-cuin stared at him. 'He was killed by an arrow meant for the deer.'

Mhirr-cuin straightened herself. For a brief pause she gazed far beyond the distant horizon of the falling sun. The green hood nodded imperceptibly as a thin smile of satisfaction momentarily touched her cowled face.

'Come Father!' Mhirr-cuin took Htorr-mhirr by the hand and half-dragged him to his feet, guiding him like a reluctant, shambling bear to where the Tribe's survivors were sorting themselves out. Releasing his hand, her waving wrists summoned the people closer.

'Hear me,' Mhirr-cuin began, taking the listening circle into her confidence. 'Do you remember how, this day, before the sun was at the top of his climb, I told you, as I have told you often before, of the Four Great Horned Ones, who created all things and rule all things? Do you remember how I told you that the Four Great Horned Ones were hungry? And that if the Tribe did not appease that hunger, they would inflict terrible punishment upon us?' Mhirr-cuin looked round the circle, staring at each face in turn. One by one, they dropped their eyes and nodded. 'Look about you,' commanded the girl. They all did so, and looked back at her with fearful eyes. 'Do you remember how Vhi-vhang magicked the deer to bring them to the Tribe?' One or two muttered, perhaps in agreement, perhaps in disagreement. 'The deer despised your magicking, Vhi-vhang.' Mhirr-cuin's finger was right in front of the older woman's tired, impassive face. 'But they came just the same, to play a game with the Tribe, to inflict the punishment of the Four Great Horned Ones on the Tribe.'

There were distinct words of agreement now.

Mhirr-cuin's finger was twisting about her wrist-joint as though she were screwing her accusation into the old witch. 'Vhi-vhang, this day you drew a stag that looked like a man with antlers on his head. Vhi-vhang, this day you drew the death arrow with your left hand. This day the man who wore the antlers in the Horn Dance, Kheila-hidd, your own man, was killed by an arrow. You killed your own man, Vhi-vhang.'

'No!' A shout from Ochy. Two women seized her, struggling. 'No! No! No!' A hand was clapped over her mouth. She bit it. The hand was withdrawn. She felt her skirt rip and the hand came back, stuffing the wolf-skin into her mouth. Ochy's splutter was cut short in a spasm of choking.

Vhi-vhang had not looked at her, had not moved. Mhirr-cuin had continued without glancing at Ochy, without interrupting her speech. 'Vhi-vhang, you drew a field of corn and destroyed it with magick.' There were cries of outrage from the onlookers. 'These things we know. What spells have you cast that we do not know, Vhi-vhang?'

Fists were being waved at the old woman, voices raised in uncomprehending demands.

Mhirr-cuin's head bobbed as she wheedled sarcastically: 'Oh yes, we know about the cures you have performed.' The hooded figure straightened implacably. 'But they were little cures, Vhi-vhang. Your curses have been great ones, Vhi-vhang. You cursed the rain and you cursed the corn, Vhi-vhang.' Again Mhirr-cuin mimed gratitude and wrath. 'Oh yes, we know of the handful of children you have cured, but how many cows, how many breasts went dry this summer? How many babies did you kill this summer, Vhi-vhang?'

The watching circle was a whirl of waving arms and shouting mouths, save for accuser and accused, a stooping and sniffling Htorr-mhirr, and Mhirr-ling, who was adding his cries of opposition to the general furore.

Mhirr-cuin kept the anger boiling. 'We were already going to our winter place fewer in number than when we left it – and now this.'

She waved her left arm around and brought it back, a green-clad shaft spearing Vhi-vhang's gaze. Mhirr-cuin was standing on her left leg only, her right drawn up under her gown. Within the shadow of her hood, her right eye was closed.

'She is the cause of all our misfortunes. I scratch her above her breath.' Mhirr-cuin stepped forward and drew her left hand across Vhi-vhang's forehead. Long nails ploughed bloody furrows.

There was a roar of delighted anger. Mhirr-cuin stepped back a pace. Vhi-vhang snuffled as the blood ran past her nostrils into the corner of her mouth. It was the first sound she had made.

The green hood turned towards a child. Mhirr-cuin pointed to a stone. 'Throw it!' He picked up the jagged limestone and flicked it at Vhi-vhang.

It hardly reached her; glanced off her thigh. But even before it had clattered to the ground, other rocks were being picked up, being thrown with jeering and raging. Vhi-vhang did not try to ward them off. A small boulder hurled two-handed hit her ear and she went down. The two excited women holding Ochy tried to join in. The girl broke free, tore the remains of her skirt from her head and ran to Htorr-mhirr, hung on his arm. 'Artzan, Artzan, save her.'

Mhirr-cuin half-turned. 'Tell me what to do and I will do it,' she reminded her father. 'Those were your very words. Do you remember them? I am telling you what to do now – not in words but in thought. Listen to me. Listen to the Four Great Horned Ones.'

Htorr-mhirr raised his head for the first time. He pushed Ochy aside and stood straight, clearing his throat. 'I am Htorr-mhirr, Artzan of the People of the Bear. The Four Great Horned Ones are our Masters. Mhirr-cuin is their Witch. Vhi-vhang is their enemy. I have decided. I have spoken.'

For a moment Mhirr-cuin's gown sagged as she let out a sigh: she had won the first, the hardest battle. For a moment she relaxed in proud relief. Unnoticed, Vhi-vhang's glance at Ochy said, 'Run!' Then she was grabbed by four women and spreadeagled.

Now Mhirr-cuin was again concentrating upon the business in hand. Yet she also noticed Ochy, backing quietly away, breathing heavily, eyes darting hither and thither before she turned and ran.

'Tschi-tschan,' called Mhirr-cuin. 'You have no reason to love Vhi-vhang. She killed Ihyself and your unborn child. Revenge yourself upon her offspring until she is as they are. Hpe-gnorr! Go with him. The child Ochy is to be sacrificed to the Four Great Horned Ones.'

Tschi-tschan was standing with Hpe-gnorr on the far side of the group away from Ochy. Tschi-tschan made to follow her retreating form, but his companion held his elbow. 'Let her run a little,' suggested Hpe-gnorr. He was flushed, excited. 'Then we can chase her!'

The two men walked over to their ponies. Mhirr-ling headed them off. 'There is no need. Let her go.' They thrust him aside, spinning him to the ground. Then they mounted and rode off. Mhirr-ling ran to his father's pony and followed them.

'Do not interfere. No good will come of it.' Did his sister actually call after him or did he imagine those words inside his head? He did not care either way. He would interfere if he wanted to. This time he would show Mhirr-cuin she was wrong. He would *make* good out of it. How, he did not know. But somehow he would save Ochy and prove . . . something.

Away behind him, Mhirr-cuin was standing at Vhi-vhang's head. Two women held the Tribe's totem, the Bear's Head stake, facing each other over Vhi-vhang's unprotesting, naked body.

'Father!' The single word of command from Mhirr-cuin.

Htorr-mhirr stepped forward, his feet responding to his daughter's eyes, to her voice. He stood at the apex of Vhi-vhang's outstretched legs.

Mhirr-cuin addressed him again. 'Father! Htorr-mhirr! You are the Artzan of the People of the Bear. Where you lead, the people follow.'

Htorr-mhirr grasped the bear stake. The circle of watchers gasped. Three pairs of arms centred the stake over the limbed crossroads below.

Mhirr-cuin began chanting. 'Air . . . Fire . . . Water . . . Earth . . . Air . . . Fire . . . Water . . . Earth . . .'

Ochy ran, Mhirr-cuin's chant ringing in her ears as though she was keeping pace with her. 'Air . . . Fire . . . Water . . . Earth . . . Air . . . Fire . . . Water . . . Earth . . .'

The Tribe had taken it up, the syllables pounding in time with her legs, her heart. 'Air .. Fire .. Water .. Earth .. Air . Fire . Water . Earth . AirFireWaterEarth.'

The words were coming louder and faster the further away she got.   'Airfirewaterearthairfirewaterearthairfirewaterearthairfirewaterearth.'

The chant ended abruptly. There was an agonised, wavering scream, and a shout of triumph. Ochy stopped as though struck, turned in one movement.

She could see every detail as though she were still in the circle instead of many paces away: the watchers, their backs, and the fronts of those on the farther side of the ring; Htorr-mhirr and two women bending over something visible through the perimeter hedge of legs; Mhirr-cuin, arms raised to the sky, her green hood thrown back, red hair flaming with her own internal fire; her arms going down, lifting again; the Bear Totem raised, blood running down it; another scream; the red stake plunging again; a great sigh from all the watchers.

Then Ochy pivoted and was running again.

8

Ochy ran along the ridge with the three horsemen in pursuit, lathering their spotted ponies. The girl ran and ran and ran and ran until she felt she could run no more; and then she ran some more. Black hair and wolf-skin cloak flying in the wind of her passing, she ran until utterly exhausted; then her mind summoned up more energy and she ran on.

She ran past familiar enclosures and fields now abandoned by the Tribe. She ran past old burial mounds, ancient even in her day. She ran across ankle-twisting tussocks. She ran over a pan of caked mud, starred with fissures and creeping plants. A patch of quagmire sucked at her ankles and then she was running across the sunbaked crust again, the heat cooking the soles of her feet. She ran on, two feet against the speed of four hooves. It was impossible for her to outstrip the horsemen; but she kept ahead of them.

Tschi-tschan rode with bitterness in his heart, determined to rid the Tribe of the last vestige of the brood that had wrought so much evil and had destroyed his woman and unborn son. Hpe-gnorr rode with ecstatic joy, revelling in the thrill of the chase. Mhirr-ling, slightly behind the other two, rode with desperation, striving to get in front and head the hunters away from their quarry. He had no thought of what he would do when he overtook Ochy; he just did not want her to be caught.

The horsemen urged their ponies on. They held the animals up when they stumbled on loose rocks, forced them to speed long-legged across level ground, steered them around patches of bramble, lifted them over logs and branches. They were right behind Ochy. She felt horse's breath, spots of spittle on her neck.

Ochy pivoted on one leg, snatched herself upright, and shot off at an angle from her previous line of flight. Hpe-gnorr and Tschi-tschan could not turn so sharply. Their mounts hurtled straight on, the ponies' heads being hauled this way and that, as their riders fought to check them and change direction, without falling off.

But Mhirr-ling was farther back. He could see what was happening. Could he cut across the corner, head Ochy off and . . .?

Mhirr-ling had never ridden so fast before and still stayed on. With a great surge of new-found self-confidence, he urged the pony even faster. He was bouncing up and down and from side to side on the heaving back, sometimes being thrown right forward onto the pony's neck. Yet he still managed to hold onto the reins. He knew now that he had at last become a horsemaster, just like Hpe-gnorr. There was nothing he could not do – even that trick he had once seen Hpe-gnorr perform. He – Mhirr-ling – would sweep Ochy up onto his horse and then he would ride off with her to safety.

'I am coming, Ochy,' he shouted between jarring gulps for breath. 'I . . . want . . . to . . . help . . . you . . . Come . . . with . . . me.'

Ochy ran on, hearing sounds but no words. Her whole body was governed by one thought: run, run, run!

Mhirr-ling gripped the pony's flanks with bare knees and thighs, released the reins reached down and grapped Ochy's flying cloak with both hands. She ran on, diverging slightly away from the galloping pony. Now Mhirr-ling was leaning out horizontally, parallel with the ground, body, arms and cloak a single taut bar of muscle and wolfskin, almost strangling Ochy as her feet raced over the grass, the horse's hooves pounding beside her.

The neck fastening was stiff. Ochy's fingers pulled at it, broke a nail, pulled again; it loosened, slipped, was free: the cloak was gone. Naked, save for the stone on its thong, she turned, twisted, overbalanced, regained her footing, and ran on. Mhirr-ling was left grasping at full stretch a shadowy, windblown piece of skin. He had nothing to lean on. He felt his legs sliding from the pony's back, tried to right himself, to grab the reins, the arching neck, the mane, anything, fell, hit the ground, bounced, rolled, and sat up – then decided to lie down again. Past him raced first Hpe-gnorr and then a little later Tschi-tschan. Ochy ran on.

She was used to running barefoot, but even calloused soles tire. Once a long splinter pierced her foot. Hopping on one leg, she half got it out, broke it, drew the rest out in one piece, and ran on. She was used to working naked in the fields, but the continual whip of branch and flick of bramble bruised and clawed her face and body. She wanted to flinch and hesitate, to reach out and hold the sapling or thorn away from her, but she forced herself to ignore the pain – and ran on.

Ahead she could now see the marshes, a flat plain of shimmering heat haze and darker reeds. Here and there silver water glistened in the afternoon sun. Floating above the mist rose The-Mountain-in-the-Sea – Htorr-mhirr. It was a marker, a magnet. She was being drawn irresistibly towards it, the mountain filling her vision as she ran.

A pony was close behind her again. Sometimes she could feel the animal's breath on her neck. Then she would turn, dodge, run around a bush or under a low tree, gain a few paces, hear the muttered words of the rider's anger. It was Hpe-gnorr. For some inexplicable reason, she felt more frightened than if it had been Tschi-tschan behind her. Her own breath rasped in her throat. She felt rivulets of sweat on her skin, icy cold on the side of her body away from the sun. Her heart ached, her sides ached, her head ached, her arms ached, her legs ached. Left foot . . . right foot . . . left foot . . . right foot . . . left foot . . . tree trunk ahead . . . one foot on it . . . flying through the air, arms wide . . . other foot landing . . . running on . . . left foot . . . hooves thudding, faltering, coming on behind her . . . left foot . . . right foot . . . air . . . fire . . . water . . . earth . . . air . . . fire . . . water . . . earth . . . left foot . . . right foot . . . water . . . earth . . . left foot . . . fire . . . hair thumping on her shoulders . . . pebble bouncing on her chest . . .

She was running along the rim of a ravine, then along the edge of a steep slope, thickly wooded with oak and hazel. There were occasional outcrops of rock, sprouting hart's-tongue ferns. Light and shade, sunny heat and chill shadow, dappled the leaf-strewn, ivy-cloaked incline.

Ochy spotted a deer-trail angling down the slope to the right, too steep for any pony to follow at a gallop. She made to swing down it, but Hpe-gnorr threw himself from his mount, his heavy body descending upon her, knocking her down, rolling her over. She kept on rolling, almost free of his grasp. But he sprang from hands and knees, smothering her, she trying to scrabble away backwards on buttocks and shoulders, the movement of her small smooth body under his rough hands and lunging torso reminding him of the motion of the horse between his thighs, the thrill of the hunt, the excitement of the capture – and now the triumph of the killing thrust. Fully charged with sensation and desire, lust and death were all one to Hpe-gnorr. He untucked his kilt, felt for her. The little vixen would not keep still. She would not keep quiet. He could not find what he wanted; her shrill shrieks dinned his ears. 'Keep still! Keep quiet!' he snarled in his own tongue, as his palms covered her face, and then his fingers encircled her throat. She choked and squirmed, a sharp stone knifing into her back, her legs and belly crushed by the continual searching thrust of his loins until . . . His lust was too impatient. Before he could enter her, he was rearing up in orgiastic paroxysm, his mouth wide open, roaring, his hands still pinning Ochy to the ground, but her hands groping, finding another sharp stone, not the one underneath her, grasping it, lashing sideways and upwards and sideways again, and Hpe-gnorr jerking away in surprise, grabbing for her flailing wrist, missing it, the jagged stone slicing between his legs, lifting him bodily, vertically, to his feet, so that blood and semen gushed upon her, as he towered upright, reaching the sky, just as Tschi-tschan's pony thundered into him, hurling him sideways, the horse turning, Tschi-tschan shouting 'She is to be sacrificed, not for pleasure!' And Ochy on her feet, running again, down that steep path she knew no horse could follow.

Without pausing, Tschi-tschan set his pony straight down the hill to cut her off. Ochy ran faster, but her legs were unable to keep up with her body. She tripped, fell, rolled once, rolled twice, regained her feet, stumbled to her knees, then upright, and ran on. She zigzagged left, then down another path to the right. Tschi-tschan cut across her back trail and was in front of her as she dodged right. He snatched at her hair, missed, seized it, twisted it, pulling her off her feet as pony and rider hurtled down the slope. Ochy fell, rolling over, dragging Tschi-tschan from his precarious perch, his other hand entangled in the reins. The spotted pony lost its footing, tried to gallop faster, tripped over its own feet and Ochy's legs, and somersaulted. Ochy felt rock sliding beneath her, sharp rock that slit and gashed, then she was flying, trees and sky, rocks and ferns, Tschi-tschan and pony, whirling around her. An arm-wrenching, ice-cold whoosh, a cocoon of silver bubbles in a green world, turning over and over, rocks beneath her feet, rising into darkness. She hit her head on rock underwater. It jolted her mouth open. She swallowed, choked, dying, opening her mouth again, breathed black air, felt gritty mud between her toes, a shelf of rock under her feet, then battering· at her knees.

Ochy lay gasping, her body out of the water, her belly and legs in it. It was black, all black, a blackness she could feel. Was she blind? No, she could see light in the distance. She crawled towards it, scraping her protesting body over rough gravel and slithery rock. She crawled for ever, mainly uphill, sometimes down. She crawled through pools of water and between spikes of stone. Her groping hand broke one of them off in front of her face.

The light grew stronger, but not bigger. It was a hole about a hand's breadth across. There were loose stones there, bound with fern roots. Ochy reached up to move one, to get into the light. Then she heard voices.

Or rather, it was just one voice – that of Mhirr-ling. It seemed far away, the universal cry of the searcher: 'Oyoyoyoyoyoyoy! Ooooooochyyyyyyy! Tschiiiiiii-tschaaaaaaan! Oyoyoyoyoyoyoy!'

Evidently he was up on top of the cliff, looking for her and Tschi-tschan.

Ochy cowered in her hole, listening. There was no answer from Tschi-tschan; no excited shout of survival; no frantic cry for help; no agonised moan of human injury, nor whinnying or thrashing of maimed pony – just silence.

Tschi-tschan had no reason to keep quiet. So, after a while it could be assumed that he and his horse had been killed, either by the fall itself, or by drowning in the pool. And if she, Ochy did not reply, Mhirr-ling and Hpe-gnorr would assume that she too had died in like fashion.

She wished it had been Hpe-gnorr and not Tschi-tschan who had gone over the cliff to his doom. She hoped she had killed Hpe-gnorr, but most probably she had only hurt him enough to make him vow angry vengeance for the humiliating wound she had inflicted.

And Mhirr-ling? His destiny linked with hers? she thought bitterly. He had not helped her. He had pursued her just like the others. He had shouted at her, tried to capture her, take her as sacrificial offering to the Four Great Horned Ones. Her mother had got it wrong again; it seemed as though their destinies were indeed linked – but only in death.

No, she decided: she would not answer Mhirr-ling. Even if he managed to climb down that cliff, she would still hide from him.

46

9

High up on the hill, Mhirr-ling clung to a branch and leaned over as far as he dared. He still could not see anything. His view of whatever lay below in the abyss was completely obscured by a thick fringe of ferns sprouting from just below the cliff edge. Already the supple fronds were springing back from where the three tumbling creatures had crashed through them. Tschi-tschan and his pony had gone over the cliff just like Vhi-vhang had foretold in her last magick painting. But had they or Ochy fallen into water, or onto trees or rocks? One of them might be still alive, but unconscious. Could he and Hpe-gnorr climb down there to search?

Mhirr-ling could see no way down; and he dared not get any closer to the supposed edge, in case those ferns concealed a sheer drop. Perhaps if he were to throw a stone – he should be able to hear it bouncing downhill if there were a slope beyond the ferns.

Mhirr-ling backed up a few paces, found a suitable chunk of rock, and hurled it out beyond the green fronds. It disappeared without a sound.

He had almost decided that it must have fallen into long grass somewhere, when he heard the tiniest of splashes far, far below. Almost at once there came a muttering roar, welling up from the bowels of the earth. He felt it in the air and through the soles of his feet. The sapling he was clinging to, trembled. Alarmed by the unknown, and physically frightened lest he lose his grip and be thrown into the invisible abyss, Mhirr-ling turned and frantically scrambled up the slope, not pausing until he was standing, panting for breath on the leveller ground where Hpe-gnorr had remained with his pony grazing nearby. Mhirr-ling had not seen his own mount after falling from it at full gallop. He had followed the chase on foot. From a distance he had seen Hpe-gnorr apparently leap into the air just as Tschi-tschan had raced past him in pursuit of Ochy. Once again, Mhirr-ling had cut corners, making diagonally down across the steepening slope to where pony, rider and quarry had all disappeared from sight. Mhirr-ling had wondered why Hpe-gnorr had not come to help him search and call. Now, as he looked down at the moaning man, he knew why.

Mhirr-ling felt faint; he wanted to be sick. He was no stranger to blood: he had participated in the hunting of animals, their subsequent butchery, and the preparation of their hides. But that was animals – not men. Admittedly, he had witnessed the carnage inflicted by the stampeding deer earlier that very day, but that had been too big a disaster for individual details to shock.

But this bloody thing lying in front of him – this was one solitary man. No, he realised – this *had been* a man. To be injured in such a way . . .

Mhirr-ling's head spun. He wanted to shout for help, run for help. But there was nobody there, nobody near; only him – and Hpe-gnorr.

'Oh Four Great Horned Ones,' he prayed. 'Give me strength. One day I will be Artzan. I will have to bear many things. Give me the strength to cope with this one thing.'

He realised as he uttered the words that it was the first time he had prayed to the Four Great Horned Ones of whom his sister spoke so knowingly. The plea came so naturally – and it was answered immediately. Not by any voice, but by the disappearance of his weakness. He found he was able to regard Hpe-gnorr and his wound dispassionately.

'What happened?' he asked, squatting down beside Hpe-gnorr.

The casualty took a long time to answer and when he did, his words were interrupted by grunts and gasps.

Mhirr-ling was only partially correct in attributing this hesitancy to the pain and to Hpe-gnorr's attempts to express himself in what was to him a foreign tongue. Hpe-gnorr was a stranger amongst these people and he knew that some tribes were particular that sacrificial offerings should be whole and perfect when being presented to their gods. And even if there were no religious significance, some tribes frowned upon the violation of girls before they had become women. Many tribes reserved especially painful and lengthy deaths for those who broke such taboos. Hpe-gnorr had not thought of that during the heat of the chase; but now – sobered by the cold fire of agony – he thought of it now. It might be better not to say that Ochy had done this to him; then he would not have to explain the nature of his assault upon her.

'It was the pony,' he gasped. 'He bucked and his backbone caught me between the legs as he threw me.'

Mhirr-ling winced at the thought; but he was also a little bit surprised. He would not have expected Hpe-gnorr to be thrown like that. The horse looked docile enough now; nor did it seem possible that any pony's backbone could be so sharp as to cause the sort of bloody injury Hpe-gnorr had received. In fact, there did not seem to be any blood on the animal at all. But perhaps the blood had not started flowing until Hpe-gnorr had actually been thrown. Still, it must have been the horse which had caused it. Mhirr-cuin had always said no good would come of riding horses; and that had certainly been proved true today: Tschi-tschan dead; Hpe-gnorr crippled; he, Mhirr-ling, suffering from the worst bruises and headache he had ever known; and from the odd snatches of conversation he had heard earlier, even the stampede had been caused by the horses and their riders. Yes, Mhirr-cuin had been right again. She is *always* right, he thought with annoyance. Nevertheless, she also claimed to know something about the healing arts; there was no one else with such knowledge now. And whether good came of it or not, Mhirr-ling could not think of any way of getting the injured Hpe-gnorr back to Mhirr-cuin without making use of the remaining pony.

Mhirr-ling cast around until he found a couple of fairly straight trees, still young, but more rigid than saplings. Jumping up, he bent them to the ground until they snapped. He trimmed away the projecting branchlets with the flint knife he always carried at his waist. The next stage took a little longer, but eventually he located enough green lengths of ivy to lash the two poles on each side of the horse's body, and then form a network between the ends dragging on the ground behind. On this he laid and secured Hpe-gnorr.

The injured man was slipping in and out of consciousness, often babbling incoherently in his own tongue. Mhirr-ling closed his ears to the noise, concentrating on the task in hand, although from time to time he could not prevent himself pondering the events of the day and what they portended. So many people had been killed or hurt, including his own father. Not that Htorr-mhirr's body had come to visible harm; but something had died inside him. And somehow, Mhirr-cuin's Ghost had taken possession of that emptiness. Yes, Mhirr-cuin was now the Witch of the People of the Bear; and apparently Htorr-mhirr would do whatever she commanded. He – Mhirr-ling – would not obey her without question if she was Witch if he ever became Artzan. He would not let her Ghost possess him. He knew what was best for the People of the Bear – or at least, he would by then: Mhirr-cuin could not be right all the time – nobody could.

He wished Ochy could have been the Tribe's Witch; he and she would have worked well together, he knew that. And she already possessed powerful magick; how else could she have kept ahead of galloping horses? He had never known anyone run so fast. Not that it had saved her in the end. No, Mhirr-cuin had won again; Ochy had been sacrificed to the Four Great Horned Ones exactly as Mhirr-cuin had commanded. Well, to one of them: the Great Horned Ruler of Water had taken her and had roared in exultation over his prey; if he chose not to share his feast with the other Three Rulers of Earth, Fire and Air – that was for them to fight over. He, Mhirr-ling, had enough to do trying to get Hpe-gnorr back to wherever the People of the Bear were now. It would be night long before he found them. He thought of the wild beasts padding along beside the path, the Ghosts of Darkness lurking amongst those rocks, the Four Great Horned Ones watching from those trees.

Mhirr-ling realised that he was holding his breath, waiting . . . for what?

It was no good. He had to do this journey alone, bear the responsibility of Hpe-gnorr in solitude. It will be good training, he told himself. One day, I shall be carrying the whole Tribe. But first, he would try one last call: 'Oyoyoyoyoyoyoy! Tschiiiiiii-tschaaaaaaan! Oooooooochyyyyyyy!'

There was no reply.

Mhirr-ling turned back to the horse, took its rein, and began leading it along the ridge towards the setting sun, the dying man on the litter crying out at every jolt and scrape along the way.

10

Far below, Ochy sat in near-darkness. The noise which Mhirr-ling had sensed as a vague rumble, had within the cave come as a harsh scream followed by a violent roar that tailed off into a prolonged slobbering snarl. Terrified, Ochy had almost cried out, stuffing her fingers into her mouth and biting them hard. Yet, that unknown horror within the cave was less immediately threatening than what lay outside. *It* might not yet have sensed her presence; but if she emerged, her fate was certain at the hands of Hpe-gnorr and Mhirr-ling. So, Ochy sat soundless and motionless. It was quiet for so long after the monster's roar, that she came to believe that it must have frightened away her pursuers. But then she heard Mhirr-ling's final searching call and, at the last, her own name, 'Oooooooochyyyyyyy!' And then silence.

Ochy sat for a long time, still seeming to imagine movement and noise long after she knew she was hearing nothing. Then she sat even longer, fearing lest Hpe-gnorr or Mhirr-ling might have clambered silently down the cliff or worked their way round from some other direction and be lurking outside.

The water gradually dried on her. She was without food or fire, and trapped in a cave with some terrible monster. She was naked, except for a pebble on a leather thong about her neck. She sat there looking at the little patch of sky, which gradually darkened to blue-black, almost as black as the blackness of the cave.

She sat there as the stars appeared and the moon came out, the last crescent of the dying moon.

She sat there fingering the pebble.

She sat there and slept.

11

It was full daylight when Ochy woke. Even without moving her head she could see the blue sky of another warm autumn morning.

She did not feel like moving her head. She did not feel like moving anything. A terrible lassitude embroiled her; despondency mired her thoughts.

Even if she had wanted to move, there was nowhere to go. Behind, the cave was black and full of horrors; in front, there was no way out.

Ochy sat there for a long time. She sat there fingering the pebble at her throat. She sat there going over the events of the previous day, trying to recreate the order in which they had happened.

At some stage she remembered that she had tried to remove a stone from the cave entrance. She sat there, looking at the obstruction more closely. Yes, there were lots of small stones, bonded by loose earth and little roots, probably the result of some landslide from above.

Ochy reached up – her arm was so stiff – and pushed at one of the stones. It fell away instantly, clattering away down the slope outside. Ochy sat there, heart pounding, holding her breath, listening. There was no other sound. Then she decided: I will go out and face whatever awaits me there. If it is my destiny to die at the hands of Mhirr-ling, so be it; I do not care any more about what happens. Dispiritedly she moved another stone and then, because it was something positive to do, she found she was kneeling, attacking the pile with both hands. Some soil and pebbles were hurled outside, some she pulled inwards. One rock, bigger than her head, proved immovable. She scratched around it with her nails, felt for a sharp, flat stone and dug away the dirt. She hacked at a tangle of grass roots, sat back, put her feet up against the stone and pushed. She pushed again. The rock gave way. A couple more scrapes and she could wriggle through the hole, slide past the upturned roots of a big oak, into the open air.

A narrow steeply banked shaped valley fell away before her. It was filled with oak and hazel and alder, and an occasional yew or elder. Many of the big trunks had toppled over or were leaning on other trees. Upturned roots groped at the slopes and shed branches littered every level patch of ground. Over all clambered ivy, bryony, honeysuckle, bramble, and old man's beard, tendrils spiralling here, shapeless mounds of greenery there. Leathery-tongued and lacy-leaved ferns sprouted from every bare bit of soil. There was hardly a stone without moss on it, a rotten log without fungus oozing from it. Behind her – she could just see without moving her neck too much – was a nearly vertical slope cloaked in the same riot of vegetation that choked the valley. Only in one place was there bare rock, a grey layered cliff dropping sheer to a deep dark pool, whence issued a river of white water foaming over boulders and under a tunnel of fallen tree trunks. There was no sign of either Tschi-tschan or his pony; presumably their bodies had been swept right away. The whole scene was one of dampness and decay, relieved only by bright sunlight filtering through the treetops which did not quite meet overhead, and by the brightly coloured leaves of autumn pattering down from the branches. Above the sound of the swirling river, Ochy could hear the rich notes of a blackbird.

A blackbird – in autumn? Ochy was puzzled. Then she noticed the speckled form of a starling, perched on a dead branch halfway up the cliff; it was imitating a blackbird. That was a good omen, to have summer song all the year round.

Ochy stood up, and immediately fell, stones and twigs digging into her kneecaps and flattened palms. She cried out with the pain. Again she tried to stand, and again she fell, this time aware of agonising pain in her back. She could not straighten herself. She was bent double, fixed in the position she had been sitting in all night. She found the only way she could move was by crawling on her hands and knees, or shuffling along on her bottom. When alongside a rock or tree-trunk, she could just support herself with one hand while her misshapen body shambled a couple of paces.

Her mother had told her of the Ghosts of Darkness that lived in caves and did such things to people's bodies. She thought she ought to be more frightened, but the dull glow of pain was too persistent to let her mind consider abstract things.

She wondered what other hurts she had, and looked over her body as best she could without moving back or neck too much. She was covered in scratches and bruises, dirt and dried blood. There was a long gash up the front of her body, but it did not seem more than skin deep and had now stopped bleeding.

But she could hardly move and she had to have something to eat and drink. This might be the last meal she would ever have, the last journey she would ever make. Well – she would enjoy it.

53

Ochy crawled laboriously over to where she could see a trailing bramble, pushing into the greenery so that it hung about her as she sat. She stripped the runners of their black berries, stuffing the fruits into her mouth as fast as she pulled them from their stalks. Having exhausted that spot, she shuffled round into another verdant corner. In the third green alcove, she found a couple of yellow toadstools. She pulled them up and munched away.

It was too much effort to try to get down to the river to drink, so she selected the fattest blackberries she could reach and let the juice trickle down her throat. If anything, it made her thirstier, but it put some sort of liquid inside her.

Ochy sat there, recovering from her efforts. The strain of moving about while crippled up had exhausted her. She wondered if she would ever be able to walk upright again, but she felt too worn out even to worry about that. She sat there leaning her back against a tree, watching the shadows lengthen and then become one entire shade. It was still afternoon in the treetops, but sunset had come to the valley bottom.

She must get back to the cave. It had sheltered her safely for one night. It would do for another night.

On hands and knees she clambered back towards the hole she had made. It was only a little slope, but it seemed mountainous, especially the last few feet past the oak roots.

She had seen no sign of bear or wolf, nor of human hunters, but she did not want anything to invade her sanctuary.

Ochy noticed a flat piece of stone of suitable size lying a little way back down the slope. She retraced her laborious journey until she had passed it. By digging with her knees and toes into the dirt, half straightening her body and pushing with her extended arms, she could slide the rock upwards without hurting her back too much. She turned round, wriggled her feet into the hole – suppose something grabbed them? – and dropped through, pulling the flat stone up so that it was wedged into the oak tree's roots, practically blocking the aperture.

The effort had reopened the gash on her body; it had started bleeding again. There was blood on her legs too. It was coming from . . . There was just enough light for her to see. She was bleeding from inside.

Ochy looked in horror. Then she remembered. Her mother had told her this would happen. Well; she was now a woman. Perhaps the power of witchcraft would now be revealed in her; perhaps not. She could not be bothered whether it was or not. All she wanted to do was sleep.

But this night, sleep would not come. Ochy was so uncomfortable. Her back would only cease complaining when she found the exact position she had taken up last night; and she could not find it. She ached so much. Her bruises cried out when she leaned upon some jutting stone. Her cuts dried, the scabs rubbed off and she bled again.

Even when she thought she was dozing off, her mind reawakened her, racing over the events of the past few days, going over all the events of her whole life. She remembered the potions and the recipes her mother had taught her, repeating the rhymes to herself over and over again, getting them mixed up with other chants and starting again. She remembered the hunting lessons her father had given her. She would have to use those skills now. She would need a bow. How would she make one? She could not think how; she could not concentrate. She thought of the old stories of her people, and fingered the pebble at her chest, the pebble with the Secret of Time. She wondered what it meant, what message it would have for her. She thought of the Ghosts of Darkness and listened to the plop-plop of water in the cavern, the murmur of the river. She thought of her people who had once lived in caves and how they had used magick to bring good luck to the hunters. She remembered what she had been told about the good days when the Tribe had learned to herd animals and plant crops, the good days when the Tribe had eaten summer and winter without fear of hunger. Magick had not been needed then, only hard work. Even the hunters then employed more skill than magick. And then she remembered the droughts and the hunger and Mhirr-cuin's stories of Ghosts and the Four Great Horned Ones.

How she hated Mhirr-cuin! Ochy pounded the cave floor with her fist. Mhirr-cuin had killed her father and mother – or had she? Vhi-vhang had certainly drawn some poor pictures. Kheila-hidd had shown little respect for the Ghosts; the whole deer-magicking ceremony had been badly done. No wonder the Four Great Horned Ones had been insulted. No wonder they demanded sacrifices – if they existed. Of course they existed: the fact that Vhi-vhang had known nothing of them, had merely demonstrated her ignorance.

In contrast, yesterday's events had been a terrible proof of the existence of the Four Great Horned Ones. And Mhirr-cuin was their Witch, speaking for them, relaying their orders, bending their magick to her command. Well, she, Ochy, would be as powerful a witch as Mhirr-cuin. She would be more powerful than Mhirr-cuin. She would gain dominion over the Four Great Horned Ones, command them, use their magick to destroy Mhirr-cuin.

But with sudden retrospective alarm, Ochy realised that she had come close to losing her magick powers even before they had been manifest in her. She had been dedicated to the Ghosts. If taken by any man, even by force, she would lose those powers. Of course, that was why Mhirr-cuin – who had always opposed the riding of ponies – had ordered Hpe-gnorr to accompany Tschi-tschan in pursuit of Ochy. She must have known that, crazed by the excitement of the hunt, he would violate before killing.

Ochy laughed aloud. Mhirr-cuin's plan had failed – just as all her plans would fail.

But would they? Ochy thought of Mhirr-cuin's Ghost. It was not bound to mortal shape like Mhirr-ling or Hpe-gnorr; it could climb cliffs, enter caves. It would be watching her here, now, in the darkness. It would tell Mhirr-cuin where she was; it would return here to . . . to do what?

For a moment Ochy felt fear, then defiance. 'I spit upon your Ghost, Mhirr-cuin,' she shouted. 'Go! Tell your mistress. I will kill her if she comes here. I will kill anybody she sends here. I will kill anybody she sends here.' Ochy took a deep breath and threw her voice again. 'Do you hear me, Ghost of Mhirr-cuin? I will kill you too if you come back here.' The words chased each other around the blackness.

Stiffly, while still sitting, Ochy raised her right foot just clear of the cave floor; she closed her right eye and half extended her left arm.

'By the Ruler of the Air
By the Ruler of the Earth
By the Ruler of the Water
By the Ruler of the Fire
By the Four who Great and Horned
Rule and live in all things ever
I vow that one day soon or later
They will have your body and
I will have your head Mhirr-cuin.'

'Mhirr-cuin . . . Mhirr-cuin . . . Mhirr-cuin . . . cuin . . . cuin . . . in . . . in . . . n . . . n . . . n . . . n . . . n'. The echoes died away.

An answering mutter came from the depths of the cave. Then there was black silence.

12

No, not quite silence. This night the darkness was not silent. Perhaps last night she had been too tired to hear, but this night there were noises. Ochy relaxed her limbs and strained her ears until her scalp muscles ached.

There was a scuffling on the earth bank outside and an owl hooted. Ochy could hear the soft wind in the trees, the patter of falling leaves, the creak of a branch. There was the murmur of the river. Far, far away, a wolf howled.

In the cave, water plopped; here, there, here again. She could hear a rapid series of quiet plips; plipplipplipplipplipplipplip-plip; almost a continuous stream. Somewhere else there were two heavy drops in quick succession, then a pause, then two more . . . plooploop . . . plooploop . . . plooploop . . . Another was a steady plop-splash . . . plop-splash . . . plop-splash . . .

Once Ochy heard a small wave break on a rocky ledge, as though something were swimming in the underground river. She shivered. She was cold. She was so cold. She had nothing to wrap around her and she was cold, so terribly cold.

But even worse than being cold, was being naked in the dark. She had nothing to pull over her head to shut out the black noises around her. If only she had not lost her winter-cloak. What was that she felt across her leg – a trickle of water? – a spider? – a snake? – a Night Ghost?

Ochy tried to bury her face in the rock, her wrists entwined over the nape of her neck so that *They* could not see her.

But *They* could see her. The ice-cold teeth sank into her spine. Screaming, she hollowed her back to relieve the pain, but the jaws pursued her flesh, biting deeper, lifting her bodily, shaking her.

She fell clear, rolling on her side, hands clasped to the small of her back, sobbing. The monstrous shape backed off, eyes glowing redly in the dark sharp teeth like points of light.

She was on her back now, the stone beneath her legs twitching chitinously, the harsh carapace of some giant insect. Her mind was petrified. She must not alarm the thing. She must keep her legs still, keep them rigid.

Too late! The beast knew she was there in the darkness. Its

fangs sliced into the muscle of her calf. Now her foot was grinding in the creature's throat, her knee locked in its jaws. She felt her kneecap grate and then fix solid as her leg was twisted this way and that, her hands trying to free and straighten the limb. Ochy rolled over and over, attempting to keep one turn in front of the beast's rotating muzzle. In vain she screamed and moaned, beat at the earth, felt sick; was sick. The phantom creature too, vomited, throwing her leg up in a sudden spewing. She was covered in filth, but the pain was gone, her leg was free, its muscles and joints flexing easily, the ecstasy of relief so acute that sweat ran down her forehead and she fainted.

A terrible blast of cold air, a wind of ice and snow, came howling across the hillside, tumbling rooks and ravens upon its upcurrents, setting stormclouds racing, tossing leaves and flowers and trees, knifing into Ochy's damp forehead. She woke, the cold aching her head behind her eyes. She moved; the frosty gale clawed at her exposed back. She moved again, the bitter wind driving her before it, until she found the shelter of an earth bank.

The earth rose up and swung round to engulf her. Beasts and insects gripped her limbs and hair, pulling her down into a bottomless abyss. Rocks landslided down, rained vertically upon her body. Her mouth was full of gravel. She spat it out, rinsed it with water. She drank. She drank again. She could not stop drinking. The water filled her mouth faster than she could swallow. She could not get rid of it. It flooded into her nose, her eyes, over her head, a tidal wave that swept over her body, drowning her in a deep ocean. Cataracts streamed off her skin, receded, left stranded fish squirming and flapping coldly in the small of her back. She shivered them off, shivered again. It made her feel warmer. She shivered again, shivered and shivered, enjoying the delicious warmth of her moving skin.

The warmth grew, glowing hotly. Smoke billowed around her, flames now leaping from her flesh. She clawed and beat at them, in vain; she was on fire, right through, a single, living, inextinguishable heat. She was screaming, her shrieks echoed by the laughter of the Night Ghosts and beyond them the mocking faces of the Four Great Horned Ones, gloating in her agony.

Miraculously, blessedly, cool delicate moisture sprayed upon her, washing her gently, entering her parched lips. The earth suddenly hollowed itself to make room for her hip, her elbow, her head, moulded a bed about her. The air was soft and warm, teasing her hair, drying her skin. The cave was full of warmth and light.

About her stood a circle of stones, great stones, warm grey stones joined at the top by heavy lintels, and stones the same colour as the pebble about her neck.

The Four Great Horned Ones were around her, corporeal yet indistinct figures, animal yet not beastlike, human yet not mortal, male and female, yet neither masculine nor feminine. They spoke, sometimes as one, sometimes separately.

'*We are the Four Great Horned Ones. We made all things. We are in all things. We rule all things. Each of us is greater than the other three.*'

'*I am the Ruler of Air. I blow out Fire, send Water as rain, and scatter the dust of Earth.*'

'*I am the Ruler of Fire. I eat up Air, turn Water to steam, and melt Earth.*'

'*I am the Ruler of Water. I stop you breathing Air, extinguish Fire, and dissolve Earth.*'

'*I am the Ruler of Earth. I make Air change direction, suffocate Fire and soak up Water.*'

'*Yet we cannot live without each other.*'

'*I am the Ruler of Air. Fire makes me move, Water gives me clouds, the flowers of Earth provide my fragrance.*'

'*I am the Ruler of Fire. I need Air to breathe, Water for cooking, Earth for food.*'

'*I am the Ruler of Water. I am made in Fire, carried in Air, found in Earth.*'

'*I am the Ruler of Earth. My creatures breathe Air, Fire shapes me, Water feeds my everything.*'

'*Air, Fire, Water, Earth, Rulers of all things, Makers of all things, Dwellers in all things, Supreme in all things, save one. We do not live for ever. We die and are reborn. We live and die and are recreated. We are all subjects of Time. Only Time lasts for ever. We all bow to Time.*'

The Four Great Horned Ones turned away, each facing his own direction, the Ruler of Air to the sunrise, the Ruler of Fire towards the hot lands, the Ruler of Water to the rain-bearing sunset, the Ruler of Earth towards the cold lands. All four made deep obeisance to the Great Stones about them. They turned back to Ochy. 'You hold the Secret of Time.'

All four beings bowed to her, and then Ochy felt the cave floor falling away beneath her. The rocky walls fled downwards. She was soaring upwards, her arms beating rhythmically as she climbed up through the clouds. Trees were like young nettles, and forests like grassland. Small clouds were like trees and big ones mountains.

Then Ochy saw a great plain, green and rolling, and in it was a circle of Great Stones, warm grey stones joined at the top by heavy lintels, and stones the same colour as the pebble about her neck.

Then Ochy saw a man walk up to one of the Great Stones and place his hand on its surface. The man was wearing short breeches and carried an axe. Another man appeared – Ochy did not see where he had come from – and he was wearing a long white robe and had a long white beard; he, too, stroked the stone. Then another man stood there with a shining tunic and a short skirt and a crested plume on his head. He patted the stone. His place was immediately taken by another, then another, and another, and another; men, women, and children, one after the other. Most wore strange clothes and some carried stranger weapons. There were animals too: dogs and sheep, horses and cattle, birds, insects and spiders, sitting on, leaning on, licking or sniffing at the Great Stones. And sometimes other men stood around the Great Stones, encircling them, keeping them secret, keeping the people away. Then dark clouds swept over the plain engulfing all. And when they had cleared, the Great Stones were still there, and again the people came, touching and feeling them, people of all sorts and sizes and ages. There were brown women and yellow men, and black faces, and red hair, and blue eyes, and more and more and more, all touching the Great Stones, some reverently, some foolishly, some joyfully, some sadly, the figures succeeding each other so quickly that Ochy's head whirled faster and faster and faster so that she was spinning round and round and falling down and down and down until she awoke lying face downwards on a bed of stone.

For a moment Ochy lay without moving. Just then she had no idea where she was, nor even *who* she was. She had been dreaming – that was obvious – the most real dreams she had ever had.

She sat up. The dreams fled, but their memory stayed. She would never forget them. She fingered the pebble at her throat. It was linked with a circle of Great Stones, that she now knew . . . but where? And how? She could not guess, but what she did know without any doubt at all was that the Four Great Horned Rulers of Air, Fire, Water and Earth really did exist. They had visited her in this very cave. They had tested her and they had approved her and one day they would tell her how her Stone with the Secret of Time was linked with the Great Stones she had seen in her dream. After all, she was under their special protection. And they had bowed to her. They were hers to command. With their power flowing through her, there was nothing she could not do. And with their power and aid, she would one day kill Mhirr-cuin. Everything until then, would be a preparation for that great triumph. But until then ... Ochy gave a little sniff of wry amusement ... even witches are subject to the same emotions and sensations as other mortals; and right then it was her sense of smell which was being violently assaulted.

13

Ochy wrinkled her nose. The cave smelt dreadfully foul. She sensed she was not in the same place where she had tried to go to sleep. That was over by the entrance; dim light was showing there.

Ochy crawled towards the greyness, sloshing through a puddle on the floor. Her stomach felt terribly hungry, but she was not thirsty. She could remember a dream about drowning; perhaps she had tried to lap up some water in her sleep.

Ochy pushed the flat stone aside and looked out. She could not tell if it were dawn or dusk. It felt like dawn. She struggled out and stood up.

All her aches and pains had gone, and that strange tiredness of spirit; but she was very hungry.

Yes, it was getting lighter; it must be morning.

She could examine her cuts and bruises and scratches now. The bleeding seemed to have stopped everywhere; yes, everywhere. All her hurts were healing nicely; most had cleared up completely. But she was filthy, and not only with dried mud and blood. She remembered being sick at some time. It also looked, and smelt, as though she had thoroughly fouled herself.

She was ravenously hungry, but first she must get clean. She scrambled down to the pool, then downstream along the bank until she could stand knee-deep in a safe back-eddy.

Ochy felt better when she scrambled out, slapping surplus droplets away with big leaves. She gathered and ate berries and the occasional toadstool until the sun was well up, then returned to the cave. Her Ghost had brought her safely back to the cavern from her journeyings in the Dream World. Well, if her Ghost regarded the cave as home, she would too.

First of all she made the entrance hole bigger so that she could get in and out more easily. Although the rubble was loosely packed, it was well bonded with small roots so that Ochy could remove individual stones without causing a general slide.

She tossed loose earth and plants inside the cave, then went out and brought back a pile of ferns. She used these materials to clean up the mess inside the cave, finally washing the area with vegetation soaked in one of the puddles, wiping it dry with more ferns. She took the soiled bundle outside and hurled it into the river below the cliff. The current carried it away.

'I am sorry to make you dirty, Great Ruler of Water', she called, and then went off to find a suitably springy hazel shoot. This she took back to the cave, together with a bundle of sticks. She went to and fro, gathering twigs, branches and logs, which she threw down inside the entrance. She ate ripe berries and toadstools whenever she felt like it, taking some of the larger fungi back to the cave. She worked slowly, still feeling weak and tired, and at one time sat and dozed in the warm afternoon sun before continuing her labours.

At last Ochy gathered up several armfuls of ferns and took them into the cave. With more light filtering through the enlarged hole, she could locate the place where she had woken up. It seemed dry, free from draughts, and quite comfortable. Ochy dumped the ferns there, then selected the driest and flattest log and dug away at it with a sharp stone until she had hollowed out a cup. Another jagged piece of rock drilled out a deeper, narrower hole and carved a channel from the little pothole down the side of the log.

Ochy undid the thong around her neck, placed the pebble carefully to one side, tied the thong to one end of the hazel branch, twisted it about a hard pointed stick and secured it to the other end of the hazel. Kneeling, she placed the pointed stick in the hole, steadying the log with her foot. Bearing down on the pointed stick with a stone in her left hand, she pulled the bow to and fro with the other. Several times she took the stick out, dug the hole deeper, added a pinch of sand and tried again, muttering the firemaking chant. At last there was a paint puff of smoke, the wood dust was smouldering then glowing. She introduced some dry bits of bird's nest, and then breathed carefully until a flame appeared. She fed it and had a fire going.

Once it was well alight, Ochy transferred some of the burning brands to another prepared site. This one would be her permanent fireplace, the first one merely serving to dry out the ground where she intended to sleep.

Replacing the pebble about her neck, Ochy looked around her. The flickering firelight revealed that the cave was more like a passage about two or three times her height, the floor gravelly with an occasional puddle of water.

Her heart leapt as she saw a tall white figure standing close behind, but even as her hand went to her mouth, she realised that it was only a natural column of stone. There were other much smaller pillars sticking up from the floor, while more stone spikes hung down from the roof. Just beyond the fire's glow, another frieze of stone teeth curtained off a black tunnel. She must have crawled up there from the river when she had first come to the cave.

That was enough looking about for the moment. Ochy went out foraging for more firewood and bedding ferns, occasionally picking and eating berries and nuts. As it grew dark, she sat at the mouth of the cave, twining a series of long pliable sticks together. This lattice-work she jammed into the cave entrance. It would not keep out a determined predator, but it would give her some warning of danger.

She then squatted by the fire, hacking away with a sharp stone at a short, fat log. Becoming drowsy, she ate one of the big yellow toadstools and smashed off a spiky pillar of stone to serve as a useful knife.

Last of all, Ochy looked out through her lattice gate, to see the new moon overhead. The new moon? Last night the moon had been dying; now the new moon had been born. Could she have slept in the cave all those days and nights, living through those momentous dreams? They had been like some terrible initiation ceremony. Her mother had told her that in the old days, girls had undergone an initiation ceremony when they became women. Well, she, Ochy, was now a woman, and she had certainly gone through a fearful ordeal. But that was behind her now. Ochy came back into the cave and sank down on her pile of bedding ferns.

The stone pillars flickered and danced, partnering their shadows. This cave was a place of ghosts but she had conquered the Ghosts. Ochy knew that she now possessed the power of witchcraft. But that did not mean that she could challenge Mhirr-cuin straight away. She had so much to learn first: how to use such knowledge as she already possessed; how to learn new skills with no one to teach her, and then perfect them with continual practice, until she knew without any doubt whatsoever that they would always work at her command, whatever the circumstances; how to subjugate her body to her will, so that she demonstrated her immunity to the pains suffered by other mortals; how to command the Ghosts, so that no one doubted her authority as a greater witch than Mhirr-cuin; and how to manipulate the powers of the Four Great Horned Ones to destroy Mhirr-cuin.

And one day, she would learn what her little pebble had to do with the Secret of Time and a distant circle of Great Stones. Murmuring a sleeping-chant to herself, Ochy snuggled down amongst the ferns and closed her eyes.

14

That Moon, by day and by night Ochy explored her valley. Its tangle of vegetation, fallen tree-trunks and river-foamed boulders effectively dissuaded human intrusion, while the near-vertical slopes above and behind her made unheralded approach from that direction virtually impossible. Satisfied in that respect, Ochy could concentrate on making her cave more comfortable for the winter. She laid in a store of firewood and ferns, gathered quantities of nuts and seeds, and dried toadstools by stringing them along a length of honeysuckle creeper she rigged up in the cave.

She finished hollowing out a log deep enough to hold several handfuls of water. She could now take stones from the fire and drop them in the water, sizzling it hot enough to mix with some roughly ground seeds as a lukewarm gruel. In a thicker paste, it could be griddled on a stick or on a flat stone over the fire.

She caught a hedgehog, drowned it in a pool in the cave, covered it in clay, and baked it. When cooked and broken open, the prickles came away with the rock-hard mud, while its innards had been shrivelled up by the heat.

She spent several nights sitting up in a tree balancing a heavy log over a badger's sett. The black and white striped snout snuffled out, then the thick body, dark against the soil in the moonlight. The branch pinned it to the ground. Ochy dropped on the animal, hammering at its head with a pointed stone. The beast shrugged off the fallen bough and turned away in an eye-twinkling movement. It was already disappearing down the sandy entrance to its hole. Ochy grabbed the thrusting back legs and the badger twisted round, its bloodied near-blind head snapping at her fingers. The girl let go and fell backwards down the slope. The badger vanished underground and she never saw any sign of it at that sett again. She wondered if it had gone somewhere else, or whether it had died alone in its dark burrow.

Ochy had better luck with a short hunting bow which she made, again using her neck-thong as a bow-string. Pigeon feathers from a peregrine's kill flighted her arrows with their chert heads. She tied the arrows to the body of the bow and slung the weapon across her back so that both hands were free. She had already investigated the hill above the cave by means of a circuitous route which began some distance down her little valley. She now set off up the precipitous slope, pulling herself up by holding onto tree roots and tufts of grass. She then scaled the birch-clad heights above, their leaves falling fast under a grey damp sky which brought no rain. She crawled into a tunnel of yew and holly, then doubled back.

Ochy was now looking across a level pasture, many paces in area. The grass was still green and a couple of adder flowers could still be seen. Ochy had observed roebuck here several days previously, and it seemed to be the sort of place they favoured.

She had judged right. As the grey sky pinkened and then darkened, two deer materialised at the edge of the wood.

Ochy held the bow at full stretch. Soon her arms were aching. The deer would never pass that small dark gap, where her arrowhead was just one more prickle, her eyes two more glossy gleams in a tumble of holly leaves. Then suddenly, one of the deer, a yearling, was right in front of her.

'Ruler of the Air, guide my arrow', she thought. But she had been waiting too long. Her aching fingers, her arms, her shoulders, were cramped, would not move. The arrow broke free of its own volition. She could not follow its flight: it was too dark. The deer bounded away; then fell before reaching the trees. The heavy rock she wielded to finish it off was not needed.

The carcass was much bulkier than she had expected, but she managed to drag it to the top of the slope above the cave and heaved it over.

In the daylight, Ochy laid the animal on its back and slit across its skin from one hind leg to the other, using her stone knife. Hacking off the short tail, she gradually pulled and sawed away at the tissues connecting the skin to the body. Near its chest, she half cut, half smashed off, the forelimbs and head, then tugged the skin right clear of the carcass. Finally, she slit open and completely gutted the beast.

Throughout her toil, she tried to keep the edge of the stone keen by continually pressing it with a pebble, but it was still a messy and inefficient business. Nevertheless, at the end, she felt reasonably satisfied with the results of her labours.

She was now able to enjoy several good meals from the grilled liver, lights, heart and brains of the animal. She dried the meat for the winter. The hide, softened in a pothole filled with her urine, then scraped and cleaned, made a reasonable night-time and cold-weather covering. With the sinews and gut, she prepared a bigger and more powerful bow of yew, while the bones served as a whole range of useful tools.

This whole task was not accomplished in a single day, nor even in a handful of days. There were intervals when she went out gathering vegetable food and fuel, or hunting small game.

She also penetrated the womb of the cave beyond the rocks and stone icicles she could see from her hearth near the entrance, carrying a bundle of burning twigs to reveal a landscape of phantasm beneath a caverned sky of perpetual night.

A few steps inside the cave she came to a platform of rock littered with small fragments of roof. The White Ghost of an obese woman floated upon a pool of grey stone, barring further progress in that direction. Low down to her right, she could sense and hear the presence of water, the underground river, not the still pools she could see about her, rippling from the plop of erratic drops. Behind, to her left, a narrow dark passage ran upwards through a tortuous avenue of rock pillars.

Ochy followed it uphill, past tiny grottos of stone flowers and trees of brown and green and red and orange. This route came to a dead end, and she was forced to retrace her steps.

Going downhill, she noticed that from this angle the level platform where she had stood earlier, seemed to continue beyond the White Ghost. Ochy squeezed past this apparition, her bare flesh sliding along its cold slippery belly. Clambering over and between giant boulders, she had to keep her head – and the torch – down to avoid hitting the roof. Then abruptly she was in a great hall, its walls towering up to meet without touching in the darkness. Again the roof lowered to a flat arch, this time over a sandy beach bordering the river which welled strongly from a wall of rock.

She could go no further. Again, Ochy returned the way she had come until she had passed the White Ghost. This time she scrambled to the left and made her way down a short slope to the river. She realised that this must have been where she had struggled ashore after falling from the cliff.

The blue-green river swirled past silently, remorselessly. However had she managed to swim underwater against that powerful current? Then, too, there were many twists and turns within the cave between here and the entrance; yet she could remember seeing daylight, and making for it. How had she been able to do that?

Then she realised that her very survival was proof that the Four Great Horned Ones had been with her right from the beginning.

The Ruler of Air had carried her over the ground faster than a horse could run. The Ruler of Water had cushioned her fall from the high cliff. The Ruler of Earth had given her strength to forge against the river into the safety of the cave. And the Ruler of Fire had shown her the light to head for in the darkness.

Ochy gave thanks to each of the Four Great Horned Ones and then to them all.

She peered across the river. She could just make out another beach there, but as far as she could tell it looked as though it led to a dead end. Her gaze came back across to the rocky wall that blocked off the stream flowing from the other sandy cave. She looked down – and started back in horror.

The living rock beside her had a straight line cut in it, a small square platform, another, and another, a flight of steps leading up from the river to – a second jump of terror – a face, an enormous face, with a great nose, and open mouth, the eyes invisible beneath brows arching backwards with evil slant.

The air was suddenly chill. Ochy felt her skin pimpling, the tiny hairs on her body and limbs rising. Who was this subterranean demon who had been changed to stone? Had it made these steps so that it could walk abroad whenever it came alive again? Was this the Ghost of Darkness?

'Are you the Ghost of Darkness?' Her voice was fearful, tiny.

There was an answering growl from somewhere deep within the mountain.

Ochy was seized by fear. It fed upon her innards, glowed, spread through her body. Fear was exhilarating. Fear was ecstasy.

Boldly she walked up the steps, pausing at each tread to savour the terror within her as the demon glowered at her and dark forces played hide-and-seek with the flickering flame in her hand. A bat flew overhead.

Standing face to face with the malignant being, she raised her left leg and closed her left eye, while her right hand presented the torch towards the mocking face. She whispered quietly so that no one else should hear. 'I, Ochy, the Deep One, The Eternal One, Witch of this Cave, Witch of the People of the Bear, Destroyer of Mhirr-cuin, Ruler of the Rulers of Air, Fire, Water, and Earth, Guardian of the Stone with the Secret of Time, do command you, the Ghost of Darkness, to obey me in all things.' She paused and went on. 'Henceforth, you are my slave. When I desire, you will walk abroad, then return and tell me all things. Do you obey me?'

There was a moan from the cave. The monstrous shape in front of her grew, filled the whole cavern. The flaming twigs smouldered and went out. The river behind her swirled and the cavern roared. The blackness was a quagmire of sensation. Ochy felt giddy with power and fear.

'I, Ochy, Witch of this Cave, command you. Obey me, Ghost of Darkness, or I shall banish you from this cave for ever. I shall condemn you to a life in the light of the sun.'

There was a whimper from somewhere inside the rocks themselves.

'That is good,' came Ochy's whisper. 'I have relented. I shall only send you forth at night.'

Ochy lowered her foot, opened her left eye and raised the branch above her head. Immediately it blazed into life again. The face before her shed its mocking smile and resumed its mask of stone.

'I do not fear your tricks, Ghost of Darkness,' asserted Ochy. 'I do not fear your power. I do not fear your darkness. I do not fear anything.'

Without taking her eyes from the stone figure, Ochy walked backwards without faltering down the steps, until her heels overhung the river. Swirling wavelets flicked at her skin. She tossed the flaming torch over her shoulder. The darkness came with a hiss and she walked unerringly back to her hearth near the entrance.

Later, Ochy thought about the full extent of the caverns she had explored. She seemed to feel more at home within the mountain than near the daylight. The shadowy pinnacles and moving rocks, the pools of water reflecting sparkling colours, the secret, eerie world of the Ghosts, that was the right place to practise her witchcraft. She could learn the steps of magick dances in the sandy chamber.

Presently, Ochy found a warm, dry spot among the boulders in the Witching Cave. She made it larger, moved food, tools and bedding there, and made a homely blaze. She stockpiled firewood there and in the Dancing Cave. As she squatted by the fire, scraping away at the roebuck's hide, she would glance at the White Ghost and the Ghost of Darkness, smiling affectionately at her fellow tenants of the dark.

15

Outside, the last leaves were being swept from the tossing boughs by salt-laden gales. Stiff-winged, the gulls raced up the valley, or hung with quivering feather just clear of the cliff above the cave. Thick clouds masked the top of the ridge. Rain lashed the hillside, rivulets poured from bedraggled moss, brooks ran in the bark crevices of mighty trees, streams flowed through limestone fissures. In the cave the river rose, was blocked, vented its wrath in unseen caverns, roaring and clashing. Breaking from its petrine prison, it flailed at the valley slopes, uprooting trees and ripping down banks.

The winds died, changed, died again, blew strong once more. The frost came, pretty and delicate at first then hardening its heart until the earth petrified without whiteness. Mud was as hard as flint, leaves brittle as fine crystal. The rocks themselves split, clattered bouncing down the cliff, shattering the thin ice suspended bridge-like over the shrunken river. From the faraway cold lands, redwings came to the ridge, searching for food. The cold followed them, they found no food and they died in their flocks. The foxes and martens and wildcats, owls and crows scavenged their corpses until the snow shrouded them. Small flakes first, then larger ones, whirling upward in freak air currents by the cliff. Prints in the snow, blood on the snow, all forgotten under more snow out of a green sky. The cliff armed itself with a belt of ice daggers. The sun came out, shone boldly for a few moments at midday, then shrank beyond the skyline again. The merry droplets grew morose, froze harder.

Then the body-aching bitter cold of the thaw. Noises everywhere, crack of icicles, swoosh of snow slides, tinkle of streams where no stream had flowed before, the swelling voice of the river.

The wind came warmer now. Again it brought the sea smell. There was rain and more rain. The lapwings tumbled up on the ridge, the geese and duck departed, the deer and wolves were on the move. A chiffchaff came to the valley. There were snowdrops and daffodils, primroses and catkins. Leaf buds and yellow butterflies appeared. Blackbird and thrush and chaffinch were singing. Each morning a crescendo of birdsong dinned the valley, thickening with fresh greenery. Now drifts of may and elder whitened the hillside. The cuckoos came, male and female, calling and bubbling. Last of all the screeching swifts.

Each summer morn, the valley mist lightened, drifted across a pale yellow disc, lifted and vanished. While he climbed, the sun shone from an empty sky. After midday he was joined by clouds of snow, whose eye-straining whiteness heightened the brilliant blue of heaven, a blue that lower down faded, met and hazed into the earth itself. Sometimes the small white cloudlets danced and merged, boiling upwards into trunkless trees of foam. When these monsters met, they clashed as enemies, roaring and ripping at each other. In mortal combat, they trampled the earth beneath, uprooting trees and shattering oaks. Sometimes their nebulous hostility hung over the ridge for days on end, threatening violence for so long that their eventual flame and thunder came as an exhilarating release of pent-up emotion.

Then the days of sun and heat would return, but the birdsong would be over, the cuckoo silent, and the swifts gone. The leaves reddened, the deer were on the move and the winter approaching, gripping the countryside, then passing on and giving place to spring.

Ochy had always watched the things about her. Indeed, she had been encouraged to do so by her father's hunting skills and by her mother's witch lore. But now she was no mere spectator, nor even a user, of the seasons. Now she lived the seasons. She knew the cold wind and the hot sun, the rain in the air and the mist from the sea. She came to know what the deer on the hill or the pigeon on the hazel would do when it too experienced these sensations. She came to know exactly where to lie in wait with bow and arrow, or where to set a snare, just by glancing at the ground. She came to know exactly where to find herbs and plants and toadstools whenever she needed them, without searching for them. The whole of nature lived in her; the Four Great Horned Rulers of Air, Fire, Water and Earth surrounded her; their gifts were hers for the taking and she never forgot to thank the Four Great Horned Ones whenever she accepted those gifts.

Ochy now enjoyed such bounty that she did not have to spend all her days trying to stay alive. Now she had time to think about her witchcraft. Sometimes she squatted outside in the sunshine, sometimes stared into the fire, or an especially crystal pool. She hoped the water would show her what Mhirr-cuin was doing, or where she would find the circle of Great Stones. But there were no present visions or future portents, just her own dark eyes frowning

71

back at her, framed by thick masses of black hair tumbling about her browned shoulders. The reflection showed a faint ring of black strands around her nipples, and a line of thin hairs just visible between her nose and her upper lip. All the women of her Tribe had hair on their limbs and their body, but was this facial hair a true sign that she was a witch?

Often she stood before the Ghost of Darkness, returning its stare as motionless and as impassively as if she too were made of rock. Sometimes she chose a spot where icy water trickled down upon her. Sometimes she pressed a jagged piece of flint into her flesh or deliberately placed the full weight of her feet upon splintered bones. How long she held her tortured stance, she had no way of telling. At first, she broke away with a cry of pain. But, as the seasons passed, Ochy willed herself to ignore the agony until it became mere discomfort, and eventually could be dismissed altogether. Sometimes she achieved this by numbing her mind with monotonous chants. On other occasions, she chewed ivy-leaves, which seemed to give her boundless physical energy. She could feel it welling up within her, beating against the prison of her body, resisting the self-inflicted hurts, and threatening to burst forth with uncontrollable violence – a violence only held in check by her rigid determination to remain absolutely motionless until she had completed some chant or until she had finished reciting her list of Mhirr-cuin's crimes.

For when all the other ways of concentrating her thoughts had failed, Ochy remembered Mhirr-cuin. She remembered how Mhirr-cuin had mocked Vhi-vhang's magick and had then organised the sacrificial death of the old witch. Now, Ochy realised that that act had been merely the culmination of a campaign of persecution against Vhi-vhang. Ochy remembered every insult the red-haired woman had ever uttered, every sneering glance the girl had made, every physical assault the child might have contemplated, every dribbling snarl that had come from Mhirr-cuin's lips as a baby instead of the anticipated cooing smile. Even Mhirr-cuin's apparent kindnesses, Ochy now realised, were but sham friendship, calculated to catch the recipients off-guard or bind them to return a disadvantageous favour in the future. Ochy could remember every one. And as she listed them in her mind, each one became clearer with each recitation, each one reminding her of fresh villainies, until Ochy's hatred boiled within her, driving out all sense of pain from whatever self-imposed ordeal she was then experiencing.

And with the hatred came desire for revenge, for killing Mhirr-cuin, annihilating everything she had touched, humiliating her in the sight of the Tribe and in the eyes of all peoples. Standing before the Ghost of Darkness, Ochy vowed that she would not rest until she had sacrificed to the Four Great Horned Ones, Mhirr-cuin and everything belonging to her, everything – except perhaps Mhirr-ling. Perhaps he was meant to be special for her. Perhaps his and Ochy's own destiny were linked in some way which did not involve the death of one at the other's hands. Perhaps Ochy was destined to be Witch to his Artzan. Perhaps she was destined to help him find that lost kingdom.

But before any of that could come to pass. Mhirr-ling would have to be rescued from Mhirr-cuin, freed from her influence over him. And to do that, Mhirr-cuin's magick must be demonstrated as feeble, her power must be seen to be defeated, and Mhirr-cuin herself killed – and once again Ochy found herself standing before the Ghost of Darkness, renewing her vow of sacificial vengeance.

But no other sacrifice would she make. This too she promised. To dedicate something which did not belong to Mhirr-cuin, would demean the value of the Great Sacrifice whenever that were made. And anything sacrificed afterwards, could not hope to match that Great Oblation.

So, although Ochy killed for food – apologising to and thanking the Four Great Horned Ones before and after each hunt – she never killed for any other reason. Accordingly, when she found little injured animals, she brought them back to the cave, quieted them, tended them, and tried out the various recipes and potions she dragged up out of her memory.

Ochy remembered that each one had its own special chant which had to be repeated a particular number of times. If certain words were left out, or extra ones inserted, or if the rhyme were not said the exact frequency, then the concoction was not ready, or was overdone, or was obviously spoiled. Ochy's memory was good, and she was training it to be better, but she found it very difficult to count and remember how many times she had gone through a chant. Still, she was able to bring some of her healing remedies to fruition, and these she tried out on injured animals, partly in preparation for the day when she would need to use these skills on the sick and injured of the Tribe, and partly because she became fond of the little cripples. One or two of her successes stayed with her, but most made their own way as soon as they could, leaving her lonely and a little disappointed.

She did not feel like eating the invalids that died and did not want to dispose of their little corpses simply by throwing them outside. It came to her that each creature ought to return to whichever one of the Four Great Horned Ones had ruled its life.

A duckling which had been swept over and battered by a waterfall, failed to respond to treatment and very soon died. The little ball of fluff was placed in the crevice of a piece of bark and floated down the river until out of sight.

A stoat, its hindquarters savagely torn by some larger predator, was still a most fiery beast and refused to be handled. When it died, Ochy cremated its body on a pile of brushwood and placed the ashes in a hollow log which she then buried in the ground.

A tiny mouse was buried in the earth with proper ceremony, but a swift was very much a creature of the air. Ochy found one that had been stranded amongst some ferns, been unable to take off again, and had thrashed about until it had injured itself. It was too proud to accept help from any earthbound mortal and was soon dead. Again Ochy made a funeral pyre, but this time gathered the ashes together and threw them high into the air. The summer breeze took them and for a moment a black crescent moon wheeled and dipped against the blue of the warm sky.

Ochy added to her knowledge of animal bodies by examining the carcasses of quarry killed for food. She had plenty of bone implements now, and so she set out whole skeletons, seeing how the bones were linked, each one contributing to the strength and movement of the living creature.

These observations also helped her to make good likenesses of animals and people when she practised magick painting on stone or hide. Over and over again – until she could work with her eyes shut – she fashioned shapes from clay or wove bodies from plant stems, making fur and hair from moss or grass. Most of all she practised making a poppet of Mhirr-cuin. If she destroyed it ceremonially, at the height of her witch-powers, Mhirr-cuin would die. But she would have to see Mhirr-cuin again to make sure that it looked right, and she would have to obtain something of Mhirr-cuin's to add to the doll. An improper poppet would have no magick power, so Ochy always got rid of the thing without using it in any spells.

Inside the farthest cave Ochy danced, mimicking the high-stepping deer, the proud-walking bustard, the belly-sliding snake. The sand retained her footprints and she compared their regularity with the tracks left in snow or mud or soft earth outside. With outstretched neck and beating arms she became a migrating goose, with stomach thrust forward, a pregnant woman. She took on the stealth of the hunter, the labour of the farmer, the patience of the horsetamer, the frenzy of the copulator. She milked imaginary cows, was delivered of imaginary babies, fashioned imaginary tools, and congratulated herself as imaginary corn grew higher and higher until it could be reaped with an imaginary sickle. Each of these was governed by its own rhythm of time, and in each she mimed her gratitude to the Four Great Horned Rulers of Air, Fire, Water and Earth.

16

As the seasons passed, Ochy found herself venturing further and further into her cave system. She discovered no rock that resembled her little pebble, but she did find several narrow crevices that led into other passages. Most of them climbed and doubled back, leading to hidden ledges overlooking the pool at the bottom of the cliff. A few tunnels proved to be back ways into once-open caves whose entrances had been completely blocked by falls of rock. Some of these contained animal skeletons, sometimes singly, sometimes jumbled together in an untidy ossuary. Ochy also found flakes of flint and a number of stone tools, so very ancient and yet still perfectly usable. She took a good collection of arrowheads and scrapers back to her own cave, together with the best skulls of long-gone deer and bear, plus several beasts quite unknown to her. She arranged them in suitable array in her Witching Cave: three bear skulls, a giant wildcat with teeth as long as Ochy's hands, a couple of creatures that had been half-wolf, half-cat with massive jaws, and a range of antlered deer. The centrepiece was a huge stag's skull, its palmate antlers spanning a distance over twice Ochy's own length. She gave each skull its own name, to be whispered secretly, quite separate from a public title which she spoke openly.

From one of the antlered skulls, she hung her necklaces, for by now she had made several as company for the Stone with the Secret of Time. For one, she selected a dark, almost black piece of stone, and a contrasting tooth from one of her kills. She made holes in both of them using the same bow-drill technique as if she were making fire. She let these two beads slide freely, whizzing them apart and then together again with a satisfying click. Ochy thought of them as Light and Dark, Hot and Cold, Here and There.

She felt that she ought to honour the Four Great Horned Ones in some way, and searched for several appropriate bits of flat stone. She drilled and chipped away at them until she had four triangular pieces, with elongated sides representing a pair of horns. She drilled their central holes and suspended them in a row, so that they lay side by side flat upon her chest.

Ochy's most ambitious effort contained one bear's tooth for each moon from springtime to springtime, a total of two handfuls plus three. In fact, the number three kept recurring in her mind and her last necklace comprised two big pebbles flanking a much smaller one. She told herself that these represented the three stages of Time: Now was in the middle, separating the huge weight of Past and Future on either side.

Ochy came to wear all five necklaces when casting spells or practising magick dances. She found her fingers straying to them, easy remembrancers of the number of times a chant should be repeated or a circle perambulated. At all other times, Ochy removed her necklaces. This was partly to prevent them being lost or falling into the clutches of evil ghosts. It was also because once, while exploring underground, she had slipped down a precipitous slope, and the leather thong carrying the Stone with the Secret of Time had looped around a small pinnacle of rock, almost strangling her, and Ochy had no wish to repeat that particular experience.

It was on that very expedition that she had entered a small round chamber, floored with soft white sand. Lying on or projecting from the powdery drifts of dust, were several handfuls of highly polished, translucent pebbles, brown and red, yellow and green, black, blue, multi-hued, glowing, flashing, changing colour in the light of the burning branch. Most were quite small, but some were as big as a starling's egg. These were of ice stone: she could see right through them, the cave walls and the torch flame changing shape, growing nearer and then more distant according to the way she held them up to her eye. Her largest treasure was bigger than a swan's egg, with shifting layers of grey-brown smoke suspended in transparent yet opaque layers of milky whiteness. When Ochy took them all back to her home cave, she soon learned that this big pebble had a curious affinity with the Stone with the Secret of Time. It seemed to reflect back the bluestone, then absorb it, so that its image remained caught in the opaque crystal after the two stones had been moved apart. Now the bluestone image became twinned, like a double-headed axe, now it was elongated, a long pile of stones different from the bluestone in colour. The image became just one of those rocks, a skull, her mother's face, grey-brown smoke in a big, milky-white, opaque, translucent pebble. Ochy put it down with reverence: it was a scrying-stone. She began pondering over what she had seen and what she might yet see in it.

Later she tried to use some of the other shining pebbles in

77

another necklace, but they proved too polished to hole and too hard to drill. It was while she was trying to work on one of the transparent ice-stones that she noticed a spot of white light moving across her knee. She wondered if something was in the stone and held it up towards the sun for a better look. The needleprick of light made her drop her arm with a cry and clap her other hand over her eyelid.

Ochy soon got over the surprise and began experimenting with the crystal. She felt the warmth of the white spot on the back of her hand as though it had drawn the sun down out of the sky. Within a few moments her hand felt as if it were burning and she pulled it away involuntarily. She tried it on a dry leaf; it smouldered and burst into flame. These ice crystals could make fire! Ochy was delighted with this discovery – 'Thank you, Ruler of the Fire.' It would make life much easier: no more working away with the bow-drill.

It did not take much exasperating practice to learn that the pebbles would not make fire in the dark, in moonlight, or even on a cloudy day – only in bright sunshine. And there was certainly no sunshine underground. But that did not matter. By now, Ochy had lost all fear of the dark – except when the old moon died and the night sky was bereft of stark light. She did not worry about it in advance, and each time she was surprised by the terrible lassitude which crept over her as the thin crescent in the heavens melted.

By the next night, all her plans had been abandoned. Even squatting made her feel tired, and she just sat or lay, weary and depressed, not bothering to wash, ignoring food, and hardly caring about the fire. She made a compress of dried woundwort, but the smell of blood lured a multitude of demons, gnawing at her belly, hammering inside her head, laughing at her, mocking her loneliness, her failure, her weakness itself. She hid her face under her skin cloaks, covered the whole of her body, but still the evil ones sought her out. Their ghostly fingers, now ice-cold, now red-hot, chased sleep away, prevented reasoned thought. She wept with despair, moaned with tiredness, and screamed with frustration. Her only comfort was the pebble at her throat. She fondled it continually, her fingers becoming smooth as they polished the Stone with the Secret of Time.

Then, suddenly, she would feel better, the demons would flee, and she would sleep, to awaken happy, determined, and strong. She looked outside the cave. There was the new moon sailing across the sky. All her fears were gone – until the next time. But perhaps the next time she would be ready for them, would overcome them, ignore them.

And so, each new moon, Ochy forgot her temporary fear of the dark, the queer rock shapes, the strange noises, the shadow ghosts that flitted just beyond the torchlight. And each new moon she set out again to explore the unknown caverns without fear. And one night, in one of the most familiar parts of her own home cave, she found a narrow crack that broadened at its top to form the shape of a double-headed axe. That crevice, just like the one she had seen in the scrying-stone, led her right into the heart of the hill.

17

Ochy soon realised that this series of caves was much more extensive and intricate than anything she had previously encountered. But she was determined to continue her underground search for rocks like her pebble with the Secret of Time and for whatever the scrying-stone intended her to find.

She therefore piled bundles of brushwood as she went, going back for more at each stage of her exploration. She wrapped them in skin to keep them dry, sometimes carrying them, sometimes dragging them through tortuous rifts by means of a thong attached to her ankle, while her fingertips groped the body-wide darkness ahead of her. In that maze below the mountain, promising pathways often proved dead ends, and then she had to retreat, somehow manipulating the firewood back the way she had come. She frequently regretted the effort involved in moving the branches, twigs and fire-bearing hollow logs. But that regret soon changed to pleasant comfort as she squatted chewing ivy-leaves before a drying fire, or held a flaming brand aloft to reveal a yawning chasm in an otherwise smooth downhill slope. And she positively rejoiced in the hard-won subjugation of her body which enabled her to withstand the rigours of the cold and damp beneath the ground.

Ochy took her time, with plenty of breaks for hunting and foraging in the open air, and for practising her witchcraft in her home cavern. But eventually there came a night when she left the Witching Cave and knew that at last, something was going to happen.

Probably the most difficult part was right at the beginning – her traverse of the double-axe slit. She had to wriggle sideways through the constricted, tortuous crevice, arms at her side and palms pressed against the rock. Calcite fingernails responded by squeezing into breast and buttock, scratching every round of soft flesh. The roof of the slit came lower. Knowing what was ahead, she began to angle her body to one side so that eventually she was sliding along on her hip. One hand reached out, while the other swam along the wall. Then her groping fingers found emptiness ahead, flanked by the familiar shapes of two rounded boulders, and she knew that she was through.

Ochy untied the thong attached to her ankle and gently tugged at it hand over hand until she felt the thin bundle of twigs. She lit them from the fire-bearing hollow log that accompanied them. Beside her was a heap of large bundles, each one containing several separate skin-wrapped bunches of firewood. Ochy swung one of these packs onto her back and set off through the mountain.

It was easy going, for the floor was dry and sandy, the gently curving passageway high and wide. Even at its narrowest, it only slowed her jogtrot to a walk. What had confused her original explorations had been the huge number of dead-end tunnels. At every junction, the wider, less steep passage that went straight ahead, had led nowhere. It was the narrower path slightly off to one side that had invariably proved the right one to take. But now Ochy knew which way to go and made good progress, often passing a stockpile of wood which she had dumped on an earlier visit.

Occasionally she ducked her head under a low ledge of rock. Sometimes her feet pattered across bare rock or were pricked by sharp gravel. Once she splashed through a stream that flowed from the rock, along its own shallow channel and into the other wall. There were chambers full of stone beasts and figures, plants and flowers. The colours vibrated in her torchlight. At one place the tunnel headed towards the grinning mouth of a human skull. Ochy clambered over the lower jaw of boulder teeth and entered a huge cavern.

The roof was completely lost to view, occasional icicles of stone seeming to hang from the very darkness itself. Tree trunks of white rose up towards the suspended spikes. Some met; delicate tracery and massive pillars together carrying the whole weight of the mountain.

Ochy waded calf-deep through waves of fine dust which lay in great drifts of yellow snow. The air here tasted stale and fusty, even without the clouds of fine particles which Ochy scuffled up, to writhe around the stone pillars and hang in heavy layers. She hawked deep in her throat and spat out the muck.

She pressed on towards a pit at one side of the great chamber. It was waist-deep in mud, but she plunged in, ducked under a rock and came up in another tunnel. This one was muddy, but she sloshed along without pausing. The miry trap was repeated after some distance and a little later she had to get down on hands and

81

knees. It was not too difficult to crawl: she could still keep the torch alight, nor did she have to remove her pack.

When she stood upright again, the passage bent sharply and then became very high and narrow. It was drier here, except for a series of potholes. These were always full of fresh, drinkable water without any obvious source of supply. Ochy jumped across them, her toes gripping the slippery rims. At last this tunnel ended as it had begun, with a crawl, and then two passages waist-deep in mud.

Now her way was upward, through a sharply twisting tunnel of rock ledges and boulders, with mud and grit and jagged stones underfoot. Two streams appeared, one tumbling from a mouth of stumpy teeth to join another welling up from under the boulders. From now on, Ochy was continually in and out of potholes, with waterfalls spraying her from her shoulders down. Miraculously, her torch still burned, illuminating an apparently bottomless pool. She scrambled around it and walked on up a waterslide, her knees pressing against the icy current. Columns of darkness pierced the roof, untouched by any sky light. The tunnel bent sharply to the left and then right again, back to the left and back to the right again, and again, its twisting further convoluted by the boulders that prevented any easy progress.

A darker passage led Ochy to a tumbled mass of fallen pillars, stone trees cast down by some subterranean gale. She clambered up this log-jam, hearing the river thundering far below. She felt one petrified trunk move and roll beneath her slipping feet, heard another creak. The first time that had occurred, her heart was in her mouth, but nothing had happened then or on subsequent occasions.

Folds of pure white stone covered the tunnel sides as Ochy crawled upwards. A vertical cliff was scaled by means of a pile of giant boulders.

The woman strode on until she reached another precipice whence a waterfall hurled itself down into a black pit that effectively blocked her path. She jammed her burning brand into a crevice so that it was clear of the falling spray. Narrow hand- and footholds were followed by sturdy projections. Arm and leg muscles protesting, she reached the top, untied her bundle, took out her fire-log and kindled warmth in one of the piles of brushwood she had managed to place here before. This was the furthest limit of her previous exploration, yet without knowing why, she sensed that she was not too distant from daylight. She squatted there chewing some of the ivy leaves she had brought for sustenance. They were never filling, but always seemed to give her boundless energy, and sharpen her senses.

The path was now dry again, although folds of brown rock dripped from the narrow roof. Ochy squeezed past drifts of petrine snow and clambered over rooted boulders. Now she had no eyes for the marvels about her. She was only aware that her torchflame was wavering. Then she, too, felt the current of air. She stopped. It seemed to be coming straight down, just where she was having to bend double under the low roof.

She fancied she could see . . . what could she see?

Ochy retreated around a couple of corners and wedged the torch safely in a crack. Feeling her way back to the place where she had stopped, she looked up. She could see light, daylight.

'Thank you, Ruler of Earth for bringing me through. Thank you, all of you, O Four Great Horned Ones.'

Ochy reached up, got her arms through the hole and hauled her body up. She was in a sort of burrow. There was just room for her to kneel. Behind her – she backed carefully round to face it – was a lacy network of twigs and grey light. Carefully and quietly, she crawled towards the spiky hawthorn and listened.

Someone was speaking.

18

'You are sure your people know what they have to do, Ahmorc?' said the voice.

The other man sounded irritated by the question. 'Do you think the People of the Wolf are fools, Mhirr-ling?'

Mhirr-ling? Ochy could not believe her ears. She had not heard another human voice since she had fallen over the cliff; since she had cowered in a hole in the ground; since she had listened to Mhirr-ling's calls as he and Hpe-gnorr searched for her and Tschi-tschan. How many winters ago was that? A handful? Or more? Or less? Now she was hiding in another hole in the ground and the first human voice she had heard was Mhirr-ling's.

She had not recognised it at first. The voice was deeper, the tone more precise, the opinions more authoritative, but the speaker had been addressed as Mhirr-ling and it was most unlikely that there were two people with the same name living up on this ridge. And now that she knew who it was, she could recognise certain cadences and accents in his speech.

Ochy marvelled at how time seemed to move in such strange circles, predetermined, yet mutable by human agency.

Suppose she had found her way through the caves last autumn? Suppose, on this journey, she had rested a moment longer – or hurried a few paces more quickly? She would have arrived just as the other person was speaking; and then Mhirr-ling's voice would not have been the first she had heard on her return to human kind. For this omen certainly seemed to indicate the end of her isolation from human affairs.

Not that Ochy was prepared to burst forth from her hiding place in rapturous greeting. In fact, she felt excessively wary of such reunion.

In her lonely cave, she had occasionally pondered on how she would help Mhirr-ling find and win his lost kingdom. But all she had to encourage such vain speculation was her mother's vague imaginings about linked destinies. Ochy's last encounter with Mhirr-ling hardly indicated such promise. Then, he had been trying to kill her, or capture her so that she could be sacrificed –

just as he was even now arranging a sacrifice to the Four Great Horned Ones.

For while one part of her mind was reviewing her relationship with Mhirr-ling, she was also listening to the conversation of the two men outside her hiding-hole.

'No, Ahmorc, the People of the Wolf are not fools.' Something in Mhirr-ling's intonation reminded Ochy of Htorr-mhirr's conciliatory manner.

'But this is the first time your people have taken part in one of the great ceremonies. You will be joining the People of the Bear and the People of the Beaver. If just one of your people stumbles, the ceremony will not please the Four Great Horned Ones; the rains will be withheld during the growing season and the harvest will fail. Then the others will blame your people. They will call upon Mhirr-cuin to search out the offender and punish him – or her,' added Mhirr-ling.

'Why would Mhirr-cuin's Ghost have to search out the culprit? If one of my people stumbles we will all see it. He – or she – can be punished immediately. The Four Great Horned Ones will see the punishment and not withhold their bounty. So my people could not all be blamed.' Ahmorc sounded indignant.

'One of your people could stumble in their heart without missing their footing. And who will then know until the harvest fails?'

'The same can be said of your people, or the People of the Beaver.' Ahmorc was half-protest, half-apology.

'That will not matter.' A new note of ruthlessness had entered Mhirr-ling's speech. 'Ever since Mhirr-cuin became the Witch of the People of the Bear, the rains have come during the planting and growing seasons, with sunshine at time of harvest. Our animals have multiplied, our people have grown fat. We have even prospered when trading with the Marsh People. Mhirr-cuin's witchcraft has done all this. If this pattern is broken, then the People of the Bear and the People of the Beaver will say that it is the fault of the newcomers. They will demand that one of them must be punished.

'But that is harsh.'

'Yes, the rule of Mhirr-cuin is harsh.' Mhirr-ling spoke coldly, then he sighed. 'Look, I only tell you these things so that you know what *may* happen. There may not be any punishments; just the ceremonial sacrifice. But Htorr-mhirr, our Artzan, has ordered that all Mhirr-cuin's words must be obeyed. And I carry out the wishes of Htorr-mhirr. For where the Artzan leads, the people follow. That is our custom.'

'Is it also your custom for the Witch of the Tribe to command your Chief – what you call your Artzan or Shepherd?'

'No, it is not,' Mhirr-ling retorted sharply, then relented. 'Well, I suppose it seems so now. It used to be the custom for the Witch to assist the Artzan, but be in obedience to him. My sister altered that. Artzan and Witch, Man and Woman, are still separate, but now the Artzan obeys the Witch. Perhaps it is because my father is an old man. Perhaps if I were to be Artzan, I should . . .' He paused, 'No, perhaps not. I suppose I should still obey my Mhirr-cuin, for my sister is always right. She says "Do this!" and it succeeds. If I say, "I will do this," and she says "No good will come of that!" then it fails. But I do not like being told what to do all the time, for I too have ideas; and sometimes I wonder "Can any one person know all the thoughts of the Four Great Horned Ones? Are they really angry and hungry all the time? Do they really rejoice in our unhappiness and fear?" Mhirr-cuin says they do, and unless we do as she commands, then there will be even more unhappiness and fear. I just wish that I could see more smiling faces around me.'

'There are no smiling faces when bellies are empty,' declared Ahmorc. 'For many seasons the crops in our fields have failed. The People of the Wolf hunger in the good times: they die in the bad times. So we have besought Mhirr-cuin to magick our crops. So we have come here this day to join in your crop-magicking ceremony.'

'You know that there can be no turning back? You know that you must accept the rule of Mhirr-cuin in all things, or else she will curse your crops for ever?' asked Mhirr-ling. There must have been some sign of assent, for he went on, 'Are your people ready to provide the sacrifice, if they are called upon to do so?'

'They will do so willingly,' asserted Ahmorc, 'for it will be a great honour.'

'Whatever it is?' cautioned Mhirr-ling.

'It is better that one dies, so that the whole tribe may live,' was the dignified reply.

Mhirr-ling changed the subject abruptly. 'Tell me again –' He must have noticed something in Ahmorc's expression – for the last time: what will happen during the ceremony.'

'I will tell you, for the last time.' Ahmorc was nearing exasperation. 'All the men of the three tribes will plough this field and sow the seed. Then all the women who have borne children will cover the seed with earth. The women will be led by my woman. She has borne me five children. She is a full woman,' he added proudly, then enquired delicately, 'You have no woman? And no children – no sons?'

'No, I have no woman.' Mhirr-ling did not seem ashamed about it: but neither did he pursue the matter, instead returning to the original topic of conversation. 'Tell me about the sacrifice.'

'The Four Great Horned Ones will send one of the Ghosts to carry off the victim they have selected,' answered Ahmorc.

'When does that happen?'

'That is not for us to know.'

'And who is the victim?'

'That is not for us to know either.' Ahmorc sounded shocked. 'It is not right for us to know the ways of the Four Great Horned Ones.'

'That is true. I see that you have remembered well the words of Mhirr-cuin. I hope you will also remember that there must be no interference with the sacrifice, however it is carried out. Mhirr-cuin insists on that,' said Mhirr-ling.

'Will Mhirr-cuin be present at the ceremony?' Ahmorc enquired.

'No. She will remain within her tent talking to the Four Great Horned Ones. But her Ghost will walk abroad to watch us.'

'Um . . . is her Ghost watching us now?' Ahmorc sounded nervous.

'I expect so.' Mhirr-ling was casual about supernatural observation. 'Mhirr-cuin already knows my thoughts for I have spoken such words to her. The Artzan of a tribe – and sometimes I feel that I am more the leader of my people than my father – must be able to speak of such matters to the Witch of the tribe, especially if she is his sister. Why should they fear each other? But I have said nothing to anyone else, lest the people's faith be shaken.'

'Then why speak thus to me, Mhirr-ling?'

'Because, Ahmorc, you are the Chief of the People of the Wolf. I want you to know everything – bad as well as good. I want you to be certain in your own mind that what you are doing, is best for your tribe.'

'It is. I have no doubt.'

'That is another reason why I have spoken to you. You have no doubts. I want to believe all the time. And most of the time I *do* believe. But sometimes I doubt. Sometimes I wonder if Mhirr-cuin commands what is best for her rather than what is best for the Tribe, or even for the Four Great Horned Ones.'

'That cannot be,' exclaimed Ahmorc. 'Mhirr-cuin would never be so selfish. She alone knows what is best for us all. She alone can interpret the wishes of the Four Great Horned Ones and devise such sacrifices as will persuade them to work for us. You must never doubt her.'

'I am glad to hear you say so, Ahmorc. Your faith has chased away my doubts. It has been good to talk to you, for you are the Chief of your Tribe, and you know a leader's lonely thoughts. And even if you were not a chief, you are still easy to talk to. You are a good friend, Ahmorc.'

The voices moved away as feet scrabbled on the slope above the burrow. They came louder as four muscular legs passed Ochy's curtain of thorns. The voices died away altogether.

19

Ochy had learned to be patient. Besides, she had much to consider. Mhirr-cuin was now not only the Witch of the People of the Bear, but also of the Beaver and the Wolf, two other small communities living on the long ridge of hills above the Great Marsh. She had achieved total dominion over her father, Htorr-mhirr, over this Chief Ahmorc, and presumably also over the so-far unnamed Chief of the People of the Beaver. Only Mhirr-ling denied her absolute allegiance – and that was only in secret.

Evidently, his doubts sprang from two sources: his own affable nature which preferred happy people and found human sacrifice repugnant; and his dislike at being told what to do all the time by his sister – especially as she was always right.

So, if Ochy could present the Four Great Horned Ones to Mhirr-ling as she herself knew them; not as bloodlusting tyrants, but as friendly dispensers of universal bounty . . . what would Mhirr-ling do? If Ochy could demonstrate that Mhirr-cuin was not always right, that she did not have command over the Four Great Horned Ones, that her magick was not all-powerful; how would Htorr-mhirr, Ahmorc and the rest of the people react?

Would they immediately transfer their allegiance from Mhirr-cuin to Ochy? If so, could Ochy use those followers in her search for the Stone with the Secret of Time, and in the quest for Htorr-mhirr's lost kingdom? That would certainly be a working-out of her and Mhirr-ling's combined destinies – although there had been no mention of that in the conversation she had overheard. So presumably, Htorr-mhirr had still said nothing about that quest.

But suppose, even after Ochy had demonstrated that Mhirr-cuin's magick was feeble, that the people's blind faith still acknowledged Mhirr-cuin's authority, so that they seized Ochy and sacrificed her to the Four Great Horned Ones?

It was still not yet time for a confrontation. Ochy wanted to know more about Mhirr-cuin and her magick, measure her own skills against her rival's. Only then would the time be right.

So Ochy waited in her hiding-place, listening for sounds of human presence before setting out to explore the immediate area.

It was nearing twilight, when she gently parted the thorns and eased herself into the open air. She was standing at the edge of a circular depression. In the centre, in front of her, a patch of ground had evidently been heavily grazed and then cut up and smoothed with antler hoes. Around it and stretching up the surrounding slopes, was moorland grass and low scrub, a couple of curlew calling, the voice of a crow. The bare earth, about a hundred paces across, was the only sign of human activity – except perhaps far over on the right, where the setting sun was lying imprisoned in a tangle of bare branches beyond the top of the slope. Ochy could just make out a humped shape, black against the golden light.

Ochy felt drawn towards this object, as though it were somehow familiar. With her customary caution, she headed towards it. The sun was well down, sitting on a level layer of black cloud, as she reached what she now saw to be a long, low stone cairn, similar in shape to the earth-mounds her people erected over their dead. It was almost completely surrounded by quick-growing thornbushes and hazels, their burgeoning leafbuds joining dusty catkins on the branches. Soon fresh foliage would hide the low erection. Indeed, even at this time Ochy would not have noticed it, if it had not been shown up by the sun behind it.

By now the sun had finally set, and a solitary star was shining bright in a cloudless sky. Frosty dew was gathering on the big stones, but Ochy knew instinctively what she had to do.

She began pulling at the stones, found a loose one, and wrenched it out, half turning to throw it into the surrounding scrub. Another rock followed, and another. Soon she was burrowing into the cairn, like a hunter diving into the innards of a slaughtered deer to escape the winter's cold.

The sky was completely dark now, a meadow of celestial lights obscuring that first bright star. The moon was coming up, an enormous full moon, that looked over the horizon, sending one silver beam straight into the hole where Ochy was toiling. It shone on one particular rock. Ochy tugged that one out, and the next, and the next – each one like a solid round skull. They crashed and clattered, breaking off branches and splintering each other as they fell. Then something like a flat stone door barred her way. The moon shone upon it. Ochy sat down on the cave-like hollow, put her feet against the surface and pushed. The slab gave way slightly.

For no reason she could think of, she stopped pushing, knelt upwards, and curled her fingers around the upper edge of the flat stone. It came away easily. She pulled it towards her, scrabbling backwards as her arms took the weight and she lowered it down.

The black and white lunar contrast revealed a square tunnel. The bones of human feet lay in the entrance. Beyond was a skeleton.

Ochy crawled into the chamber, every movement occluding the silver moonlight. She crawled between the legbones and found herself facing a grinning skull.

Ochy raised her eyes, looked over the skull. Beyond pelvic bones and rib cage, the skeleton was headless. A shattered wooden stake protruded from splintered bones. Ochy glanced back at the skull. It was ossified no longer: it had the face of Vhi-vhang!

No, it was a naked skull again.

This was her mother's grave. This was what she had seen in the scrying stone. This was why she had been drawn here. Ochy picked up the skull and kissed it. 'Greetings, Mother. I have come to free you from the power of Mhirr-cuin.' Then she backed out into the moonlight.

Ochy had almost regained the entrance to her underground highway when she sensed footsteps nearby. She paused, melting into some loose bushes so that the bright moonlight rippled across twig, hair, branch and skin as one. Ochy heard a woman's low voice as several legs brushed through the undergrowth from behind her. 'Who could have done it?'

Without moving Ochy could not see who spoke, nor the woman who replied, 'Wolves did it.'

'But wolves could not throw stones about like that,' protested the first speaker, who went on with a plaintive whine, 'Now the dead witch will walk abroad and ruin the crops.'

'Hush. I do not believe that Vhi-vhang was deliberately bad. If her Ghost does spoil the crops through her artlessness, it will be the fault of the People of the Wolf. Their wolves let Vhi-vhang out. Mhirr-cuin's Ghost will find and punish who or what is to blame. Now, quiet!' The last word was a whisper.

The speakers moved on and all was silent again. Ochy waited. She was about to step from her concealment when she noticed a movement to her left.

20

From where she was standing, Ochy had a perfect view of the bare ground flooded with moonshine. To her left a line of men stood along the edge of the clearing. Each one carried a stick and appeared to be wearing some sort of apron. Otherwise they were naked. In front of them with arms raised, stood Htorr-mhirr.

He had aged considerably since Ochy had last seen him on that dreadful day. He had grown terribly thin, stringy skin hanging where muscles had once bulged. His hairs were sparse; tiredness and doubt stooped his tall frame. His voice lacked enthusiasm as he tried to lift his head to the night sky.

'O four Great Horned Ones . . .
Hearken to the People of the Bear . . .
O Four Great Horned Ones . . .
Hearken to the People of the Beaver . . .
O Four Great Horned Ones . . .
Hearken to the People of the Wolf . . .
O Four Great Horned Ones . . .
Come to this our corn planting . . .
O Great Horned Ruler of the Air . . .
Breathe life into this our corn . . .
O Great Horned Ruler of the Fire . . .
Give late sunshine to ripen this our corn . . .
O Great Ruler of the Water . . .
Give early rain to swell this our corn . . .
O Great Horned Ruler of the Earth . . .
Give food to strengthen this our corn . . .'

There was a long pause between each phrase, as though Htorr-mhirr were repeating the imprecation after somebody's instruction. Perhaps he was only rehearsing each set of words to himself first, to make sure he got them right.

'O Four Great Horned Ones . . .
Send Thy Ghosts of Darkness to this our field . . .
Command them to ward off . . .

The deer, the bird, the worm . . .
As this our field prospers . . .
So let all our other fields prosper . . .
O Four Great Horned Ones . . .
As we sow our own seed . . .
So we sow our corn seed . . .
As we would eat . . .
So we would that Thou shouldest eat . . .
O Great Horned Ruler of the Air . . .
Thou delightest in the scent of blood . . .
O Great Horned Ruler of the Fire . . .
Thou delightest in the warmth of blood . . .
O Great Horned Ruler of the Water . . .
Thou delightest in the flow of blood . . .
O Great Horned Ruler of the Earth . . .
Thou delightest in the redness of blood . . .
O Four Great Horned Ones . . .
Send Thy Ghosts of Darkness amongst us . . .
Command them to take . . .
Whomsoever Thou choosest . . .
Drink their blood . . .
Eat their flesh . . .
O Four Great Horned Ones . . .
Do what Thou wilt with us . . .
For we are Thine . . .
For ever.'

Htorr-mhirr's shoulders sagged. Then he bent his body forward, letting his arms swing back. As one, the line of men leaned forward, each holding the stick between his legs so that the end jabbed into the ground.

Htorr-mhirr stepped forward a single pace, swinging his arms as he did so. Behind him, the men also stepped forward, furrowing the soil with the stick. There was some sort of hand movement, which Ochy assumed to be seeds dropping into the scrape from the apron fold.

Then Htorr-mhirr moved again, and the ritual sowing was repeated.

The line of men moved silently across Ochy's vision, their passage marked only by the shuffling of feet, the scrape of sticks through the dirt, an occasional deep breath. It was so quiet that Ochy could hear the little rattle of seeds dribbling into the soil. Once, only once, someone coughed; Ochy felt the tension, the angry fear that rippled along the rank of bowed backs.

Then the line was at the righthand edge of the clearing, was melting into the scrubland, was gone. There was no indication that anything had happened. Or was there? Yes, the moon was almost at its zenith. Its light picked out a whole series of parallel grooves cut from left to right across the clearing.

The lunar beams also illuminated another line of figures that had silently materialised from the adjacent bushes. They were kneeling down, women, naked on their hands and knees. One woman was standing upright. Like Htorr-mhirr, she was in front of the row, and like him, she had her arms raised to heaven. Even at this distance, Ochy could see that her hair was fair, so fair as to be almost white, shining silver in the moonlight, only darkened where the tumbling mass of tight curls shadowed her shoulders. This must be the woman of Ahmorc, Chief of the People of the Wolf.

'O Four Great Horned Ones
Hearken to the People of the Bear
O Four Great Horned Ones
Hearken to the People of the Beaver
O Four Great Horned Ones
Hearken to the People of the Wolf
O Four Great Horned Ones
Come to this our corn planting
O Great Horned Ruler of the Air . . .'

She was uttering the same prayer as Htorr-mhirr, but unlike him, she spoke with conviction.

'. . . As this field prospers
So let all our fields prosper
O Four Great Horned Ones
As our bodies accept our own seed
So we help the earth
To accept this our corn seed
As we would eat
So we would that Thou shouldest eat
O Great Horned Ruler of the Air . . .

The calm unhurried voice rang out clear and sharp against the night air, each word pronounced perfectly, each emphasis correct.

94

'O Four Great Horned Ones
Do what Thou wilt with us
For we are Thine
For ever.'

As the blonde finished, she lowered her arms to her shoulders, holding them right out sideways in wide embrace. Then, beckoning to those behind, she set out across the clearing at a slow and measured tread. At each step she took, the women behind crawled forward, brushing the soil with alternate hands, hiding the corn seed in the womb of the earth. The work was done in uninterrupted silence.

The full moon was right overhead as the creeping line reached the edge of the field. For a moment they all paused as though expecting something to happen – but nothing did.

One of the women, perhaps more uncomfortable than the others, perhaps with palm or kneecap bearing heavily on some sharp stone, seemed to move slightly as if preparing to crawl on into the bushes.

But then Ochy saw that it was a shadow just this side of the kneeling line.

No, it was not a shadow, it was more of a formless shape, a solid shape, rising from the very soil the women had just covered, the men had just ploughed through.

The shape was crouching; it was on four legs; it was a wolf; a wolf, right behind the unsuspecting women.

Ochy opened her mouth to cry out in alarm, to shout a warning, she knew not what. But before any sound came, one of the naked figures glanced round, saw the wolf and leapt to her feet with a shriek. Already tense with horrible anticipation, the other women were jumping up, screaming, running. The wolf, too, was upright, on its hind legs, amongst them, its head lunging this way and that, yowling and snarling in bestial rage. Running every way in panic, the women crashed into each other, fell over, lashed out, tried to get away. Everywhere they turned, the wolf was there, barring their path, harrying their backs as they recoiled.

Some were ecaping into the thick undergrowth around the clearing, but one girl bolder or more frightened than the rest, stood her ground, facing the slavering jaws. Arms slightly spread, she seemed to be offering herself as sacrifice, accepting the fate of a chosen martyr. The wolf did not hesitate. It knocked her flat, trampled over her body and face, and grabbed another woman by the wrist. The wolf spun her off her feet and swung her round, her bottom bouncing and scraping on the rough soil. The woman cannoned into other flying figures, all going down in a shrieking heap. As each fought clear she was grabbed again into the maelstrom of arms and legs.

The wolf was straddling a couple of squirming women, tearing them apart. In one mighty heave, the wolf reared up, its forelegs hoisting one of the women right above its head. Now its jaws were lifted towards the full moon in a long ululation. Again and again, the blood-chilling howl rose and fell, wavered and grew, echoing from the distant trees, drowning its burden's screams.

The woman struggled and twisted, her blonde curls hanging straight down from her head. Ochy saw that it was the woman who had led the corn-covering ritual; the woman of Ahmorc; that Ahmorc who had boasted of his woman's fullness; that Ahmorc who had sworn his readiness to accept any sacrifice.

The howling ceased abruptly in a sharp snap of jaws as the wolf hurled the woman towards the centre of the clearing. She fell with a thud and the crack of bones in the still night air.

The two figures were alone now in the silent cornfield. The blonde woman's shrieks had given place to a faint, intermittent moaning.

In one bound the wolf was on her, its dark shape grovelling and tearing and snarling at the white form which occasionally jerked and darkened. From time to time, Ochy heard the mushy click of stone on bone, the messy slavering of a feeding animal.

Now the wolf was standing on its hind legs again, facing towards Ochy's left.

'O Great Horned Ruler of the Air,'

That was Mhirr-cuin's voice: muffled, excited, older, but Mhirr-cuin.

'I, Witch of All the Peoples
Have tasted the blood of this sacrifice
And it is good.
Breathe life into this our corn
And make all our crops prosper.'

The wolf-woman was already holding a roundish object by its blonde hair. Now the head of Ahmorc's woman was being whirled round and round. Now it was sailing high into the air.

There was a sigh from somewhere above, the merest hint of a dark shadow across the stars – and the head was gone.

Now the wolf-woman – it must be Mhirr-cuin – was facing

directly away from Ochy, calling on the Ruler of the Fire to enjoy the still-warm innards that were being trailed across the field.

The corpse's arms were thrown in the direction of the sunset, while the legs and what was left of the torso was dragged across towards Ochy, with an imprecation to the Ruler of the Earth. The wolf-figure dropped to its hands and knees and melted into the soil.

Next instant it was standing outside Ochy's hiding-place looking straight at her.

The creature had the body of a woman, but the head of a wolf. The back and limbs were completely covered in coarse grey fur, springing from the bone-white human skin of the front of the torso. That whiteness shone even more unnaturally in the eerie moonlight, a whiteness streaked with the dark blood of the wolf-woman's victim. Bits of bloodied flesh still stuck to her breasts, were matted in the fur, or were impaled upon the long flint claws that projected above the wolf-creature's hairy hands. Dark spittle drooled from sharp canines and lolling tongue as it peered into the tangled thicket. Its ears moved forward, listening, then back flat against its head in apprehension.

Ochy knew that this wolf-woman was Mhirr-cuin even before the familiar voice again uttered from deep within the creature's throat.

'I, Mhirr-cuin, Witch of All the Peoples
Know you desecrated the grave
Of the false witch Vhi-vhang
Come out
That you may be punished.'

The voice was low, whispery. Ochy suddenly realised that Mhirr-cuin was frightened and that though Mhirr-cuin knew that whatever had broken into the long cairn was hiding in this thicket, she could not see *what* sort of thing was there. That was why Mhirr-cuin had not struck into the thicket: that was why she had not invoked some terrible curse. Mhirr-cuin's vision could not penetrate the shrubbery – she feared the physical strength, the magickal power of that lurking being.

Ochy realised that she was now a witch as powerful as Mhirr-cuin. She was tense from holding her breath, from the excitement of the ritual, the slaughter of the sacrifice, at the very time that Mhirr-cuin's power was being drained from her.

Ochy felt ivy-inspired energy and hatred boiling up inside her.

She knew that she could kill Mhirr-cuin now. In spite of the wolf-woman's claws and fur, Ochy knew that with her bare hands and teeth she could rend Mhirr-cuin in a welter of blood just as the sacrifice had been torn asunder.

Ochy braced herself like a bent bow for her lethal lunge from the thicket. She started to open her hands to drop the skull she was clutching to her breast. The smooth round shape seemed to grow warm.

'Not now,' came her mother's voice. 'This is not the time. If you kill her now, who will know that it was you who did it? Victory must be recognised by the people to be successful.'

Ochy listened inside her head. She did not move, holding in check her mounting lust for physical violence. She would make no reply. She would not let Mhirr-cuin know what being had robbed Vhi-vhang's grave.

'You can go on wondering – and fearing – about that, Mhirr-cuin, Witch of All the Peoples,' Ochy sneered mentally, then almost jumped as the wolf-woman let out a teeth-edging howl. Far away came an answering chorus of yelps and growls.

Mhirr-cuin reverted to human speech. 'Did you hear that? I have told the wolves that they have been blamed for what you have done. They will inflict their own punishment upon you.'

The wolf-woman dropped on all fours and vanished into the ground.

Arrogant in her own powers, Ochy immediately pushed through the coarse vegetation and stepped out into the open.

21

Ochy made a bag for Vhi-vhang's skull out of one of the skins covering a bundle of firewood and set off on the trek back to her home cave.

Once there, she put down the skull and tossed some brushwood onto the fire. She heard a little whimper and looked round just as the wolf's foreclaws rammed into her chest, sending her flying backwards to crash against one of the white stone pillars. She thudded against the unyielding rock, jolting her head to and fro. A myriad sparkling lights winked and danced, piercing the gloom of the cave, instantly coalescing into the glowing eyes of the beast snarling at her throat.

Ochy had struck her head at the base of an obese pinnacle where it joined the floor of the cave. Her head was forced onto her chest so that the wolf could not seize her throat at its first onslaught. Its teeth worried at her chin and chest, its foreclaws raking at the upper part of her body. Ochy could feel its hind legs straddling her thighs, working to and fro with each lunge of its jaws. This was a she-wolf: the bare skin of its full dugs brushed against the witch's belly. It must have been sent by Mhirr-cuin to punish her for desecrating Vhi-vhang's grave; perhaps it was Mhirr-cuin herself.

Ochy punched at the she-wolf's throat; tried to fend her off with forearms and hands; brought her knee up into her opponent's belly. She dug her fingers into the thick neck fur, trying to haul the lupine head away. The slavering teeth snapped at her face, claws ripped at her shoulders. Ochy lifted the beast slightly: her bottom slipped on the ice-cold stone, her head slid down into a shallow pool of water that lapped her ears as her hair floated about her. Snarling with anticipation, the she-wolf plunged her muzzle towards the witch's unprotected throat. Ochy felt the cold skin of the wolf's snout under her chin, the spittle of its jaws flecking about her. She clawed at its head, her left hand found its ear, ripped at it. She dug her thumbnail into the ear cavity, scraping at the soft membranes. With an agonised yowl, the she-wolf whipped her head round, her jaws fastening in the witch's arm.

A wolf never lets go, Ochy remembered. She would make it let go. Her other hand anchored itself about the animal's other ear; her right thumb gouged into its eye socket, twisting under the eyeball. Again the wolf swivelled its head, snapping and snarling.

This time Ochy was quicker. Her right fist caught the pointed jaw, then her knees thrust its body back; her hands heaving at the grey shape. She felt the claws sliding down her body, then she was standing upright, putting all her strength into one kick after another. The she-wolf left the ground, her body somersaulting backwards, the heavy dugs flopping.

Ochy vaulted a pile of stones, raised her foot again. The beast cowered; the kick missed. Its canines fixed in Ochy's thigh, bringing her to the ground, the animal's hind-legs trampling her face. Ochy locked her other leg around the wolf's head, hoping to break its neck. Its dugs brushed her mouth, she bit hard, felt her teeth meet, pulled hard, tasted blood and milk.

She-wolf and woman rolled over. Ochy seized the beast's hind legs and twisted them in opposite directions, trying to rip the struggling creature asunder. The wolf released her leg, and writhed about. Ochy grabbed its throat and stood up, swinging the beast towards the river below. She slithered on a patch of blood and went over, dropping and snatching at the wolf. The two furies bounced and rolled down the slope in a tangle of hair and skin. Both were on their feet, animal snarls bubbling in their drooling mouths as they gulped for breath. Both were stained with the other's gore, their own wounds oozing blood with every movement of their heaving lungs.

Ochy moved faster, locking her arms about her opponent's throat. The she-wolf reared up and sank her teeth into the witch's breast. Screaming and growling, the two figures pirouetted around the cave, their shadows clambering up the walls, wrestling across the ceiling.

Now Ochy was on her back again, the cold unrelenting rock forcing her body up towards those merciless teeth that snapped and worried, seized and shook. Her flailing hand hit one of the thin pinnacles of stone and broke it off. She groped for it, knocked it further away, found it again and jabbed the jagged spike into the wolf's bloody eye socket, twisting and scraping.

Now Ochy's right wrist was in the beast's jaws. Now her head was in the river, water covering her face. The witch locked her calves over the wolf's back and straighened her legs. Her thigh muscles bore down on the creature's spine. The she-wolf's bleeding dugs were flattened against Ochy's belly and breasts, the animal's legs spreadeagled on either side. The wolf's head was raised, twisting this way and that as it yelped and yowled.

Now Ochy was on top, almost kneeling, still paralysing the she-wolf between her thighs, her fingers throttling its windpipe, forcing the snarling teeth underwater until bubbles and blood rose silently and filtered away into the darkness.

Ochy wanted the fight to go on. Heaving the she-wolf's carcass above her head, she hurled the grey bundle at the foot of the Ghost of Darkness. The tail still twitched. Ochy seized it in both hands, swung the body from side to side, smashing the dead wolf to and fro against the rocky pinnacle until the stone was spattered with blood and flesh and hair. Ochy tore at the corpse with her bare hands, hacked at it with pieces of stone. Her tongue lapped blood, her teeth chewed lumps of raw, warm meat. She caressed her naked body with bloodied palms. She garlanded skeins of innards about the misshapen pillar, daubed it with gore.

> 'Eat and drink your fill
> O Ghost of Darkness
> I have tasted this she-wolf
> And she is good.'

Laughing and chattering, Ochy released her embracing arms from about the stone and raised her head. A long unearthly howl uttered from her slavering lips.

> 'Hear . . . me . . . O . . . She . . . Wolves.' She filled her lungs
> between each word. 'Go . . . tell . . . Mhirr . . . cuin . . . that . . .
> I . . . Ochy . . . the . . . Witch . . . of . . . the . . . Cave . . . will
> . . . slay . . . her . . . just . . . as . . . I . . . have . . . slain . . . the
> . . . she . . . wolf . . . she . . . sent . . . against . . . me.'

Again the howl echoed around the cave.

It was only later, after Ochy had pranced yowling around the cave until the ivy-induced frenzy had burnt itself out and she collapsed exhausted by the fire that she heard again that little whimper, smelt again the scent of wolf, and felt a little furry cub snuggle towards her for warmth; it was only then that reaction set in, the agony of her injuries suddenly struck home, and she huddled freezing cold under all the winter skins she possessed, shivering with shock and pain.

22

It took a long time for the fever that fell upon Ochy to pass, and for her wounds to heal. Even then, her scarred body and limbs remained stiff and tender, only gradually resuming their former suppleness and strength. But from now on, she was no longer alone: she had her mother for company, although she did get irritated each time she found that the skull had moved from where she had last placed it. And by the time Ochy had fully recovered, she realised that Vhi-vhang was telling her that she did not want to stay in the Witching Cave. Accordingly Ochy carefully followed her mother's whispered instructions.

By the light of the fire burning in the Dancing Cave, Ochy could just make out the underwater mouth from which the river swelled. She took a small piece of wood from the pile and fastened it to the end of several exceptionally long leather thongs, which she knotted together and wound round and round her waist. Ochy then paced back along the sand, took a deep breath and ran forward. She hit the clear water in a dive, a silver arrowhead penetrating the black tunnel. It bore right and her head hit the roof. She dived deeper and kept forging against the current. Now her limbs were tiring and her lungs bursting. Her head was splitting, but still she kept swimming. Her head broke into fresh blackness. She gulped thankfully.

The Ruler of Air had let her breathe again and now the Ruler of Earth was laying out a bed of sand for her to rest on.

Presently Ochy began crawling along the water's edge. Then she fingered the walls about her, feeling a faint current of air coming from a small round hole slightly bigger than her fist. She found a pinnacle of rock in the darkness, lashed the thong to it, floated the piece of wood downstream, and lowered herself into the racing water. The current whirled her back into the Dancing Cave, where she saw that the thong and piece of wood reached well into the lighted cavern. By this means, she could haul waterproofed bundles of firewood, food and her mother's skull upstream against the current.

And so, when the last crescent of the moon began to fade, the witch dived under the arch and swam upriver to the Far Cavern.

Given breath by the Ruler of Air, warmed by the Ruler of Fire, and protected by the Rulers of Water and Earth, Ochy waited out the bad times until she knew that the new moon would have returned. The only way the demons could get at her, was via the little air hole, but this was guarded by her mother's skull.

Often Ochy heard Vhi-vhang whispering to her, calming fears, reminding her of forgotten spells, suggesting fresh adventures, and recalling the villainies of Mhirr-cuin. At other times, Ochy occupied her mind by using combinations of necklaces to retell all her chants and charms. And then, at the end of the period of the dead moon, Ochy washed the darkness away as she plunged back towards the Dancing Cave and a rapturous reception from the wolf-cub, Dhogh.

For by now Ochy had repaired the entrance barrier forced aside by the she-wolf when looking for a den to rear her cub. Most of Ochy's injured or abandoned pets either left when fit or remained undemonstrative and she expected this new arrival to repeat the pattern. But this soft bundle of fur responded to her affections with licking and jumping and leaping after her every movement. He tried to follow her everywhere.

Ochy taught him to keep himself and the cave clean, how to find and fetch things, when to stay until summoned. To demonstrate to the Wolf-Ghost and to Mhirr-cuin that he no longer belonged to them but had been tamed by the Witch in the Cave, she called him "Dhogh", with enough dignified emphasis to show that it was a name and not just a word.

By now the promptings of her mother's skull and the scrying stone had persuaded Ochy to begin adventuring beyond the confines of her cave and the ridge immediately above. She still maintained the stockpiles of firewood along her underground road, but now the valley became her main highway as she embarked upon an exploration of the Great Marsh and the world beyond. Sometimes Dhogh came with her. His ears picked up distant sounds and he communicated the information to his mistress. She replied in wolf-tongue, sent him off to intercept the prey and drive it towards her. Sometimes she despatched Dhogh on a much wider-ranging exploration, to act as her Ghost and report what he had seen and heard. Sometimes she went out alone across the Great Marsh.

She learned to find her way through waving meadows of tall reeds, through its expanses of treacherous bogs, its hidden ponds of clear water, its deep channels with violent currents, and its secluded islands with moss-shrouded oak, alder and hazel. She learned to look for deer tracks on the soft margin, sure guides to those invisible pathways that led through the swamps to deep lagoons and safe islands. She waded thigh-deep in mud and water amongst rushes and sedges twice as tall as she, relying on her ears to guide her through the whispering maze. She learned to mark those slight discolorations where mud firm but damp, became a bottomless quagmire. She came to depend upon the sense of touch in her toes to tell her what unseen surface was underfoot and underwater. Her ankles knew the prick and slash of dead reeds, their cone-like roots and skeleton stems bleached white in the scorching sun. At night their jet moonshadows rippled across the deathly landscape, each step releasing the black smell of rottenness.

She learned where stinging insects swarmed or bloodsucking leeches wriggled, although neither seemed to bother her much. She knew the runnels where salty water came swirling silently and regularly, only to drain away just as mysteriously, leaving shelving banks of deep brown mud. She felt the fiery heat of sunlight burning her shoulders, her back, her whole body, as she trekked across a sucking desert, the only living creature beneath the eye-aching blue. She plunged in lonely meres of crystal green. She stood on islets of golden sand and watched the water creep across the ground until the seabirds clustering about her rose in a thunderous piping snowstorm and she was left forging against the foaming waves with all her strength. She felt the savage pull of mighty rivers when all the waters about her were calm and still to the far horizon. She learned the disguise of floating vegetation when stalking her prey. She acquired the skills of steering a buoyant tree-trunk. She learned how to lash several logs together to make a raft. She learned to catch fish with baited hook; learned to stand motionless until silvery forms darted about her and a single spear-thrust earned her food. She learned how to hide underwater, breathing through hollow reeds.

She saw how the deer munched seaweed in the winter; how the beaver stored up food against hard times. She came to learn the ways of coot and moorhen, knew the sandpiper, oystercatcher and shag, watched heron, crept up on bittern, and looked for the coming of flamingo, pelican and stork. When they departed, geese and duck took their place, bitter cold air swept the reeds, the distant seas thundered, and ice fringed the lagoons. Occasionally wrapped in her own little world of warmth, Ochy ventured onto the hard sheets of stony water, but most of the cold time was usually spent in her cave.

But she also worked along the flanks of her home ridge, watching out for boar, wolf and bear, noticing how some valleys remained warm, sheltering plants that throve even in the coldest weather. Then the heat and the sun would return and she would set off on another expedition.

On one day of high summer, when the trees were heavy with sap-dripping foliage, Ochy worked right across the marsh. She skirted the conical peak of Htorr-mhirr – the Mountain-in-the-Sea – where the Marsh People lived, climbed over a narrow ridge, and descended to more swamps on the other side. It had hardly rained since winter and the going was easy. Reaching the top of the rising ground beyond, Ochy scaled what looked to be the tallest tree in the forest and was soon swaying in her elevated perch. Some illness seemed to be affecting this, the highest, bough: there were few leaves just here and she was able to survey the whole of the countryside.

Looking back the way she had come, the witch could see the Mountain-in-the-Sea, and behind that her own home ridge, its wooded slopes screening the thinner vegetation on its crest. Tongues of greenery thrust out into the surrounding marshland; solid coppices heaved themselves from the hazy swamps. Looking ahead now, Ochy could see that the marshes ended. To be sure, she could make out a watery gap in the hills ahead, leading to a great bay of reeds. The swamps made a similar but wider inroad slightly to her right, while looking even farther round in that direction, the level wastes merged in the lighter sky over the sea. She turned her head more until she was looking right back over her shoulder. Then her gaze swivelled to the front once more.

Ahead, the hills swept round in a vast semi-circle like the waves of the ocean, their green caps composed of countless trees, branches and leaves, marching onwards until they merged into the arc of the sky. There was no sign of any clearing or of human activity, save for a couple of thin columns of wispy smoke on the far ridges. Everywhere the air was draped with droning heat and mist. A fishing eagle shared the tree, preening quietly, not bothering to exert itself on such a day.

The witch jumped violently: the eagle looked at her reprovingly. Ochy had closed her eyes for just a moment. It would not do to fall asleep this far from the ground, but it would be nice to have a doze rocked in a swaying tree.

Ochy clambered down the branches and descended the slope to the very edge of the marsh. She found a big oak, its huge boughs so wide that they formed natural hollows. She swung herself into

105

one and found suitable places for her bow and pack. Warmed by the sun's reflections from beneath but shaded by the foliage above, she sprawled on her belly and was instantly asleep.

The sun was well down when the light step of a roedeer woke her. Through some trick of the air, the shy creature had not scented her. Not had it been alarmed by the suntanned arm dangling from the branch just above its ears. Ochy's head was cradled comfortably in the crook of her other arm. Without moving, she could see every hair along its russet back, could hear its faint breathing.

The deer waited warily for a moment, then stepped a half-pace forward and lowered its neck to drink. Its muzzle dipped into the water with barely a ripple. Not a whisper of wind stirred the reeds; the evening mere seemed perfectly still, a reversed reflection of the world above.

Ochy noticed the deer's eyes shining in the water, saw her own face and black hair just above the deer's head. At the same instant the deer too saw the crystal picture of the woman in the tree above. A look of puzzlement, perhaps half-remembered recognition, seemed to pass behind the deer's eyes.

Ochy smiled, her white teeth bright in the water and then a floating tree-trunk erupted in foam and teeth, teeth, so many teeth – sharp pinnacles of stone fringeing a floating cavern that snapped shut about the deer's head. The creature's legs braced against the pull, then collapsed. The fawn carcass whipped through the shallows into deep water. Ochy glimpsed a long, long body the colour and consistency of rock. Eyes glinted atop its facial carapace, a serpent's tail exploded in foam and the pond was again rippleless, the remains of a rainbow pattering down through a gentle mist of spray.

Ochy found that she had backed up against the bole of the oak, no longer over the water, trembling. She had never seen such a monster, not even in the bones of those long dead beasts in the cave.

For a moment retrospective fear chilled her blood as she realised that this dragon could have seized her at any time during her exploration of the marshes. Then she remembered that she was a witch, with power over beasts and ghosts. She had no cause to fear anything. She would stalk this weird creature, find out all about it. No, she did not fear anything, not even a dragon like this.

As immediate proof of her confidence, she braced herself against the rough bark, thrust herself upright, raced along the branch and

106

dived straight into the water, her body making a loud smack as she struck. She kept well down until she could hold her breath no longer. Surfacing, she gulped air and bent her body towards the bottom again, twisting amonst the waving fronds and the grotesque shapes of waterlogged timbers. Above the surface again she cruised slowly across to a wooded island, waited until it was completely dark, then returned just as leisurely without further incident.

23

Ochy soon found that the dragon kept to its own part of the
marsh, near the place where she had first seen it, an area where
several arms of swamp converged. At first she only noticed it after
it had gone; the swirl of something submerging, the alarmed
squawk of a drowning coot, a floating log that was no longer
there. Then Ochy began looking for the two lumps which were its
eyes, unwinking in the middle of a still pond. Confident in her
own powers, she would swim towards it, diving underwater to
watch the lizard-like body twisting through its own length as the
gaping mouth snapped and bubbled at fish and wildfowl. At other
times it lay in thick mud at the water's edge, its scaly tail ready to
sweep some unsuspecting animal into its nightmare jaws.

Yet so many fish teemed in the deepwater channels, so many
birds skulked in the tangled reeds, so many beaver lived within the
security of dam and lodge, that the dragon's depredations had no
visible effect on the myriad denizens of the marsh. Indeed, for
most of the time, the monster was replete, lolling comatose in the
sun on some mudbank. It was on these occasions that the witch
was able to observe it closely.

The dragon was very similar to the little lizards that ran along
the rocks or made tracks in the sand on hot days. But it was much,
much bigger than those harmless reptiles. Its skin appeared hard
and bony, with a double row of vertical scales running along its
back and down its tail.

Ochy was fascinated by its jaws. Bordered by knives of flint, the
gaping mouth seemed to be laughing eternally, a welcoming
entrance to a fiendish death. Yet starlings and sandpipers hopped
unconcernedly close. Once Ochy thought she saw a little bird hop
right inside, peck at something between the dragon's teeth, and
out again, but the movement was so quick she could not be sure.

Although its gait on land appeared clumsy, the monster could
bound along at a surprising gallop if it wanted to and Ochy took
good care to keep out of its way then.

Sometimes she shied little stones and bits of wood at it in an
attempt to find its weaker parts. They just bounced off. Once with
legs wrapped around an overhanging tree, she hung head

downwards poking at the sleeping dragon with a stick. There was no reaction – except for the swivelling of an eye.

Towards the end of the long, hot, dry summer, a change came over the dragon's behaviour, and it began an orgy of killing. No sooner had one animal been dragged floundering and baying into the water, than the monster was returning and lying in wait again. Once, Ochy saw it hold a young ox underwater until it drowned. The dragon then seized one of its victim's legs in its jaws and rolled over and over, until the limb was torn off and the gory carcass dismembered.

Nothing was excluded from its menu: frogs, small fish, birds, everything was snapped at and seized; if wounded, pursued until overtaken. Even the little friendly birds kept well away at this time.

The only thing that bothered it for a short while, was a swimming grass-snake that appeared longer than Ochy was tall. The dragon managed to seize the serpent's tail in its jaws, but the next instant the monster's head was wrapped with scaly coils. Mud and foam boiled as the dragon dived deep, then reappeared shaking its constricted head from side to side above the surface and trying to scrape the snake from its jaws with its foreclaws. The embattled reptiles surged towards the swampy bank, burrowing into the quagmire under rotting treeroots. Shortly afterwards Ochy saw the dragon with a long creeper-like body dangling from its mouth as it made off towards its lair which was not far from this encounter.

Once it had been a little wooded valley, just a depression, an indentation in the hillside bordering the marsh. The small brook had been dammed by beaver, who had moved on once they had exhausted the most suitable trees near the water. The brook was too tiny and too close to its source to sweep away the obstructing logs. Eventually, the valley had silted up, only distinguishable from the rest of the marsh by being a couple of hands higher than the main swamp, and by being more stagnant and lifeless, quite unlike the lush marshland.

This dank backwater was surrounded by a thick growth of hazel and alder. Rotting trees lay part in and part out of the pond. Ivy and old man's beard clambered over the trunks and bushes; thick moss deadened every sound. The air was silent, as motionless as the black water, covered with green scum so dense that it supported leaves and twigs, and even little pools of brown liquid. In the middle was the long-abandoned beavers' lodge, draped with many seasons' layers of leaf-mould, dead moss and rotting sedges. Even though the sun was well up, the forbidding shadows of this place so chilled the air that wisps of steam could be seen rising from the decomposing midden. This was the dragon's lair and Ochy had found it.

As she watched from the dark trees, there was a slight swirl from the base of the piled vegetation. The dragon's eye-lumps appeared, paused for a moment, then surged through the green slime. Its long body clambered over the moss-covered remains of the dam, and slithered into the open marsh.

Ochy sat on the edge of the pond and watched her feet and calves disappear into the slime. Bracing herself with the palms of her hands, her bottom slid forward into the mud, soles of her feet touched the bottom, went through it and sank until they were resting on hard sand. An open pool of black water lapped the witch's groin.

She took a hesitant step forward, then another. At first the ring of water moved with her, occasional black leaves floating to the surface, accompanied by bursting bubbles of marsh gas.

The slime grew thicker; her body was pushing against it, making a solid wave of muck as her feet felt their way over entrapping obstacles. The water was getting deeper; she was wading with her arms stretched sideways, making a half-crablike progress through the morass. As the scum reached her breasts, the witch drew her legs up and glided noiselessly towards the reeking island in the centre.

Ochy circled the heap, diving down and feeling for the entrance in the smooth blackness. Her hands brushed sodden twigs, more twigs, a gap, then more bits of wood. That was it!

Twisting through her own length, she located the space again, wriggled through a narrow, tortuous tunnel, and broke surface in a stygian furnace.

Ochy gasped with the fiery stench, held her breath, opened her mouth, and again felt her gorge rise. She started to retch, forced the vomit back down her throat, and felt all round the hole she was floating in. Her fingers identified the head of a deer, several deer, the skin of a beaver, a wolf. Something moved under her hand, fat grubs writhed, flies buzzed around her face. Her palm went through something like a swollen leather bag and the stink of putrefaction exploded in her throat. Ochy opened her mouth wide and gulped in one of the bluebottles. It whirred at the back of her throat and she spewed violently, her head bent to the surface of the invisible pool.

Deliberately she felt for a solid ledge, put her palms on it, hoisted and twisted herself up until she was squatting in the midst of that malodorous larder.

She waited, waited in the noisome dark until the dripping sounds of her withdrawal from the water ceased, waited until the disturbed flies had settled again, waited until the soft rottenesses about her had stopped giving way under her body, waited until the invisible pool plopped quietly: something big had entered the pond surrounding the lodge.

Ochy waited a moment longer – 'I am not afraid of you, Dragon of the Marsh' – and roll-dived into the unseen muck-filled tunnel.

She came out of the tunnel just as the dragon was entering it. The monster was too close to turn or snap, as invisible in the murky depths, woman and reptile brushed past each other. Ochy felt its back scales scrape her belly and knees and toes, then she surfaced in a dazzling green maze.

Brushing the slime from her eyes, Ochy gulped air; even this dank place smelt fresh and good compared with the vile prison she had just left.

The green scum parted before her hands and mouth as she breast-stroked across the pond, her black hair floating in the black wake that bubbled behind her and was then lost in the coalescing mass of slime.

As she reached dry land – or at least mud that was not so sticky – the dragon surfaced behind her, the legs of some hoofed animal still protruding from its jaws: it had not even waited to deposit its latest victim before pursuing the intruder.

Ochy stood, legs apart, hands on hips, her body leaning slightly forward. Green ornaments decorated her skin and hair, necklaces of slime dangled at her throat. She had survived this self-imposed ordeal.

'I do not fear you, Dragon of the Marsh,' she taunted. 'You frightened me the first time I saw you, but I do not fear you any more. I do not fear anything,' she emphasised. 'I am the Witch of the Cave. I hold the Stone with the Secret of Time. The Four Great Horned Ones protect me.' And then, not quite an afterthought, she whispered, 'Thank you, Four Great Horned Ones for being my friends.'

The dragon eased itself slightly in the water. Now only its eyes were above the surface. They stayed watching her for a very long time, sinking lower and lower until just the lumps showed. Ochy's return gaze did not waver. She did not blink. But even so she could not tell the exact moment when the thick

111

slime was again an unbroken sheet of green.

Ochy did not see the dragon again until the following spring. She assumed that it slept in the torrid ordure of its nest, feeding from its putrefying store if woken by hunger before the hot weather came.

24

Returning through swamp and woodland to her cave, Ochy skirted Htorr-mhirr – the Mountain-in-the-Sea – at the same time as the Marsh People were arriving from their summer journeys. By now she had had plenty of opportunities to observe this tribe without being seen herself.

Like the dragon, the Marsh People stayed in their own part of the swamp and kept to their own seasonal routine. They came to Htorr-mhirr as the leaves began to change colour. They cut bundles of reeds and slabs of turf to stack around a framework of stakes, covering holes in their huts with lumps of earth or worn skins. There they dwelt during the winter months, working on their belongings and trade goods. On fine days they repaired their boats or built new ones of long oak planks. Each timber had a series of holes bored around its perimeter so that it could be lashed to its neighbour and the joint made watertight.

When the sun shone and the water was calm, they fished or paddled over to the islands in the marsh. They killed red deer by stampeding a herd into the water, pursuing them until the swimming animals were exhausted and had their throats cut. Sometimes the carcasses were towed back to the camp; often just the antlers were hacked off and piled in the boats. They obtained beaver skins by setting the lodges on fire and slaughtering the terrified creatures when they emerged.

When the wooded slopes of Htorr-mhirr were studded with golden petals, the People of the Marsh set out on their expeditions. Some went by boat, towards the setting sun, their craft laden deep with flint sickles, axes, knives, barbed heads for arrows and spears, decorated pots of rough and finer finish, and a variety of ornaments. Others travelled on foot in the direction of the sunrise, their baskets packed with polished stone axes. There were deer antlers for picks and hoes, bone combs for scraping skins, and tight bundles of fur robes. All these burdens were slung from twin poles lashed to the shoulders and wrists of slaves.

Men, women and children, all sallied forth on both overland and sea journeys, only a few, very old or sickly folk being left behind to keep the huts and boats in good repair. This they never

113

did – at least not to the satisfaction of the travellers – a cause of bitter recrimination when the trackmen appeared over the wooden causeway – something else that was always there but was never mended – and the boatmen came surging through the reeds.

Then there was much feasting on meat traded from the People of the Bear. They savoured their favourite delicacies, shellfish, snails and slugs. They made merry – and got argumentative – on drink brewed from corn, also obtained from the tribes up on the ridge. They compared flints from the sunrise, polished stone tools from the sunset, and strange materials from they knew not where, but which they had acquired on their travels. They haggled over these exchanges, fierce debates which sometimes ended in violence.

Perhaps the oddest thing about them was that they were all different in shape and colour and clothing. They were short and stocky, or tall and thin, or tall and broad, or short and thin. One full-bearded man was only the height of a child, but he had the strongest hands Ochy had ever seen. One of their womenfolk was of an immense obesity. To see her get up was to watch a mountain arise with much puffing and blowing, obviously incapable of further activity before it was time to lie down again. Yet over a long march, she outlasted everybody else in the tribe – and could move through dense undergrowth more quietly than they.

Their hair was dark, curly, fair, straight. Some of the men had beards; some were bald. A few were brown-skinned, one or two so dark as to be almost black. Some went completely naked even in the coldest weather. Others were clad in long fur coats and breeches in spite of the hottest sunshine. Between the two extremes were infinite variations of dress. A number, both men and women, wore fine ornaments at all times, even when performing the filthiest tasks. Some were scarred or painted with intricate markings that seemed as incomprehensible as their tribal organisation.

As a child, Ochy had witnessed their bargaining with her own tribe, and was therefore familiar with many of their words and phrases. Now, with an ear accustomed to assessing strange noises, she was soon able to follow most of their speech. Even so, she could not work out who their chief was, nor even if they had one at all. If they did, he certainly did not make decisions which everybody else then had to obey. Instead, each individual task seemed to have its own particular organiser. Everybody deferred to him or her when that work had to be done; but he was

114

perfectly willing to accept somebody else's leadership in any other situation. For example, the man in charge of the boats had a merciless temper if the paddling rhythm were disturbed; yet ashore, he was reduced to washing the women's cooking pots. Another man was always laughed at when they went hunting, being ordered to keep well back out of the way; yet when strangers were encountered, he was the one who stepped forward to argue with them in their own tongue. And if a situation arose for which no one seemed responsible, then the whole tribe argued until they came to a decision – or until the crisis went away.

Yes, everyone seemed of equal standing during the winter; yet in the spring, for no obvious reason, several men and women, boys and girls, were roped up for the overland trek. And yet the same people did not always return as slaves. Sometimes it seemed that the Marsh People took it in turns to act as human beasts of burden; indeed, sometimes there were many fresh faces in the group when Ochy saw it next.

Once the witch shadowed one party that set out across the causeway. After several nights, the travellers met up with a similar file of itinerants. A short exchange of words resulted in a fierce, but almost bloodless, fight. The party Ochy had been following proved the losers; they were made the others' pack slaves, and were led off along the victors' line of march.

Ochy realised that the black and brown men and women at the village by the Mountain-In-The-Sea must have been acquired in such a violent interchange, or perhaps in more peaceful bartering, or perhaps in a whole series of encounters right across many lands. For Ochy sometimes heard both them and the white people telling tales of great waters, immense snow-meadows and sandy wastes. They spoke of strange ghosts, some with and some without fear, each man or woman worshipping in whatever manner their own little group thought best – at least they did until Ochy began to notice frequent reference to the Witch of All the Peoples.

The Marsh People were not happy: their voyages by land and sea were not prospering. There was talk of the witch who lived on the ridge above the Great Marsh; how she could make it rain in the growing season and bring sunshine during harvest – but only for those tribes who accepted her rule and the worship of the Four Great Horned Rulers of Air, Fire, Water and Earth. These deities demanded sacrifices, but so did most gods and ghosts. Was it not worth making sacrifices if Mhirr-cuin – they whispered her name lest she should hear them talking about her – if Mhirr-

115

cuin could still the waves of the sea, make their arms strong in the fight and their tongues quick in barter?

The outcome of this debate was that a tall young man with piercing blue eyes named Onta, volunteered to go to the People of the Bear and ask Mhirr-cuin to help the Marsh People. He returned with an unsmiling blonde girl who introduced herself as 'Ihtar – Acolyte of the Witch of All the Peoples'. She selected two younger children, a dark girl and a black boy. She demanded, and was provided with, a specially built hut where the four of them lived from then on and where Ihtar began instructing the others in the correct ceremonial for the worship of the Four Great Horned Ones. Soon they were assisting Ihtar in her public casting of good luck spells on the boats of the tribe, each stage of construction having its particular imprecation. There was also the ritual cursing of those members of the Marsh people who did not turn immediately to the worship of the Four Great Horned Ones. And always afterwards a baby died, or a leg was broken, or a fishing net split so that a great catch was lost; and always it happened as Ihtar said it would – in the name of the Witch of All the Peoples, of course. Of Mhirr-cuin herself, there was no sign. She remained up on the ridge, making her wishes known through the thoughts and words of her Acolytes. She did promise that she would come in person to perform the Great Sacrifice which would guarantee success to the Marsh People on their sea voyages. But that would only be after they had fulfilled their part of the bargain.

Mhirr-cuin made it known that she had heard of an old man named Wheg-ling. He had no home, but wandered from place to place seeking – and sometimes finding – Magick Stones which held the secret of power over other people. Only he knew how to use them. If the Marsh People could find this man, and force him to use his skills to enable Mhirr-cuin to make good her name as Witch of All the Peoples, then Mhirr-cuin would herself place spells of good fortune upon the boats of the Marsh People. As proof of her good faith, Mhirr-cuin instructed Ihtar to cast immediate spells of good fortune upon the paths the Marsh People took during their inland travels. In return for that, the Marsh People had to take with them more of Mhirr-cuin's acolytes to spread the worship of the Four Great Horned Ones.

That winter, Ochy brooded in her cave, resentment and bitterness festering within her. She was a greater witch than Mhirr-cuin, she knew that. But it was Mhirr-cuin who was known as the Witch of All the Peoples, and was well on her way to wielding power over every tribe. And what was she, Ochy? She was the Witch in the Cave; well on her way to old age without ever being known by anybody. Well, it was time to make her name known, time to demonstrate to all peoples that Mhirr-cuin was *nothing*, that she – Ochy – could command the Four Great Horned Ones. If it came to a choice, the Four Great Horned Ones would choose her, Ochy. They would fight on her side, they would help her to humiliate Mhirr-cuin, help her to kill Mhirr-cuin, help her – Ochy – to become the Witch of All the Peoples.

Yes, it was time to command the Four Great Horned Ones to obey her, to come at her bidding . . . as Dhogh came when she called him. She looked at the wolf, excitement stirring within her. She needed a witness to her powers; why should it be human?

'Come on, Dhogh,' she called – and together they stepped out of the cave.

Outside, the catkins were blowing, their companion leaves swelling from the bud. The whole winter had been very dry, frosty but with no snow and hardly any rain. But now the blue sky was darkening. Thick grey clouds were surging in from the sea. Their bases were already coalescing, obscuring the sun in murky haze. One opaque layer glowed red and orange. The whole heaven was covered now. A chill wind blew, rattling bare twigs, rustling the dry leaves of last fall. Ochy felt a strange exhilaration charging her bones. Her skin tingled, her heart beat faster.

25

The sky was completely overcast now, a dark grey pelt that deepened suddenly to blue-black. Golden sunlight flooded the valley; every stone, every twig, every hair on the wolf's fur, every line of the woman's body stood out in stark relief.

Then the sun was gone. Once again the clouds were grey. Now they were low as well, touching the trees, resting on the ridge above. Unbidden, the words flew into Ochy's mind and she shouted them aloud, flinging her arms upwards at each salutation.

'O Four Great Horned Ones
Hear me
I am Ochy
The Witch of the Cave
I command you
Come
Show yourselves to me
Hear me
O Great Horned Ruler of the Air
Come
Anoint me with your Air
Hear me
O Great Horned Ruler of the Fire
Come
Fill me with your fire
Hear me
O Great Horned Ruler of the Water
Come
Cover me with your Water
Hear me
O Great Horned Ruler of the Earth
Come
Strengthen me with your Earth.'

Down the valley, the dark clouds descended, lengthened, pillared. A black swirling tail dropped, its tip invisible below the level of the treetops. There was a crash of thunder. Ochy saw branches and rocks whirled into the air.

Swaying from side to side, the ethereal column marched up the valley. There was the bellowing of countless bulls and the nerve-jangling squealing of numberless boars. Whole trees were being sucked up; gouts of water exploded from unseen meanders of the river.

The aerial serpent burst through the last curtain of trees and leapt across the open space in front of the cave. Its tail was just over head height above the ground. Ochy felt her lungs empty, the walls of her body cave in. An irresistible wind swirled around her and Dhogh, pulling their hair into vertical strands. Ochy's head was wrenched skywards and she looked straight up into the very body of the Ruler of the Air.

Coils of solid atmosphere formed his skin, writhing and twisting and interspersed with trees and boulders, animals, spurts of water and running fire. At the very top of the column a mouth opened and closed, a voice thundered:

'I am the Ruler of the Air
You are part of Me
You are part of Each Other
We are all part of Everything.'

The black snake was gone, smashing into the cliff over the cave and withdrawing into the murk above.

Ochy's hair was still streaming upwards as rigidly as if frozen. Every hair on her body stood away from her flesh. Dhogh was twice his normal size, his fur erect like the prickles of a hedgehog. The spiny tips were quivering, flickering in some trick of the light, were alight themselves.

Streamers of blue-white flame flowed outwards from the wolf, met the cold blaze radiating from Ochy's hair and fingertips. Coiling and swirling, more flames danced from the trees about them, the catkins dripped blue light. Fire ran to and fro across the river, wreathed the mouth of the cavern, mounted into the air. Now the witch and her wolf were surrounded by a cold crackling conflagration. Now a ball of white fire hovered before them, its mouth opening and closing in thunderous words:

'I am the ruler of the Fire
You are Part of Me
You are part of Each Other
We are all part of Everything.'

119

With a final deafening thunderclap, the hail descended, stinging Ochy's bare skin, numbing her head, making Dhogh tremble with the chilly impact. Lightning cracked across the sky as hailstones bounced and popped on the rocks, shredded fern leaves and flattened the wavelets on the river.

More and more fell. The first were melting, plastering the witch's hair and the wolf's fur, making their bodies stream. Runnels carved shapes in the white drifts, forming a face with a mouth that opened and shut, its voice a susurration of syllables:

> '*I am the Ruler of the Water*
> *You are part of Me*
> *You are part of Each Other*
> *We are all part of Everything.*'

Abruptly the hail stopped: there was a muttered roar from above, then a vicious crack, and a rain of sodden earth and pebbles. Trees and boulders were moving on the slope above. They stepped out valiantly, jumped into space, hit the river, threw great fountains of water into the air. One gnarled trunk was ignited by a thunderbolt just as its roots snapped and it was hurled across the valley like a flaming arrow. Shapes came and went in the cliff, a mouth opened and shut, the very soil screamed:

> '*I am the Ruler of the Earth*
> *You are part of Me*
> *You are part of Each Other*
> *We are all part of Everything.*'

The clouds lifted, almost disappearing altogether. The sun came out, shining lower but stronger. A skein of rooks flapped across the join between pale blue sky and golden puffs of cloud. It was a fine, clear evening.

Dhogh braced his paws wide apart, thrust his neck forward, curled his lips back, and shook, shook, shook. A rotating fan of droplets sprayed outwards from his flying hair. His body was a silver-grey blur revolving around a sharp cone of white teeth.

'No, no, no!' laughed Ochy, holding her arms before her averted face. 'No! Stop! Come in the cave. I will rub you dry with ferns. You like that. Come on Dhogh. Good Dhogh.'

The wolf stopped shaking and looked at her. The witch grabbed for his neck fur and he leapt aside. Ochy called softly, beckoning with her finger, smiling. 'Come to Ochy. Good Dhogh. Come,' then jumped at him.

The wolf ran round in a circle, his legs bunching and stretching, his tail just beyond the reach of the witch's snatching hand. Ochy cut across the circle, the wolf doubled in his tracks, and they raced around in the opposite direction, sloshing through molten hailstones, stumbling over branches and rocks. Ochy clutched the flying tail, pulled hard. Dhogh whipped around in his own length, and stopped. Ochy still running, tripped over him, and went sprawling. The wolf sat on his haunches, watching her, his head on one side, tongue lolling between his teeth.

Now kneeling, Ochy reached for a thick stick, picked it up, brandished it, and hurled it into the cave entrance. Dhogh was off in pursuit even before it had left her hand. Ochy hurried after him – 'Good Dhogh.' Then, 'Come here,' as the wolf hurtled out of the tunnel, feinted and dodged round her. He turned, trotted towards the woman and dropped the stick at her feet.

Ochy picked it up and threw it down the valley. Dhogh spun round, ran several paces, stopped and looked back. The stick was still in the witch's hand. Again she pretended to throw it, the wolf jumping stiff-legged in the direction of her aim. Emitting snarling yaps he leaped up when Ochy's arm drew back the next time. As she staggered, laughing and admonishing the wolf, Dhogh's teeth sank into the bark, and Ochy had to grip it tightly with both hands.

Witch and wolf spun around, the beast with its legs tucked up clear of the ground, the woman's long hair flicking black and glossy in the golden sunset. Dhogh was growling happily. Ochy shaking so much with merriment that she had to let go. The wolf hit the ground and rolled over, dropping the stick between his paws.

Ochy walked across to him, leaning over with her hands on her knees. 'Good Dhogh,' she said, and made a lunge for the stick. The wolf seized it, crabbed sideways, and released it again. His jaw cowered against the ground, panting, daring. His eyes swivelled upwards.

Ochy gently put out a hand and patted his head, caressed his ears, stroked his back and flanks. Her fingers reached under his belly. Dhogh rolled over, whimpering slightly. Squatting down with his outstretched throat between her legs, Ochy tickled the wolf's chin, then worked her fingers up and down his underparts. His back legs vibrated whenever she touched some sensitive nerve. He dribbled and licked at her.

121

Then she had whisked up the stick and was racing into the gloom of the cave, Dhogh leaping and yarling at her, and trying to snatch his bone-like treasure.

As the tunnel widened, Ochy tossed the stick in front of her. Dhogh hurtled after it, his forepaws hit it, his nose bounced it to one side, and he somersaulted beyond his turning point. Ochy kicked it farther away, and dived on it just before Dhogh got his jaws there. She held the saliva-slippery stick between her breasts where the wolf could not reach. He circled her recumbent form, then dug his nose under her body, his paws scraping, his head tunnelling and heaving. Ochy clung to the earth, but she was still lifted up laughing, the licking tongue searching her flesh for the familiar stick. He got it in his mouth, then lost it again. Again, he burrowed and lunged. Now the stick was under his body, both figures wrestling the other away from the elusive prize. Ochy rolled over onto her back, hauling Dhogh after her so that he could not retrieve the chewed stick. But the animal was no longer interested in that piece of wood. The woman too, forgot its existence. Now the struggle itself was all-important, their bodies tingling with every contact. Hands and paws tangled in fur and hair, their tongues tasted the other's saliva and scent. Now Dhogh's agitation became more urgent, Ochy's movements more frantic, until wolf and woman coalesced in a coupling of human and animal sensation.

Later, Ochy squatted at the cave entrance chewing ivy-leaves and meditating her relationship with Dhogh and the wider realm of nature. She had been dedicated to the Ghosts and now that dedication had been sealed with physical bonding. Human intercourse would have joined her to one man only, focussing her magick arts upon him, or at the most upon their family. Even if several men had taken her at the most mystical level of physical experience, she would still thereafter have only been responsive to human sensations and emotions. But because the Ghosts had possessed her, she was now and forever at one with all the Ghosts, at one with the whole of nature.

The Ghosts could not all have coupled with her, and Ochy found special significance in the fact that their chosen representative had been the Wolf Ghost in the shape of Dhogh. Did this mean that her future destiny was linked not only with Mhirr-ling, but also with the People of the Wolf? But her Stone with the Secret of Time . . . how did that fit into the great scheme of things?

And so Ochy squatted there, watching the countless stars drift across the firmament of night. She knew that other sleepless witches were watching those same stars with her. So were other people, and animals, plants too, and rocks. All were looking up at the stars at this very same instant of time. All were united, in this same immediate experience, in this one Present, with the infinite Past and Future stretching out on either side.

Yes, she was part of Everything. Everyone was part of Everything. 'We are all part of Everything.' That was what the Four Great Horned Ones had said. 'Yes, Everything is part of Everything', she muttered to herself, '. . . except . . . except . . . Mhirr-cuin'.

There was no place for Mhirr-cuin in Ochy's great scheme of things. Her rage and resentment boiled up afresh and without realising where her feet were carrying her, she found herself again hurrying along her underground highway.

26

Once again Ochy was ducking under lumpy ceilings, vaulting rocky outcrops, scrambling over precarious boulders, squeezing through narrow passages, dodging icy waterfalls. Once again, hidden by branches and ferns, she was looking out across a levelled field under a bright full moon. Once again she listened to the prayers and watched the corn-planting ritual, the naked men sowing, the crawling women covering the seed.

But this time Ochy saw that the ceremony did not end in panic-stricken slaughter. This time the kneeling women stood erect, silently waiting. From the bushes returned the men. Behind them came a shambling line; old people and children, wizened crones and bent men, cripples and toddlers, a few carrying babes in arms.

The lines coalesced and appeared to form up in families, the youngest of each group standing in front. They began to move, a high-stepping pace, each one first pausing to allow a slight gap to open. They looked neither to the right nor the left. Their arms were motionless and rigid at their sides, except for those hobbling along with the aid of a gnarled stick or carrying a child too young to walk. The last person, a tall man, waited until the leader, a child of some four summers, was almost behind him, then he too started out.

The whole circle of figures rotated slowly in a trance, alternately bone-white and jet-black as they passed in and out of moon-shadow. It was only after Htorr-mhirr had passed twice, that Ochy identified the person she assumed to be Mhirr-ling; and that was only due to his logical proximity to his father. Htorr-mhirr was still recognisable, though older and wearier than at the last ritual Ochy had watched. But Mhirr-ling! He looked scarcely younger than his aged parent. To be sure, his muscular frame was as powerful as his father's had once been, while his black hair and beard were as thick and wavy as his parent's former red locks. But the way he breathed, the way he walked ... The Mhirr-ling she had overheard speaking to Ahmorc had had a clear voice and confident step. This Mhirr-ling could hardly shuffle past, phlegm rasping in his throat as he fought for breath.

The night had been clear and still, yet now Ochy could hear the rushing of a mighty wind. Several large bushes on the far left swayed to and fro. Twigs and last summer's remaining leaves were projected through the air.

'Stop!' The woman's voice rang out. 'He has chosen. The Great Horned Ruler of the Air has chosen.'

The voice seemed to be coming from a dark-clad figure outside the circle. The voice was that of Mhirr-cuin.

Every participant in the ritual was as still as if they had never moved. No head turned in that direction. The only ones who could possibly see what was going on, were those on Ochy's left, who happened to be facing that way. Ochy herself could only shift her neck very slightly lest even that tiny disturbance be heard by the nearest worshipper a few paces away. Two of the figures, a young woman and a boy, advanced upon the curly-headed boy separating them. As if in a trance, they took him by the arms and steered him towards the cowled witch towering above them.

The two children resumed their places. Mhirr-cuin pivoted her prisoner towards those now-still branches. Even though Mhirr-cuin's face was turned away, Ochy could still hear her words:

'Come O Great Horned Ruler of the Air
Come taste and eat.'

There was the merest flicker of something sharp in the white moonlight and Mhirr-cuin had disappeared.

The young boy stood there alone – headless. He took two deliberate paces forward and fell. The wind rushed through the trees again. The circle was moving once more.

Even with her retentive memory, Ochy found it difficult to recall how many times the ring of figures passed her. Once, twice, a handful of times? Htorr-mhirr, Mhirr-ling, People of the Bear, People of the Beaver, People of the Wolf, blonde hair, thick black beards, crippled oldsters, grave children, white skin, black shadow, all silent save for an occasional flick of toe on stone, a harsh half-cough, a belly breaking wind, small noises that in that tense silence rang like thunderclaps. When they came, the whole circle hesitated, waiting for retribution, fear leaping from one to another.

Where did it come from? Was it over there? Was it near me? It is me. Don't breathe. It might not happen.

Then after an eternity, the circle moving away.

Twice more, death and Mhirr-cuin interrupted the dream-like sequence.

125

On the opposite side from Ochy, a fire blazed up, its crackling flames drowning whatever Mhirr-cuin was saying. There was the nearest thing to a struggle among silhouetted figures and a tiny squalling doll arched into the bonfire, its wail stifled in an explosion of red and gold.

Solid coils of thick blackness still looped across the stars and moon, a miasma of burning smells still clung to the marchers at their third halt. This time the sounds of sacrifice came from the right, choking and gurgling as of someone being held down in a pool of water.

The last victim would be dedicated to the Ruler of the Earth; Ochy knew that. She also realised that the ritual would be conducted very close to her watching-place. She was ready for something to happen. Her very anticipation made her jump of alarm more violent when the shock came and the soil opened with a roar right in front of her, with Mhirr-cuin standing just beyond the hole.

'He has chosen. The Great Horned Ruler of the Earth has chosen.'

Mhirr-cuin's arms were raised in demonic stance. Now she had turned round and was facing the worshippers.

The young woman who had already assisted in the night's first sacrifice, was now gripping the arms of a much younger girl. She looked just over a handful of summers in age. Her other elbow was held by an old man, his wispy-haired head jerking spasmodically.

The two acolytes thrust the child forward towards the witch, who seized the golden curls, bending her head down to face the ground.

'Come O Great Horned Ruler of the Earth
Come taste and eat.'

A sharp push sent the little girl sprawling into the pit. A rumble of earth covered her, Mhirr-cuin vanished, and the people melted away.

Ochy burst through her screen of thorns without feeling their taloned claws. She spaded the soil with both hands, shovelling earth to each side, raking swathes of dirt with interlocked palms. Her fingers encountered skin, rounded flesh, the girl's buttocks. She moved her digging a fraction farther over, a flatter part of body, shoulder-blades. The small head was bent forward. There were stones there. They flew out of the way. A mass of earth-

126

matted hair was exposed. Ochy worked down each side, past the little ears, feeling for nose, mouth and eyes. There were more stones here, small ones, but perhaps they had trapped a little more air in their interstices than if the face had been rammed into soft sand. The child's hands were underneath; they would come free quite easily. Ochy swept the dirt off the girl's back and made sure her legs were free. Briskly she ran her hands over the fragile frame, checking for broken bones, and lifted the little child out of her grave.

The sudden weight took the witch by surprise, caught her off her kneeling balance and pulled her down into the pit.

The child could not be that heavy. No; one foot was still caught by something that had looked like a shadow in the moonlight. It was a big flat stone. Ochy levered and pushed it to one side. She flopped the child onto her back. Her eyes stared sightless into the full moon. Her chest was still.

Ochy felt the little rib-cage: it seemed intact. She stuck a finger in the girl's mouth, felt around and hooked out the dirt stuffed about the tongue. There was a bit of gravel in one nostril; that came out. The other was bleeding; perhaps it was only a cut and not coming from inside.

Ochy tilted the child's head back, leaned over and covered the mouth with her own lips. Slowly she breathed into the lifeless body, taking her mouth away to inhale herself. Again and again she repeated this action. Her own breath was coming back at her; that was not right.

Once more her middle finger probed the girl's oral cavity: grass, roots, soil, her fingernail caught one of the green blades, fed it to one side of the open mouth. She gripped with several fingers, broke the grassy tip, seized it a little further down, wriggled it into a better grip, and out came a small clod of earth from the back of the girl's throat.

Again the witch bent her mouth over the child's forcing life-giving breath into the lifeless body. The little girl's chest rose. Ochy took her mouth away: it fell.

Once for the Ruler of the Air
Once for the Ruler of the Fire
Once for the Ruler of the Water
Once for the Ruler of the Earth
Once for the Ruler of the Air
Once for the Ruler of the Fire
Once for the Ruler of the Water
Once for the Ruler of the Earth.

127

She paused – 'Ruler of the Air, help me' –

Once for the Ruler of the Air
Once for the Ruler of the Fire
Once for the Ruler of the Water
Once for the Ruler of the Earth.

Each time she blew in, the child's chest swelled in sympathy, flattening each time she took her mouth away. The little girl took no breath unaided.

Ochy placed her hands on the lower part of the child's chest, pressing down.

Once for Then
Once for Now
Once for To Come
Once for Then
Once for Now
Once for To Come

Then her mouth over the child's, breathing in again.
'Ruler of the Air, help me.'
Now the pressure again.

Once for Then
Once for Now
Once for To Come

Sweat was running off the witch's body. She felt the coldness trickling between her breasts and down her spine. Her knees ached with pressing into the soil.

Again, her mouth closed over the child's. Again she forced her own warm air into those cold lungs. Again she withdrew her mouth to suck in breath.

As she did so, she felt an involuntary puff against her own nostrils, saw the child's eyes close, flicker open, then shut tight in agony as the little body heaved. Ochy turned the golden head to one side and vomit spewed out. The child tried to turn onto her belly, retching bile and crying. She was alive.

Ochy picked up the lightweight form in her arms, holding her sideways to avoid the worst thorns at the secret entrance to the caves. She cuddled the child in a winter robe that she had brought and fed her warm herb drinks by the fire that was soon alight.

She had robbed Mhirr-cuin of one of her victims, and now she had physical proof that what the Witch of All the Peoples could kill, the Witch in the Cave could bring to life again; undead evidence that the sacrifices of Mhirr-cuin were not acceptable to the Four Great Horned Ones.

27

'My sister!'

Ochy was hunched up, squatting by the fire, trying to realise the nearly forming shapes of flame and glow that flickered before her mind.

'My sister!'

The little girl's words broke the witch's concentration. 'Ssh,' she rebuked, then glanced round in surprise. The child had spoken for the first time since being delivered from her sacrificial entombment.

Not once while being revived with warmth and food, not once during the long trek through the caverns, with frequent halts by brushwood fires, not once during the few nights since her arrival in Ochy's home cave, not once had the little girl uttered a word. Not once was there a nod of thanks, or headshake or refusal, or any sign that she comprehended or cared who Ochy was, what she was doing, or what was going to happen next. Ochy had soon given up asking her name, while more detailed questioning would have been hopeless in the face of that wide-eyed thumbsucking. Eventually Ochy went about her normal activities as mutely as the still figure squatting by the fire. At one time, she wondered whether the shock of being buried alive had rendered her speechless. Perhaps she had been dumb since birth. Well, she would find some way of making contact just as she had with the other invalid creatures she had succoured in the cave.

But now the child had spoken, clearly and purposefully. She was lying on her belly, snuggled up against Dhogh, so that her face and arms were cradled in the wolf's back. She was staring at the pulsing opacity of the scrying stone.

Ochy came over beside her, her long hair brushed the child's shoulder, flicking the strange brown blemish there. It was an odd shape, something like two stone axes placed back to back. It reminded Ochy of the outline at the top of the crack that marked the pathway through the mountain. The child did not stir although Ochy's raven hair must have been tickling her. The witch bent her face even closer to the child's cheek to see exactly what she was looking at.

The centre of the scrying stone was swelling with light, white light – no, more yellowish, but almost white. It boiled and swirled, became a tangled mass, of near-white curls, surrounding a girl's face. Was it the reflection of the child in the cave? No, the face was different; the girl in the scrying stone was older; she was the Acolyte whom Mhirr-cuin had sent to teach the Marsh People about the Four Great Horned Ones.

'Ihtar, my sister,' pronounced the child.

The image expanded to the girl's head and shoulders, a hand on one shoulder, a man's hand, a man standing behind her.

He, too, had very fair hair, his beard a curly fringe encircling his face. Besides the customary kilt of skin, he was wearing a necklace of animal teeth. Ochy thought they looked like wolf's teeth.

'Ahmorc, my father,' explained the child in the cave without prompting.

A third figure was standing before the other two, a green-clad form whose hem and hood brushed the scrying stone's rim of shimmering light.

'Mhirr-cuin,' said the child and spat.

Now other people were standing there, mostly men, a couple of women. One or two had dark skins, the others appeared white. All were clothed in a variety of fashions. Ochy recognised them as some of the Marsh people.

'The People of the Marsh,' commented the child, and spat again.

Ahmorc released his hand from Ihtar's shoulder, the fingers spreading to fill the whole of the scrying stone. The fingers merged, misted and reformed. They became dark boats gliding across the marsh. They slid into a low swathe of dawn mist, so thick that the boats and paddlers were hidden. Only one figure remained visible, a green-gowned shape standing erect and motionless, yet moving effortlessly and soundlessly across a meadow of pure white, pricked through with occasional dark tips of reed.

Again the scrying stone changed its viewpoint. Behind Mhirr-cuin came another gliding figure, Ihtar, naked now save for chains of primroses which crowned her blonde curls, fell between her small breasts and girded her waist. Her wrists were bound by a more sinister girdle, a leather thong that extended tensely to the lashings about her ankles.

The boats were in open water again now, all clearly visible. The crew of Mhirr-cuin's skiff came alongside the one they had been towing, fumbled with it and then cast it loose. Ihtar was now alone in the centre of a ring of watching canoes, themselves imprisoned by a wall of mist.

131

Mhirr-cuin was still standing erect. She stretched out her hand. There was a flicker of white in the still water. The Marsh People held their breath.

Ihtar did not move.

The water moved. It was seeping into Ihtar's boat. Already the craft was lower. The water was over the girl's ankles. She made no sign that she sensed it. The boat's bulwarks were level with the water; the boat had disappeared, and the girl's knees, and her thighs.

Mhirr-cuin's rigid finger had extended into an invisible rod, gently but inexorably forcing Ihtar beneath the rippleless mere.

Now the water was lapping her shoulders. There were two heads now, the inverted reflection clearer than the air-misted face it met on the watery threshold. The red lips opened, perhaps to speak, instead to drink. Ihtar's eyes were still open as they passed beneath the surface. Blonde hair swirled slightly, a few petals floated momentarily. Then they too were gone and the scrying stone went blank.

'I hate Mhirr-cuin.' The vehemence of the child's utterance was given added venom by the innocence of her expression. 'I hate her and I hate the Marsh People.'

Her fingers twisted in Dhogh's fur: he grumbled and lifted his head, then dropped it again, too lazy to do anything about such a small irritation. The witch reached out and disentangled the child's locked fingers.

Ochy had never felt any emotions about the Marsh People except wary curiosity. Certainly, she had never hated them. But then, she had not just seen her sister being sacrificed by them. But why? Ihtar was the Acolyte Mhirr-cuin had set over them; why should she be sacrificed?

'I will tell you why,' said the child, listening to Ochy's thoughts. 'My people used to perform dances to make our crops grow. Sometimes we did not dance well, the Ghosts were not pleased and the crops were not good; but we hoped we would dance better next time and were happy. Then came Mhirr-cuin, who told us of the Four Great Horned Ones who rule all things. First *their* hunger must be satisfied, she said. So my mother was sacrificed, and my three brothers. And it is all my father's fault. Mhirr-cuin cast a spell over him and he handed the People of the Wolf to her.'

'Ahmorc did what he thought was best for his tribe,' calmed Ochy, deliberately taking an opposing view to establish the little girl's reaction. 'Mhirr-cuin's magick gives good crops and full bellies.'

'It does not – not for us,' retorted the child. 'When the People of the Wolf had bad harvests, the People of the Bear and the People of the Beaver fed well. That was why we accepted the rule of Mhirr-cuin. Oh yes, from then on, the rains came only in the growing time with sun at the season of harvest. But our crops still spoiled. And the other tribes said that that was because we stumbled in our hearts and if the Four Great Horned Ones were not offered our bodies and blood as food and drink, then other people's harvests would be spoiled also. So always the sacrifices are taken from amongst our people. And my father Ahmorc said to Mhirr-cuin, "Take one of my daughters and teach her to commune with the Four Great Horned Ones, so that she may turn their wrath away from us." And I wanted to be a witch, to cure and kill, curse and bless, sacrifice and say who should live. But Mhirr-cuin chose Ihtar, because she knew that she could spellbind Ihtar to her, but I shall be spellbound by nobody. And when Ahmorc thought that Ihtar had become a great and powerful witch with dominion over the Marsh People, then Mhirr-cuin invoked her spell and Ihtar gave herself as sacrifice in the great ceremony for the Marsh People's voyages. And Onta is now their Acolyte and he has found Wheg-ling. And I hate the Marsh People because they chose Onta and I hate Mhirr-cuin because she rejected me and I want to see her dead.'

It was an incredible speech for a child just over a handful of summers old. The witch was silent for a moment before commenting, 'You speak of Mhirr-cuin's rule. What of Htorr-mhirr? Is he not the Shepherd of the People of the Bear, and so of the other tribes also?'

'He is Artzan, yes.' The little girl shrugged. 'But whatever Mhirr-cuin wishes, he commands.'

'Does not his son, Mhirr-ling, speak as one who will be Artzan one day?' asked Ochy. 'Does he not speak about these matters?'

'He did once,' affirmed the child. 'Once he said that the hunger of the Four Great Horned Ones would never be satisfied, no matter how well they fed. So the sacrifices should cease and the people be happy again. Oh yes, Mhirr-ling spoke about these matters before all the people – once.' The irony of the child's speech was bitter. 'But never again.' She looked squarely at Ochy. 'Mhirr-cuin made him an old man, and he remained an old man until he took away the words he had spoken. And now, if he is not the first to shout agreement with Mhirr-cuin, she sends her Ghost to turn him into an old man again, and he remains an old man until she calls her Ghost away and restores his youth.' The child finished her narrative and resigned herself to morose contemplation of the lifeless scrying stone.

Abruptly it began to glow with light again, silently yet with such an intensity that the changing colours seemed audible in the quiet cave. There were two figures, Mhirr-cuin and Htorr-mhirr, the father pleading with his daughter, then arguing, finally drawing himself up to his full proud stature – and demanding. For a second the cowled woman seemed to recoil, then anger stiffened her frame. She stretched out her left hand, the index finger pointing. Horrified disbelief froze on Htorr-mhirr's face. Was that a flicker of light leaping from Mhirr-cuin's finger to his heart? Htorr-mhirr clutched at his chest, staggering, falling to the ground. For a moment he looked straight out of the scrying-stone. Ochy read the words 'Help me' on the lips and then it became Mhirr-ling's face calling 'Help me'. Then it was Ahmorc: 'Help me' ... a succession of faces: 'Help me ... help me ...' multiplying and chorusing 'Help me ... help me ... help me ...' countless faces that merged into a bluish-grey mass which became a circle of great stones, coalesced into the pebble with the Secret of Time – and vanished.

Ochy sighed. Sometimes she wished that the scrying stone could be a little more explicit in its guidance. Htorr-mhirr needed help; that would help Mhirr-ling, Ahmorc, and a whole lot more people, and would eventually lead her to a circle of Great Stones with the Secret of Time – that was what she gathered from this revelation. But somehow these things never worked out as she expected.

Ochy sighed again, her thoughts turning to Htorr-mhirr and the place where something had happened to him. She thought she recognised the rocks in the background; she believed she knew where she could find him. Evidently the old Artzan had at last refused to be dominated by his daughter and she had cursed him. Suddenly Ochy no longer saw him as the powerful leader who had driven her away from the tribe and killed her mother. Now he was just a lonely old man, dying far from his homeland and betrayed by his daughter.

Ochy levered herself upright by leaning on Dhogh's recumbent frame. He half-grunted, then stretched his stiff legs. Ochy took the child by the hand and raised her up too. The woman pointed at the animal. 'Mhirr-cuin sent a she-wolf against me. I killed the she-wolf and made a pet of the cub. He is my Ghost and runs hither and thither at my bidding.' Then she pointed at the child.

'You are of the People of the Wolf and I have taken you from Mhirr-cuin. You shall be the Acolyte of me, Ochy, the Witch of the Cave. I shall teach you all my arts, you shall run hither and thither at my bidding, and together we shall kill Mhirr-cuin. What is your name?' The little blonde head looked up at her. 'Ahtola,' she replied. 'I have never heard of the Witch of the Cave, but I am prepared to be your Acolyte, to learn all your arts and to run hither and thither at your bidding – as long as *I* choose to do so. For I shall be spellbound by *nobody*. But you hate Mhirr-cuin – and together we shall kill the Witch of All the Peoples.' And with that she skipped out of the cave.

28

They found Htorr-mhirr in a narrow gorge not far from the home cave. His bluish pallor showed that his heart had stopped once and had then begun to beat falteringly again. It could not keep going for much longer. The heavy notes of a blackbird's new song ended in a clumsy clacket and yellow pollen drifted from tremulous catkins, as Ochy and Ahtola supported the old man, put a cloak about his shoulders and tried to moisten his lips with a herb drink.

'I am Htorr-mhirr,' he whispered. 'I know you.' Ahtola nodded. 'I know you too.' He looked at Ochy. 'You are . . . Vhi-vhang.'

Ochy opened her mouth in denial, but declared flatly: 'I am the Witch of the Cave.'

'Ah yes . . . Vhi-vhang. You were a good witch . . . once upon a time. Listen . . . I am the Artzan of the People . . . of the Bear. My daughter . . . Mhirr-cuin . . . is now the Witch of our people. She has done good things too . . . good harvests . . . But now . . . now she wants to use her . . . power . . . for herself and not for the people. She calls herself . . . the Witch of All the Peoples . . . Already she is the Witch of the People . . . of the Wolf and the . . . Beaver . . . and the Marsh. And the Marsh People . . . have brought the man who knows about the Magick Stones which will give power over all peoples . . . and Mhirr-cuin wants those stones . . . and the Marsh People . . . they trample our crops looking for the Magick Stones . . . and I told Mhirr-cuin that they must not do this or . . . our peoples will starve . . . and . . . she . . . laughed and said "Let them starve . . . they are my . . . people . . . I will do what I want with them" . . . But I told her "They are my people . . . I am their Artzan . . . their Shepherd and after . . . me, Mhirr-ling will be Artzan." . . . and she laughed again and said . . . "You will die here . . . alone . . . and no one will take the Bear's Claw to . . . Mhirr-ling . . . and he will never be Artzan . . . and even if he is . . . I will send . . . my Ghost against Mhirr-ling . . . and make him do as I say . . . Mhirr-ling is mine . . . the People of the Bear . . . are mine . . . and the Wolf . . . and the Beaver . . . the Marsh People are mine . . . I command the Four . . . Great Horned . . . Ones . . . and I shall command . . . all Peoples . . . I shall do

. . . what I . . . want with them . . ." That is what Mhirr-cuin said . . . and she said that the Four Great Horned Ones . . . would take me . . . and tear . . . me.' The old man caught his breath and groaned.

He was in an agony of mind as well as body. Ochy had to think of something to say to comfort him. She remembered the words of the Rulers of Air, Fire, Water and Earth, revealed to her in their very persons. 'Do not fear,' she said. 'The Four Great Horned Ones are not as you dread. They will not rend you. They are already part of you and you are part of them. You are already part of Everything and Everything is part of you. Do not be afraid.'

The dying man seemed calmer, then remembered something else and became agitated again. 'Promise me that you will take this Bear's Paw . . . from around my neck . . . and put it around the neck of Mhirr-ling . . . then he will be Artzan . . . for it is not our custom . . . that a woman should rule as Witch . . . without a Shepherd . . . to lead the people . . . Promise me.'

Ochy nodded. 'I promise, Htorr-mhirr.'

He gulped and belched. She rubbed his chest again. 'Promise me . . .' he repeated. 'That you will take out the bracelet . . . sewn inside the Bear's Paw . . . Mhirr-ling must wear it . . . its mate will be found . . . in the sunrise . . . When Mhirr-ling wears both . . . he will be King of a great tribe . . . Shepherd of a great people . . . promise me.'

'I promise, Htorr-mhirr,' agreed Ochy.

Htorr-mhirr relaxed, then opened his eyes in alarm. 'Promise me . . . this . . . one . . . last . . . thing.'

Ochy held his hand as he clutched at her. 'What is it you want?'

'Promise . . . me . . .' The words were coming singly now. 'That . . . you . . . will . . . bury . . . me . . . in . . . the . . . soil . . . of . . . my . . . home . . . land . . . then . . . I . . . shall . . . know . . . that . . . Mhirr . . . ling . . . has . . . become . . . Art . . . zan . . . of . . . a . . . great . . . peo . . . ple . . . Pro . . . mise . . . me.'

'I promise.'

Htorr-mhirr settled himself and smiled. 'Yes . . . the Four . . . Great . . . Horned . . . Ones . . . are . . . my . . . friends.' His voice was suddenly clear. 'But Mhirr-cuin . . . Mhirr-cuin, my very own Mhirr-cuin . . . Mhirr-cuin,' and died.

Ochy gently untied the thong around Htorr-mhirr's neck and handed the Bear's Paw to Ahtola, who weighed it curiously in her hand. 'He was a good man,' said the witch, straightening the old man's grizzled hair and beard.

There was no response from Ahtola. The child had wandered off down the path. She retrieved something from an overhanging thorn and returned in reponse to Ochy's call. The witch repeated her comment while the child stood by impassively, twisting a red strand of hair about her fingers.

'Perhaps,' was her cold comment. 'But I did not come here to help him. I came here to help my father, Ahmorc.' She pointed at Htorr-mhirr. 'He was not of my people. He was the father of Mhirr-cuin. His last words were of Mhirr-cuin. And I hate Mhirr-cuin. I will not help you with his body. I shall take the things back to our cave. Come, Dhogh.'

Ochy's hand scythed against Ahtola's face, lifting the child clear off the ground, hurling her amongst the boulders. 'I am the Witch of the Cave,' she shrieked. 'You are my Acolyte. You will do as I say. That . . . is . . . your . . . first . . . lesson.' Ochy snapped out each word separately.

Ahtola regained her feet and regarded her assailant without apparent rancour. 'I am the Acolyte of the Witch of the Cave,' she declared flatly. 'I will do as you say.' Ochy started to turn away, but froze as she heard the child's next words. 'But I shall not learn much. The Witch of the Cave has a scrying stone; she lives alone with a wolf; and she weeps over dead men. That does not make her a great witch as Mhirr-cuin.'

Ochy seized the child's upper arms and shook her backwards and forwards until Ahtola's teeth rattled; the witch shrieked at her with each head-jerking shudder. 'How dare you speak thus of my enemy in my presence. You are mine. You owe me your life. I brought you back from the dead.' Ochy released Ahtola so violently the child staggered backwards. 'Mhirr-cuin can only kill. She cannot bring alive that which is dead as I have done.'

Ahtola shrugged. 'She can. There was a man, many winters ago, before I was born, on the day Vhi-vhang was sacrificed to the Four Great Horned Ones. He rode a horse, and the horse injured him in his manhood. He bled so much and was in so much pain when Mhirr-ling brought him back, that the People of the Bear — who had suffered much that day — said "Why did you bring another dead man here?" Mhirr-cuin said "I have always said no good will come of riding horses. The surviving pony is to be slaughtered and its body burned because it is unclean. But as proof of my magick and to show that the Four Great Horned Ones also do good things, I will bring this man back to life." And Mhirr-cuin took him into her tent and brought him back to life. But he never walked again. Mhirr-cuin sat him in the dust outside

138

her tent. And she carved a little stick bearing the symbols of the Four Great Horned Ones and put it into his hand. And he sat there all day waving it in the air so that it makes a noise as continuous proof that the Four Great Horned Ones have given him life again. But he is very old now and his hand often tired. And when the sun hurt his eyes, he cried out and tried to seek the shade inside her tent. So Mhirr-cuin has tired of him and sent him to dwell among his own tribe, the Marsh People. And he sits forever within the Hut of the Acolytes, twirling his stick as living proof of the magick of Mhirr-cuin.'

'And this man's name – it is Hpe-gnorr?'

For the first time, Ahtola registered surprise.' Yes. How did you know this?'

'Because it was not a horse, but I, Ochy, the Witch in the Cave, who killed him in the beginning.'

'That may be. But Mhirr-cuin, the Witch of All the Peoples restored him to life, and all Peoples know it. Now, if I were the Witch of the Cave, and wanted to demonstrate to all the world that I were greater than Mhirr-cuin, I should destroy that which she has brought to life, destroy her spells, destroy her Acolytes, destroy everything that is hers, destroy everything that she has done, destroy everything that she intends. And then I should destroy her.'

Once again Ahtola was knocked flying, as Ochy fumed: 'How dare you voice the secret thoughts of my mind. Those thoughts are mine and mine alone.'

Ahtola shrugged contemptuously as Ochy's hand lifted again – then waved dismissively. 'Go! Go back to the cave! Await me there. I wish to be alone.'

Ochy stared at the child's retreating back as she picked her way through the rocks. For a moment a beam of sunlight illuminated the golden curls, then she was gone.

Ochy had promised Htorr-mhirr that she would cover him with the soil of his homeland. Where that was or how she would accomplish that, she had no idea. But for the present, he must be placed safely away from marauding beasts and Mhirr-cuin's vengeance. Ochy smiled as she realised that for once Mhirr-cuin had made a mistake; she had failed to remove the Bear's Claw. It was true that without it, no man could wield authority as Artzan, so Mhirr-cuin's power over the Tribe could never be challenged. Obviously she had believed that Htorr-mhirr's body would never be found – she was wrong!

Earlier Ochy had noticed a small hollow in the side of the

gorge, and there she laid Htorr-mhirr. At last she placed the final stone over the entrance; yes, the whole site looked exactly like a natural rockfall. Mhirr-cuin's Ghost would never think of looking there. As extra safeguard she stood all that day and all night until the sun rose again, reciting funereal chants, protective spells – and death curses against any disturber of the tomb of Htorr-mhirr.

But that was with one part of her mind. Her other thoughts . . . As she turned away, Ochy was conscious of a growing warmth in her belly, the flames of anticipatory excitement leaping up as the great scheme took shape in her head.

29

Coldly and deliberately, Ochy began preparing for a demonstration of her power, which would prove to all people that she was a greater witch than Mhirr-cuin. First of all, she and Ahtola – an eager and encouraging accomplice in this campaign – set out to catch as many fish as they could. Any sort and any size would do, including inedible ones. The witch and her pupil scoured the tideline, looking for the decomposing bodies of fish and birds abandoned by the receding water. These too were gathered up and taken back to be dumped in a pit exposed to the sun outside the cave.

Soon there was a growing pile of rotting scales, heads, feathers, fish-eyes and slimy matter. While Ahtola continued fishing, Ochy went out hunting, draining and wringing the blood of her quarry into the midden. Any carrion was a welcome addition, and so too was the cave-dwellers' own excreta.

The vile pool slopped over its wormy lips at every stirring. Its stench permeated the cave and clung to the trees in the upper valley. Flies buzzed eagerly and maggots writhed from half-submerged lumps of putrescence.

Early one morning, when steam was rising from the foetid cesspit by the cave, Ochy and Ahtola sank waterskins into the scum-encrusted pool. They watched the liquid gurgle in, while brown bubbles burst in their faces. They held the skins under the surface until the last whisper of air had been forced out, and then tied the neck so tightly that the full skin bulged tautly transparent.

Skin after skin they filled until they had a mound of smooth orbs. The last one had to be crammed by hand, Ahtola clambering down into the pit to scrape the last vestiges of corruption from its sides. The golden-haired child revelled in the filth, smiling coldly as she contemplated the fate in store for the Marsh People.

At last the pit was empty. They filled in the hole with antler shovels and sprinkled sweet-smelling herbs and flower seeds over the soil.

The two had to make several journeys down the valley with their burdens, taking care not to puncture the skins on projecting rocks and thorns. They also carried down one of the transparent crystals and various other items the witch thought necessary. All were stowed aboard a raft of logs and disguised with bundles of reeds. Witch and pupil waded into the water, pushing the raft before them. When it was deep enough, they began swimming towards Htorr-mhirr, the Mountain-in-the-Sea, where the Marsh People lived. They would only just be in time.

On several occasions since deciding on her plan, Ochy had made opportunity to observe the Marsh People's preparations for their present season's expeditions. The trackmen had already gone, and now the boatmen were putting the last cargoes aboard their craft. They were too busy to notice a mass of waterlogged vegetation drifting slowly past their huts.

On the side of Htorr-mhirr away from the home cave, was a thin elongated hill stretching across the mouth of a creek that ran right into the wooded ridge of the mainland. One part of this backwater was very narrow, almost blocked by tree-trunks. They steered the raft through, their legs and feet banging and scraping on slimy bark. Eventually the craft grounded in the upper shallows. They unloaded the skins, carrying all but one up the incline and down the other side to where another raft was lying hidden. The remaining skin full of putrefying liquid was left near the first raft. Two others were deposited at the top of the hill and close to the second raft's mooring.

Woman and girl then cast off again and at intervals across the next stretch of mere, set down further skins. Most were half submerged in the water, tied to a stake driven into somewhat firmer mud. One was suspended from the bare branches of a dead willow that stuck up from the swampy wasteland. Another was balanced precariously on the edge of the old dam near the dragon's lair.

The last was carried over the tangled obstruction, along the side of the scummy pool and into the mire. Ahtola swam pushing the slippery ponderosity – the little child seemed tireless – while Ochy tried to keep it from sinking. The weight of it continually pushed her under the surface so that she came up swallowing and coughing green slime. They wedged their burden just above the entrance to the dragon's lair, and returned to where they had left their first raft. Ahtola helped to set this one afloat, and then settled down to wait as she had been instructed.

It was almost sunset as Ochy paddled the camouflaged raft into a thick clump of reeds close to the Marsh People's camp on Htorr-mhirr. She saw that the canoes were fully loaded now, and knew that there was never any carousing before a trip. One or two figures flitted about moving things from hut to hut, conversing in low murmurs, or squatted at the side of the marsh. Most were indoors getting ready for sleep as soon as daylight had faded.

Ochy watched carefully as the last golden rays played across the thatched roofs and were gone.

'Get out, you great guckoos, get out!'

The angry shout shattered the cool evening air. A duck near Ochy quacked in alarm. Other voices were raised, apparently in apology.

'Get out! Leave me be!'

The altercation was coming from the nearest hut, a square building of rather more substantial construction than the usual dwellings of the Marsh People. Even in the darkening light, Ochy could see that a series of vertical posts with horizontal timbers lashed to them, had been hammered into the ground. The roof, too, was of wood, a sloping layer of thinner poles also bound together. The hut was not watertight or windproof, but nothing could get in or out except through the narrow slit of a doorway, which could itself be barred by a gate of hefty logs.

A figure retreated from the doorway; Ochy recognised him as a brown man called Ngaro. He stood there bent forward, peering back into the hut.

There was a murmur from inside and then the irascible voice again: 'Magick Stones! Magick Stones! These are not Magick Stones! These are dirt! Do you hear me – dirt!'

A couple of jagged rocks bounced out of the doorway. Ngaro skipped from side to side avoiding them. Heavy thuds sounded against the timbers and there was a muffled yelp.

Another man backed hurriedly out of the shadowed hut. Called Rodac, he evaded the next stone by shouldering into Ngaro who saved himself from toppling over by putting his foot right into the path of another rock. He hopped about on one leg, holding his toes and complaining.

Rodac put his head round the doorway, keeping the rest of his body and limbs well to one side. 'We are not to blame,' he expostulated. 'We do not know what the Magick Stones look like.'

'We do not know what the Magick Stones look like,' whined the mimicking voice inside. Exasperatedly it went on, 'Of course you do not know what the Magick Stones look like. I know what the Magick Stones look like. I could find them if you let me out.'

'But you would not come back.' Ngaro sounded aggrieved: he was still massaging his toes.

143

'That is true: I would not come back. I would find somebody to feed me well. I will use the Magick Stones for anybody who feeds me well – and you do not feed me well.'

Ochy could not hear what was said next, but evidently it outraged the unseen prisoner. 'Whaaat,' he shouted. 'I do not call slugs and bad water, feeding well.' There was a pause and the voice went on: 'No, once I leave here, I will not come back; I promise you that.'

'And then the Witch of All the Peoples would be angry with us,' came the reply.

There was a snorted laugh from within. 'She is angry with you now. I know all about it. Your sea journeys did not bring you luck. You asked this Mhirr-cuin to make sacrifices for you. And she agreed, provided you found someone who could use the Magick Stones to give her power over all the world. You found me, and she made a sacrifice for you. No one can use the Magick Stones better than I, but I can do nothing without them. No one can hunt the Magick Stones better than I, and I know they are up on those hills . . .' – the two men glanced round at his words – '. . . but you keep me here, go out yourselves, and come back with dirt. For two moons you have delayed your departure, and I still have no Magick Stones to give power to Mhirr-cuin. So she is angry. You will depart tomorrow, and she will be even more angry by the time you come back.' There was a cackle of laughter. 'That will be a nice welcome for you to return to – if this Mhirr-cuin lets you come back. Perhaps she will send her ghosts to sink you all on the great waters.'

There was another jeer, and then, 'Yes, laugh, old man.' The two Marsh People were exasperated with the conversation. 'You can laugh in here all the time till we come back, and if we never come back, you can laugh in here for ever.'

Ngaro protested, 'It is not good to say that,' but the other man shrugged. Together they secured the heavy barricade against the doorway and then stalked off into the gathering gloom.

30

Ochy watched until the village was completely silent, and then waited. At last, the moon began to rise, a waning half-moon, but still bright enough for her to see what she had to do.

The witch crawled out of the water, pausing after every movement to watch and listen. The beach here was muddy, thick in places. As though swimming, she buried her hands and arms into the mire, silently sweeping it past her while bellying forward. At one deep patch, she pushed her face under its surface, hollowing her back and following the dipping contour of the harder sand, so that the liquid dirt flowed over her. Stealthily she stood up, a black shadow in the moonlight, and moved towards the nearest hut which held that irascible prisoner.

The witch peered through the cracks between the logs. Strips of moonlight fell across a sleeping form. He stirred, began snoring a series of choking grunts that ended in an abrupt explosion. He rolled over, chop-chopped his lips and tried to snuggle down again under the winter-cloak which he had fidgeted off onto the floor beneath his feet.

Ochy could see his face now. He was old. A scraggle of grey hair encircled his bald scalp. His face was stubbly, as though he had long spent the energy needed for growing a beard. His body and limbs were thin, as far as she could tell, for he was wearing a long leather tunic and kilt.

His exposed arms were skinny. Yet the stringy sinews connecting his bony joints were as strong and supple as leather thongs. Ochy had seen lots of ancient men with equally powerful muscles. There was nothing obviously special about this one to warrant his wrists being tied together, or to justify his legs being anchored to the log wall.

Ochy decided to deal with him later and moved towards the main collection of huts. The first one had turf walls, but the next was constructed completely of reeds. She knew that this one was used by Mhirr-cuin's Acolytes. Inside, someone was chanting monotonously.

The witch pulled to her front the little bag that was slung around her back, felt inside, and took out one of the transparent pebbles she had found back in the Sandy Cave. Standing on tiptoe, she reached up and tucked it into the thatched roof just above the eaves.

Ochy then retreated all the way to the water's edge and looked back towards the village. She stood for a long time, stepping one pace this way or that, squatting down, leaning her head at odd angles. She was still not satisfied.

A black wraith, the witch slipped through the moonlight, stretched up, removed the crystal, and tried to replace it a little higher up the roof.

'O Ruler of the Earth,' she thought. 'Make me taller.'

It was no good: she could not reach. She had all night to do her work. She would take her time. She would do it carefully. She must not fail.

The chanting had stopped now and all was quiet within. With forefinger and thumb, Ochy made a small gap in the reeds. There was the faintest glimmer of a dying fire. Before it sat a slumped figure, evidently entranced in sleep. Two other, much smaller shapes, were totally recumbent, rising and falling somnolently.

Against the far wall was something like a bundle of old skins, with a raised twig-like extremity. That must be crippled Hpegnorr, she thought, his cramped muscles still trying to keep Mhirr-cuin's foolish prayer-stick aloft, even in sleep. Ochy smiled to herself at the fate she had in store for him: he would not escape her vengeance this time.

Slowly, silently, using the fingers of both hands, Ochy parted more of the dry reeds, twisting them together so that the sides of the hole remained firm. Another hole was made higher up, then another. Gently she placed her foot in the first gap, raised her other leg, groped and found her next foothold.

She was leaning over the edge of the roof now, making handholds in the sloping bundles of thatch. These did not need so much attention, and she soon hauled herself upwards. She selected the exact place she had previously noted, pushed the crystal into its new position, and started edging down again.

As her weight began to leave the roof, the transparent pebble popped out, slithered and rolled off the thatch. Ochy whipped out a hand and caught it just as her foot shot through the reed wall up to her knee.

The witch felt an exhalation of breath on her invisible skin; an arm brushed against her as somebody turned over. She heard a muffled voice complaining in its sleep, and then there was silence again.

Ochy had one good handhold. She popped the crystal into her mouth, and sought a purchase with that empty hand. Then her free leg found a foothold. At last she could work her trapped calf out.

Once again she ascended the roof. Once again she located the transparent pebble in its appropriate place, wedging it this time with knotted reeds, but still not covering its principal face. Then came the descent again, filling in each of the holes she had made during the climb.

On the hard-baked earth once more, Ochy sagged exhaustedly. She had only scaled her own height above the ground, but the necessary stealth had tired her. Much of her mud coating had been rubbed off onto the thatch, but fortunately the huts were already so dirty that it would not be noticed. What was left on her skin was caked hard and cracked, or being melted away by runnels of sweat. Even so, her black and white patchwork was still an effective moonlight camouflage.

On the far side of the village, a giant oak had been felled and trimmed so that it jutted out from the shore into a patch of reed-sheltered water. To this trunk were moored the Marsh People's canoes. Now they were laden with trade goods and personal belongings, ready for the morning's departure. The first one Ochy came to, contained several baskets full of ornaments. Her hands sifted through them. A necklace of jet beads slithered between her fingers like a black snake. An armlet made from a boar's misshapen tusk coiled whitely in the moonlight. Small pieces of coloured wood had been delicately carved, drilled and threaded to make earrings and bracelets.

Ochy passed along the tree trunk looking for one particular canoe, the one belonging to the Acolytes of Mhirr-cuin. There would be nothing in it, the Acolytes keeping their magick safe in their own hut until it was time to go. And here it was, richly decorated with the symbols of the Four Great Horned Ones.

The witch had already picked up a flint knife from one of the other canoes. Now she cut the lashings and eased the craft clear of its berth. She secured lines to two other canoes and slashed their moorings. then she paddled out across the mist-flecked mirror of the marsh. Occasionally a duck quacked or several waders called invisibly across the starry sky. The heavy boom of a bittern carried over the mere. Once she heard the distant squawk of a night heron.

Ochy stopped paddling in the main channel which led towards the sea. The other canoes tugged at her boat. Deftly she leaned over them, cut a lashing here, hacked through a thinner piece of timber there. Then she chopped at the towlines, and the doomed craft swirled away into the darkness.

Ochy lost count of the number of journeys she made; perhaps four, perhaps more. Usually the boats were still just afloat as they passed beyond the range of her night vision. One, weighted down with flint tools and already with only a handful of fingers of freeboard, sank while still attached to Ochy's boat, almost submerging her at the same time. Another capsized, throwing its load of pots into the water so that they floated away, slowly gurgling under the surface. The canoe itself drifted towards the sea, bottom-upwards, like a waterlogged tree-trunk. Yet another pot-carrier upended violently, avalanching its cargo in a crescendo of splintering disintegration and fountaining spray.

When the last foundering canoe had passed from sight, the witch paddled her own vessel back towards her original hiding-place. The prison hut was a few paces away. The flint knife soon cut through the stout lashings securing the door in place, but the heavy timbers themselves were quite a different proposition. Ochy could not get enough grip with her fingertips to lift it to one side. There was a slight crack at both top and bottom. Ochy got her palms first in one gap, and then in the other. She tried pulling it towards her, both upwards and downwards, accepting the risk that it might fall on her.

Nothing happened; the door remained immovable.

She felt all round the rough wood, seeking a purchase, to no avail. In silent desperation, she leaned forward, legs wide apart, trying to force the obstruction inwards. Then weak and sweating, she relaxed against the timbered wall, feeling the harsh bark against her back.

'Ruler of the Earth, help me. Make your trees move for me.'

Her fingers toyed with the door beside her and it swung open. She peered at it suspiciously; she had never seen latch and hinges before.

'Thank you, Ruler of the Earth,' she thought and stepped inside.

Waking with a hand over his mouth, and a flint knife at his throat, the prisoner could only nod or shake his head.

'Listen, old man,' whispered a soft voice in the dark. 'I am the Witch of the Cave. I am taking you away from the Marsh People and from Mhirr-cuin. I do not care whether I take you away alive or dead. Do you understand, old man?'

Ochy repeated the question. The knife drew blood. The bald head nodded vigorously.

'Do not make a noise when I take my hand away or I shall slice off your head. Do you understand, old man?'

Again the grey hairs jerked up and down.

While he gasped for breath, Ochy cut through the bonds securing his legs. She did not release his wrists, wrenching him to his feet by that looser thong. He could hardly stand, having been bound for so long, but Ochy gave him no chance to recover. She flipped the door shut and stepped briskly along to the canoe, dragging the limping figure behind her.

Once he started to say something, but the sharp flint flickered close to his eye and he contented himself with a complaining grunt, undistinguishable from the noise any night animal might have uttered. He fell into the boat with enough thudding clatter to waken the whole village, but when Ochy looked back from her paddling, nobody seemed to have heard them.

Presently the witch broke the misty silence. 'I know your name, and that you know all about the Magick Stones, Wheg-ling. Tell me, and do not lie to me, are they the Stones with the Secret of Time?'

'Why should I tell you anything?' came the truculent reply.

Ochy's white teeth smiled in the darkness. 'Because I can swim well. I do not know whether you can swim at all, but you would certainly not be able to swim as well as I, with your hands tied together, when I upset this boat. Besides . . .' her tone became abrupt. 'You do not care who you use the Magick Stones for as long as they feed you well.'

'Will you feed me well? I hate snails – especially raw snails. I wish all snails were taken from the earth. Aagh . . . the very thought of them makes me feel sick.' He spat over the side with more venom than Ochy had ever known Ahtola use against Mhirr-cuin. He looked back at Ochy shrewdly. 'Are you asking me to use the Magick Stones for you?'

'Perhaps.' Ochy pursued her own line of questioning. 'Do your Magick Stones hold the Secret of Time?'

'The Secret of Time?' he repeated. 'Some tribes bow down to stones and some carry them for good fortune and some use them as markers for hunting grounds . . .'

'Yes, yes, I have known about all that since I was a child,' Ochy broke in impatiently.

'Wait a little: give me time to think; I cannot think if you hurry me.' The boat drifted in silence; somewhere a water animal plopped. 'No; I have heard no story about any stones with the Secret of Time. Now, my Magick Stones give power, power over

149

other people, power over the whole world,' he went on proudly while Ochy concentrated on steering the boat through the thickening reeds.

'So I have heard,' she retorted, and ran the canoe up onto the beach. The old man was jolted backwards by the impact. Before he could recover, the witch was yanking at his wrists and he found himself standing on the bank.

He was not as tall as Ochy, and seemed to be leaning over. For the first time she noticed that his right leg was shorter than the other. No wonder he had made such hard work of getting down to the boat.

'Follow this path and you will come to my cave,' commanded Ochy. 'There you will find food, good food. And there you will stay and use your Magick Stones for me.'

'And suppose I do not wish to use my Magick Stones for you?' sneered Wheg-ling. 'Suppose I eat your food and go away? Suppose I do not even choose to follow this path to your cave?'

'Dhogh will show you the way,' smiled Ochy, then snarled something in wolf-tongue, as a shaggy grey shape materialised out of the darkness. 'He will also make sure you do not leave the cave until I return.'

There was the faintest growl from the wolf and a glimmer of teeth. Wheg-ling sniffed contemptuously, then thumped off up the path, with Dhogh loping in friendly fashion a few paces behind.

31

The stars just before the expected sunrise seemed just a little paler than their companions of the night, as Ochy moored the canoe in its customary berth and settled herself into her secret watching place among the reeds. Almost at once a slight sound began, growing in intensity and more insistent than the first notes of early summer birdsong from the distant wooded slopes. It was a low moaning; coming from the Hut of the Acolytes. It was evidently their morning chant to the Four Great Horned Ones. Now a woman's voice could be heard from within another dwelling, questioning softly, soothing. A shadowy child flitted from the dark bulk of one hut into another dim mass. There were more voices, larger figures emerging from and coalescing with the outlines of buildings. More and more people were moving about, their skins showing as light and dark blurs in the grey dawn. The whole village was astir now, greetings being exchanged, opinions about the prospects for the coming voyage. Then cutting through the growing hubbub, a great shout: 'The boats! The boats have gone!' And the first humped sliver of sun slid over the hill, outlining the village roofs with gold.

The whole village congregated on the foreshore, staring at the empty water as if eyepower alone could replace the missing craft. 'Only the boat of the Acolytes remains?' Somebody made a statement which had all the implications of a question. 'Yet Mhirr-cuin placed spells of blessing upon them all. That is why we did not need to guard them last night. Who could have done this thing? *What* could have dared defy the magick of the Witch of All the Peoples?'

While the Marsh People debated the crisis with growing alarm, some of the men ran about searching in reedbeds and under bankside thickets trailing over the water. Others waded into the mere, feeling along the bottom. Several proposed walking right round the island of the Mountain-in-the-Sea, in case the canoes had drifted away and fetched up on another beach; one or two actually set out to do that. Most just stood, undefinable resentment against somebody or something gradually drilling into their hearts, until another shout: 'The old man! It must have been

Wheg-ling! He must have escaped and taken all the boats!'

'One man?' The suggestion met scorn from some quarters, but already several men and children were running towards the stout hut near the marsh, going in, coming out, and gabbling excitedly: 'He has gone. The old man has gone!'

'But why did he not take one boat to flee in? Why did he take the others?' queried a woman.

'To prevent pursuit, of course,' scoffed her husband.

'In that case,' she pointed out. 'Why did he not take them all? Why did he leave one boat, the Boat of the Acolytes?'

'I will tell you why.' The crowd fell silent, turning and bowing to the figure who now addressed them. 'I, Onta, Chief of the Acolytes of the Witch of All the Peoples will tell you why.' He had changed since the sacrifice of Ihtar, since his assumption of authority over the People of the Marsh. His body, limbs and leather kilt were decorated with a variety of necklaces, bracelets, small skulls and bones. His own head had itself been shaved as smooth as a skull and was crowned with horned headgear. Yet the most terrible features of his mien were his piercing blue eyes, which seemed to penetrate the very soul of each of his hearers. At the same time, the quiet smoothness of his voice was more menacing than a blustering bellow.

Behind Onta stood the other two acolytes, small children, the dark girl and the black boy. They too wore nightmare ornaments – though not as elaborate – and both regarded the People of the Marsh with an arrogance far beyond their years.

'Only the Acolytes of the Witch of All the Peoples remained faithful to her during the night,' said Onta. 'She told us to recite chants of good fortune during all the dark hours – which I did while these little ones –' he smiled formally at the two children, 'slept ready for their journey today taking the worship of the Four Great Horned Ones across the Great Water. But you two –' Onta pointed at Ngaro and Rodac 'were told to guard Wheg-ling. And you did not. So he escaped and straightaway, Mhirr-cuin's Ghost told her. So Mhirr-cuin sent her Ghost to punish the Marsh People for the sin of these two men. Mhirr-cuin's Ghost has made the canoes of the Marsh People disappear as Wheg-ling has disappeared. Only the boat of the Acolytes remains as proof of the obedience of the Acolytes of Mhirr-cuin, so that the rule of the Witch of All the Peoples can be spread abroad while the wealth of the People of the Marsh is lost – all through the neglect of those two men, Ngaro and Rodac.'

'He liiiiieeeees!' The wailing shriek made everybody whirl in alarm.

Ochy stood on the ledge above the muddy beach, motionless, her right foot raised, her right eye closed, her left hand pointing at Onta. Her black hair was lank and glistening in the morning sunshine; silver droplets and runnels coursed down her skin; her calves were dark with mire. 'I am the Witch of the Cave. My Ghost sees everything. My Ghost saw Onta not chanting but sleeping. But even if he had kept watch during the night, Mhirr-cuin's magick would not have protected your village against my magick. For I am a greater witch than Mhirr-cuin. The Four Great Horned Ones obey me, not Mhirr-cuin. They have promised me that, at my command, they will destroy Mhirr-cuin and all who associate with her, to punish all who offend me or mine. The People of the Marsh sacrificed Ihtar of the People of the Wolf – whom I favour. So, at my command, the Great Horned Ruler of Water took the boats of the Marsh People. The People of the Marsh spoiled the fields of the People of the Bear, the Beaver and the Wolf – whom I favour. So, at my command, the Great Horned Ruler of Air took away Wheg-ling.'

Ochy's finger made a series of jabs in Onta's direction. 'He is the Chief of the Acolytes of Mhirr-cuin. At my command, the Great Horned Ruler of Earth will take his body and rend it in pieces. At my command, the Great Horned Ruler of Fire will take his hut, all that is within, even those two little ones, and consume them utterly. For the Hut of the Acolytes has given shelter to Hpe-gnorr, who – at Mhirr-cuin's command – attempted to violate me when I was but a child. All these seasons I have waited and now I have come to wreak vengeance upon him. Do not move him from the Hut of the Acolytes for wherever you take him he will die and the Hut be destroyed by fire whether he be in it or not.'

Ochy's finger momentarily picked out each member of the Marsh People. 'Leave the Acolytes of Mhirr-cuin, shun them, forsake them, lest similar punishments fall upon every one of you.'

Terrified, they all shrank back except for the tall figure of Onta. In a blur of movement he snatched a bow from the hand of the man nearest him, an arrow from its quiver. Nobody saw the arrow leave the bow, but all saw the slight shake of Ochy's head as she plucked it from the air with her teeth. They all heard the crack as she bit the shaft in half, the two parts dropping either side of her jaws.

'Aaaah,' they gasped in wonder.

Ochy was holding the arrowhead in her right hand. In one swift stroke, she ran it down her left arm. Droplets of blood started, coalescing into one crimson. Once again, she adopted her cursing stance, that gory left hand pointing at Onta – and then beckoning him.

'Come, Onta. Come and see what the Great Horned Ruler of Earth has prepared for you.'

Stepping forward, he retorted: 'What bleeds, dies!' and loosed another arrow.

But Ochy had gone.

They saw her head appear beyond the hidden beach. She was swimming out across the marsh.

'You men,' pointed Onta. 'Bring your spears and paddles. You will take me in the Boat of the Acolytes. I shall catch that woman, whoever she is, bind her, take her as a gift to the Witch of All the Peoples, for her to sacrifice to the Four Great Horned Ones. Then Mhirr-cuin's Ghost will return our boats to us.'

'No, no!' Ngaro shook his head, backing away. 'That woman . . . did you see the way she took the arrow. She is no woman. She is a witch, a Ghost. Leave her be. Who knows what harm may befall us if we anger her further?'

For the third time, an arrow left the bow in Onta's hands. Ngaro was lifted off the ground, crashing onto his back, the shaft of the arrow pointing from his right eye.

'I have never heard of the Witch in the Cave,' shouted Onta. 'I know only Mhirr-cuin, the Witch of All the Peoples. She alone commands the Four Great Horned Ones. And I, Onta, am the Chief of her Acolytes.' He pointed at Ngaro writhing and screaming in agony. 'See how speedily pain comes to those who reject Mhirr-cuin and her Acolytes. And death . . .'

Ngaro's shrieks ended in a gurgling fountain of blood as Onta's flint knife severed his throat. In the sudden silence, the chittering of Onta's bone ornaments could clearly be heard.

Then in a quiet, soothing voice, he went on: 'Meliod and Sela –' He pointed at the boy and girl acolytes, 'will remain within the Secret Hut chanting Mhirr-cuin's spells for safe protection and for good hunting. No further harm will come to the village and I shall return with this unknown woman who has dared to challenge the mighty power of Mhirr-cuin. Now – let us depart.'

Some men still held back, but enough to form a crew piled into the canoe. Seizing their paddles, they backed water away from the big tree-trunk, swept about in a wide circle and came past the village.

Their chanting led by the child-acolytes, those left behind waved and shouted in unison:

Kill her!
Kill her!
Death to the Witch in the Cave!
Kill her!
Kill her!
Death to the Witch in the Cave!'

'Faster, faster!' urged Onta in the canoe.

Rodac was giving the stroke: 'In . . . in . . . in . . . in . . .'

The villagers, now silent, heard the paddling chant die away as the boat forged into the distance.

32

The sun was well up the sky before Ahtola woke. She was in no hurry and took plenty of time getting ready for her part in the day's activities. When she had eaten and refreshed herelf, she made her way down to where the tight skin of putrefying offal bulged ominously in the morning sunshine. Carefully she slackened the neck fastening. A jet of foul-smelling liquid shot out spattering her feet. Immediately she tightened the knot again, so that a thin smear of ordure oozed from the tiniest aperture. The little girl checked the fastening and made her way up the hill.

Halfway up, she stopped, turned back and wrinkled her nose. Perhaps the odour was still lingering in her nostrils; perhaps it was still coating her legs. She checked the wind again; no, she could definitely smell it in the air.

The next skin was wedged between several stones at the brow of the hill. She dealt similarly with this one and with the one on the far side of the ridge.

Out across the marshes went the blonde child, easing the knots on every skin that she and Ochy had secreted. This was the second day they had been exposed to the sun and the gases of putrefaction had swollen the skins to near bursting-point. A slight relaxing of the pressure permitted the expanding filth to trickle and ooze across the marsh, its vile smell going before it on the faint breeze.

Ahtola coped with most of the skins quite easily, but the one dangling from the withered willow almost proved too much for her. She had to scramble up the trunk, hang on with one hand, and loosen the lashing with the other. The thong gave way suddenly, allowing a thread-like stream of green matter to plop and dribble into the marsh. Ahtola could not get two hands to it, and she had to leave it running out much faster than she had intended.

None of the other skins presented any problems, not even the one at the dragon's lair itself. She ripped the lashing on this one clear away, so that its entire content whooshed out.

Her task completed, Ahtola clung to the mound of vegetation itself, feeling the heat of the sun beating down on her shoulders, the warmth of decay hugging her chest, and the chill of green slime gripping her belly. With her ear to the rotting tangle, she could just sense faint movement within. The water moved slightly as though displaced by some invisible force.

Ahtola pushed away from the steaming midden. She had not yet reached the bank when the dragon surfaced behind her. Ochy had told her what to expect, and the little girl stopped swimming to turn round and regard the monster unemotionally.

The eye lumps slid towards her, hesitating, came nearer, then turned away, came in her direction and then turned away again, as though casting about for something of greater interest than the little head a few strokes distant.

Then those stony eyes and scaly protuberances were moving purposefully away from her, the green slime opening and closing in a black wake behind them. The long, ponderous body heaved itself over the old beaver dam. As it did so, a sharp claw chanced to touch the taut waterskin wedged there. A geyser of fine-tasting offal exploded into the beast's eyes and nostrils. It waited for a moment, its huge mouth questing from right to left, a fragment of skin bag hanging from its lower jaw. Then it slithered over the rim of the dam. The scaly tail snaked out of the slime, its tip flicked into the air, and the dragon was gone.

33

The chase went on all day as the sun climbed over the marshes, passed its zenith, and began to roll towards its rest. Sometimes Onta and the paddlers saw Ochy as a speck in the watery waste. Sometimes her black hair streamed into the cresting bow-wave as the canoe rode down her back. Then she would twist and dive, while the boatmen backed water in a flurry of spray, turning their cumbersome vessel as they saw her reappear astern, or to one side, or even dead ahead.

Once they thought they had her, in the narrow entrance to a small mere surrounded by dense bulrushes. They scanned the shimmering water, wiping their eyes with the backs of their hands, waiting for her to come up. They swept the edge of the reeds, searching for any ripple or movement of wildfowl that would reveal some disturbing presence. They waited, cooling sweat evaporating from their bodies. One or two chomped food or gulped drink, and were promptly shushed by their comrades. Still they waited for their breathless quarry to burst into view or drift lifeless into sight.

And all the time Ochy hung motionless beneath their feet, clinging to the bottom of the hull and breathing through a hollow reed hidden by the overhang of the stern.

Still they waited, until convinced she had been trapped by clinging weed – and then Rodac's paddle was wrenched from his grasp, fierce blows from its edge stung wrists and hands and more paddles were dropped. One man made a grab for her black hair and fell overboard, getting another man's spearthrust through his arm. Onta was shouting; Rodac was yelling; all the others were giving orders.

By the time organisation had been restored, paddles recovered, the injured man brought aboard – almost upsetting the canoe – and treated, Ochy was well away, and swimming as strongly as ever.

Once they saw her wade ashore on a small islet of hard-packed sand, bare save for a tiny clump of reeds and a tangled bush right in the centre. As the boat grounded, they leapt out, followed the heel prints and encircled the witch's hiding place. Shoulder to shoulder, around the little mound of undergrowth, the first spearhead penetrated the vegetation.

Out burst two swans, snowy wings flailing, orange beaks hissing. Valiant hearts quailed before these unexpected assailants. Most fled back to the boat, but one or two evaded the furious birds and saw that their green lair was empty, save for a heaped-up nest, and several balls of down. A cheerful voice was calling, and there was Ochy waving to them out in deep water.

With angry words they got their canoe afloat again – they had run it well ashore in their previous eagerness – and set off in pursuit. Now their hunt was not just a matter of destroying a dangerous enemy: they had been outwitted so many times, made fools of so often, that now they were resolved to avenge their wounded pride – no matter how long it took.

Onta was giving the stroke now: 'In. In. In. In. See, she is tired. She swims no more. She floats on a raft. Now we have her.'

On their right the falling sun was hidden behind bars of slate-grey and fiery red. The marsh was already darkening. Ahead of them the kneeling figure paddled inexpertly, the clumsy raft yawing from side to side. They saw the fatigue in her arms. Often now, they saw her black head become a white blob as she peered anxiously over her shoulder. They were closing fast. They were right behind her.

She was making for a narrow inlet in the low ridge opposite Htorr-mhirr. No doubt she hoped to be able to hide in the thickets on the hillside, but she would not get there in time. They heard her cry: 'Come, O Great Horned Ruler of Earth. Accept the sacrifice I bring thee. Come and eat!'

In the bow of the canoe, Onta pointed with his knife, mocking her. All could now see what the witch had noticed too late: the little creek was blocked by several big tree-trunks fallen across its entrance. She was cut off from the densest woodland. She tried to turn the unwieldy raft and make for another shore, but the boat was surging up right behind her.

The woman abandoned her plan, leapt for one of the big trunks. As she landed awkwardly on the slimy bark, the canoe rode up onto the little floating platform of logs, so that its bow reared high into the waterlogged branches and its stern began to fill. Onta was catapulted forward, half-thrown and half-jumping out of the boat. He got a foothold on the bark, grabbed a dead twig which broke, flailing wildly backwards, regained his balance and half-ran, half-skipped along the trunk. The rest of the crew tried to shove their craft clear, or jumped into the water to lighten it. These made for the shore to join in the chase.

Their assistance would not be needed. Their quarry was limping. Onta was right behind her, his grasping hand a pace away from her flying black hair.

34

The dragon was angry, angry and hungry. His reptilian intelligence had realised at last that some indefinable being was playing a trick on him. All through the winter he had slept in the foetid heat of his lair, with occasional awakenings and nibblings at his decaying store. Now the hot days had come again and he had arisen to an empty larder.

On this, his first venture outside, his tastebuds had been stimulated by the choice aroma of corrupting meat. He had tracked down the putrid slick to its source until his eyes recognised a ripely swollen carcass and his teeth found emptiness. But the scent persisted and his saurian brain could not resist its call.

Again and again he had located a fine meal: again and again he had been disappointed. One decaying body had been suspended from a dead tree. He could only reach it by leaping out of the muddy water time after time, foaming the marsh, standing on his lashing tail in a frenzy of lustful gluttony. At last his teeth caught in it and he hung clear of the mire like some strange bird. Then the skin ripped and he thundered back into the swamp with the merest trickle of evil-smelling liquid to show for all his efforts.

He could not fill his belly on taste and smell alone, no matter how appetising, but still those lures drew him on.

Towards the end of his journeyings, the trail led the dragon overland, but this did not worry him. It was the very last carcass that finally disillusioned him. Through some quirk of exploding gases, the skin was blown inside out when he punctured it. It covered his nostrils and eyes, and encircled his jaws so firmly that he could not open his mouth. Blinded, he barged to and fro, bumping his snout on solid oaks and entangling his legs in dense brambles. At last, by a chance combination of rubbing against rough bark and scratching with his foreclaws, he removed the constriction, saw some water and slid in.

A barrier of trees at its mouth enabled the shallow creek to retain its midday warmth slightly longer than the rest of the swamp. The dragon lay there, nursing his resentment. He was far from home, in an alien part of the swamp. He was very hungry, and he was very, very angry.

35

Ochy ran along the shore and dodged to the right. Onta overshot her by a pace as she made to cross the creek. Her left foot landed on a floating log, her right foot farther along it, pushing off, and then she was landing on the far shore. Onta jumped. The log had gone. In its place a whirlpool of foam, a bottomless cavern filled with teeth.

Onta screamed, tried to retrace his steps in midair, came down in the water on his side, his leg penetrating that dread jaw which clamped about his thigh. The scaly beast revolved. Onta tried to roll with it, but he could not turn fast enough. The horrified watchers heard his pelvic bones grinding and snapping as his leg was torn off. Half hopping, half floating, he tried to drag himself out of the water. Now his other leg was seized. Again his screams became choking gurgles as his head dipped under the surface and then screams again as legless he was thrown into the air. He still had the flint knife in his hand, as the jaws fastened on his waist and belly. He beat at the pitiless snout until the waters closed over him and the muddy creek was still.

Ochy was racing along the opposite beach, all signs of fatigue and limp gone. At a slight rise she stopped, stood on her left leg and pointed at the sunset sky with her left hand. If any of the boatmen had been close enough, they would have seen that her right eye was closed. But even at a distance, they heard her words: 'Come, O Great Horned Ruler of Fire. Destroy the Hut of the Acolytes of Mhirr-cuin and all that is within. Destroy Hpe-gnorr. Come and eat.' The distant greyness parted, the last arc of the sun showed above the far horizon, a fierce brightness which lit up the whole landscape. Ochy's hand traversed to the right, lighting on the golden roofs of the Marsh People's village. Instantly a sliver of smoke rose vertically into the air, the sun was gone, the sky was grey again and the swampland dark, save for a strange flickering that grew, faded, and burst into glorious life.

'The village!' wailed Rodac. 'She has set the village on fire.'

The men on the beach forgot all about the dragon as they scrambled into their canoe and paddled with new-found energy towards the flames that threatened their thatched homes.

Ochy retrieved her raft, recovered the paddle that was floating nearby and set off towards that beckoning beacon.

The lurid framework that had once been Onta's hut was no longer a nest of flames; now it was the pulsating heart of a living monster that shot out fiery tentacles to lick at dry thatch or flicked out of doorways to entangle the legs of people running by.

Encouraged by the rising wind, the fire attacked hut after hut. Sometimes it leapt across a wide space to trample down a house with feet of flame. Sometimes a single spark caught a loose piece of straw. A child could have snuffed it out between forefinger and thumb; but, ignored, it gradually ate along the dry grass, munching its way through walls and roof until the whole building gently floated away in fine grey ash, leaving the framework of poles almost untouched.

Ochy saw another hut, one of those made from old skins, completely surrounded by blazing buildings. It smoked fiercely, thick tendrils of black snaking from every seam and billowing into the night sky. A high-pitched wailing was coming from inside. A man, his naked body cringing from every fiery embrace, waited until the surrounding flames rose vertically for an instant, then dashed blindly towards the darkened hut in the centre. Again the circle of flames parted momentarily and Ochy saw him pull aside the skin flap covering the doorway. Immediately the little house exploded in a ball of fire, flattening the surrounding buildings upon a crippled woman dragging herself along the steaming ground. The roof spun into the air, a spark-showering nebula that scythed into the distant trees at the foot of Htorr-mhirr. For a moment the undergrowth seemed to extinguish the fire, but then Ochy saw tongues of flame jumping up between the branches and bracken, like golden hunters leaping from ambush. There was now no escaping the conflagration that way.

A black boy – the Acolyte Meliod – staggered from a collapsing house with a baby in his arms, his legs framed by a network of black poles that flamed up towards his groin and tripped him. The trap held them both just long enough for a wall of red-hot turf to avalanche upon them.

And here came the other Acolyte – the little girl Sela – running screaming towards the water with a tree of flame mounting from her head.

A naked pregnant woman trod heavily towards the safety of the solitary canoe, slid down the little bank above the beach and collapsed in the mud. Her cries of pain as her labour began went unheeded. The mother delivered her child, and both died untended in the mire.

Most of the boatmen had got ashore to try to help, but the narrow craft was soon swamped by fugitives from the advancing flames. People were shouting, screaming, punching and pulling. Ochy saw Rodac begin to effect some sort of order around the boat when another canoe seemed to rear beneath it, throwing it high into the brilliant night air. There was a flash of white, an animal bellow, a man screamed in pain, and the water, red with fire, became red with blood. Drawn by the heat and light, by the cries of alarm and by the scent of fear, the dragon had come to find the Marsh People. Now he could vent his anger upon these tantalising creatures. Now he could play games with them, just as tricks had been perpetrated upon him. Now his claws ripped children's flesh; now his teeth mangled flailing limbs; now his tail crushed bones.

One man, his spine broken, drowned in water two fingers deep, unable to turn his head to breathe. Swimmers spared by reptilian anger were pulled down by non-swimmers. Babies, the old, the crippled and the pregnant stood no chance at all. A few survivors clung to the upturned boat until that too was seized in the monstrous jaws and snapped like a twig in the foaming water.

Ochy looked with horror upon the carnage she had wrought. Hpe-gnorr, Onta, Meliod and Sela had died exactly as she had planned, but she had expected the dragon to return to his own lair, not venture this far into another part of the marsh. She had intended to demonstrate her power only by destroying the Secret Hut of the Acolytes and if the fire spread to the rest of the village then that was as the Four Great Horned Ones wanted. But she had not intended this awful loss of life – Oh, not this.

The witch paddled the raft in closer, taking alternate strokes to steer around the occasional body floating head downwards in red reflections. Judging by the screams, the dragon was now somewhere over to her left. A thick wall of smoke suddenly rolled across the water. There was splashing nearby. Ochy called, 'Over here! Come over here!'

A face appeared, framed in dark brown hair. The woman was swimming on her back, clutching something to her breast. Ochy turned the raft alongside her and rolled the baby onto the rough logs. She reached down, grasping the woman's wrists to pull her aboard. For a moment the edge of the raft was underwater, then the smoke rolled away and in the light of the flames, the woman recognised Ochy.

'You! You!' she choked. 'What did we ever do to you? Get away from us! Let me go!'

She pulled her wrists loose and dropped back, accidently sweeping her baby into the water with one blow of her arm. The infant sank like a stone, the smoke descended again and the woman disappeared.

Soon there were no more human cries; in their place there were the panic-stricken squawks of nesting waterfowl, as flames swept through the reeds. Now there was cawing above as fire spiralled around Htorr-mhirr, and rooks and daws soared in the fiery vortex until their feathers shrivelled and they plummeted down to burn or drown. Now the whole of the Mountain-in-the-Sea was an erupting volcano of red and gold and orange and black, floating on a lake of seething fire.

As grey dawn broke, a thin rain began to fall. At first it was hardly more than a mist condensing upon the smouldering slopes of Htorr-mhirr, where an occasional tree stump still blazed defiantly. It fell upon the charred roots of reed and sedge. It streaked the sooty skeletons of what had once been little houses. It pattered upon the ashes carpeting the surface of the marsh. It glistened upon the singed bodies huddled on some patch of bare ground where they had hoped in vain for safety. It chilled the skin of the woman, kneeling, breasts and mouth pressed to the earth, her arms covering her head to shut out the sight and sound and smell of what she had wrought.

There were feet beside her, a voice from above, the old man's voice. 'Look at it!' he commanded.

Ochy felt her head pulled up and back: he had both hands in her hair; powerful hands – even distraught, she still noticed that. 'Go on! Look at it. Look at what you have done,' insisted Wheg-ling.

Ochy tried to shake her head, sobbing.

'No, no, no!' Ochy managed to get out a string of words. 'I never meant all that to happen. I only wanted to hurt them a little bit. I promise I will never again use my powers to wreak my own vengeance. I promise I will try to use my powers only for good. I will only do what people ask me to do for them.'

The old man was merciless. 'I do not know what good things you have done or will do, but that out there is what you will be remembered for. And even when that deed has been forgotten, the evil you used will be remembered. When people speak of the Witch of the Cave, they will only remember the bad things; they will speak with fear and loathing in their hearts. It is too late for new promises.'

'No,' moaned Ochy. 'I shall never kill again, except to eat.'

Wheg-ling sneered at her. 'That is what they all say. Priest, king, witch or chief, they all say "I shall never kill again, except to eat," and then they ask me to use the Magick Stones to give them power over the whole world. And I say, "But this power kills and you have promised never to kill except to eat." And they say,' he simpered, ' "Aah, but you see, if we do not kill these other people they will steal our food or our women or our cattle or our sunlight, so give us power from the Magick Stones so that we may continue to eat and sit in the sunshine." So I use the Magick Stones to give them power and they kill each other. But I eat and drink well, so why should I care? Anyway, if I did not use the Magick Stones for them, one day someone else would . . .' He gave a sideways wink of pride. '. . . although not as well as I can.' Then his harsh tone returned. 'I will use my skills to give you power from the Magick Stones, I promise you that. Because I can see that you will never shrink from using them, nor from ordering other people to use them. Go on, wallow in remorse: enjoy your guilt – for a while. The mood will not last for ever. And then you will remember the fire and flame, the screams of pain and the begging for life. You will remember the fear in people's eyes when you killed them. You will see the fear sitting in people's eyes when they remember what you did. And you will note the speed with which people leap to obey your command – even to kill other people at your command. You will have power, power over other people – and you will want more. And you will crave the power which only my Magick Stones can give. You people are all the same. And you all make me sick.' With a final exclamation of disgust, Wheg-ling flung Ochy's head forward so violently that it struck the ground. He turned and limped off up the track towards the cave.

Ochy remained huddled and weeping by the water's edge. Soon the steady rain was falling so thickly that it was impossible to tell what was sky and what was water, what was marsh and what was moisture-sodden land.

36

It rained all that day. It rained all the next day. It rained all the day after that. It kept on raining. It seemed as though it would never stop. Sometimes there was a heavy drizzle that soaked through the skin, waterlogged the flesh and chilled the bone. Sometimes there were a few spits of rain from a pale grey cloud that almost – but not quite – let through the sunshine. Sometimes there was a violent downpour with raindrops as big as fingernails out of a clear blue sky. Sometimes the rain was driven horizontally by fierce gusty gales from the sea. Sometimes, just occasionally, it did stop raining – for a little while. But through the rents in the cloud, could be seen those frosty white whirls high up that told that more was on its way. Soon all would be grey and wet and glistening as the rain began to fall again.

The plants loved it. They drank greedily, filling their leaves, pushing out roots and branches. Their tendrils writhed across paths untrodden for one night. Their flower petals expanded, soaking hollows and dells with heady scent. New seeds hidden in the ground and about to die for lack of moisture, sprouted and sprang forth. Within days they made up the growth of a moon or more of drought. Even the charred wasteland of Htorr-mhirr was shot with bright green, the new blades lush and attracting wild cattle from wooded islands and hillside.

Ochy, dejected and morose, haunted the cave, spending much of her time alone in the Far Cavern. Eventually it rained so much and the water-level rose so high that she was forced out into the main caves, taking her mother's skull with her. Even then, she hardly listened to and certainly took no part in the conversations between Wheg-ling and Ahtola. Nor did she pay attention to the ease with which the old man made friends with Dhogh. However, she could not help gathering that Wheg-ling was quite interested in the fact that Ahtola was the daughter of Ahmorc. He had heard the name during the reports made by the Marsh People after their searches for the Magick Stones. And without giving anything away to them, he had come to think – from their descriptions – that Ahmorc's land was where the Magick Stones were most likely to be found. He explained to Ahtola that because he knew exactly what to look for, he would not need to trample down any crops. He persuaded her to explain where the fields of the People of the Wolf were, and stumped off into the pouring rain without further ado, taking Dhogh with him.

Ahtola seemed content to be left alone all the time, but her presence irritated Ochy. The witch tried to ignore the girl's solitary games, her clumsy attempts at carving, her incorrect use of herbs when preparing some concoction. A faltered step in a childish dance or a mangled rhyme in a chant infuriated Ochy beyond reason. She grabbed the swishy sapling that rarely left her side during these moons, and cut across the child's bottom or leg or face. Then she made Ahtola start again, meting out similar treatment at the next mistake and starting again and again and again, until the little girl completed the most complicated manoeuvres and intricate spells without fault. Only then, could Ochy relax, the tension draining away from her – until another recurring error grated on her mind, and witch and pupil began another struggle of wills and intellects.

And then one day the rain stopped and the sun shone hotly for day after day after day. It was just in time. For over a moon it ripened the fruits on the trees and yellowed the seeds on the corn.

And now Wheg-ling returned – he had been gone for at least two moons and they had almost forgotten him; he returned nearly delirious with the excitement of the discoveries he had made.

'I have found them
I have found them
I have found the
Maa-gick Stones.'

Ochy and Ahtola heard his tuneless singing echoing down the tunnel. He bounced off the rocky walls into the Witching Cave, grabbed Ochy's arm and lurched around with her. Dhogh was leaping up and down, yelping with delight.

For a moment the witch resisted, objecting, then, laughing, entered into the dance, whirling Wheg-ling faster and until his crippled leg lagged behind the other three speeding feet. He stumbled, tripped, and Ochy let him go. He gyrated once more and sat down heavily on the only patch of soft sand in the Witching Cave. His head rolled happily from side to side as he waved his arms in time with his chorus.

'I have found them
I have found them
I have found the
Maa-agick Stones'

He tried to focus on the witch's face, coming and going in the firelight. 'And . . . and . . . not only have I found them . . .' He emphasised his words with little movements of his forefinger. '. . . I have used them as well. And . . .' He grinned at them. '. . . I have found some new friends – beavers or wolves or something – and they fed me well.'

'Did we not feed you well?' chided Ochy.

'Oh – oh, yes, but this was a great feast, with lots to eat . . .' He hiccoughed. '. . . and lots to drink. They have had a good harvest. They were celebrating. They asked me to share their food.' He pursed his lips knowingly; 'and their drink.' He nodded. 'They are good friends. I think I will use the Magick Stones for them.' He closed his eyes and smiled. 'Lots to eat and lots to drink.'

Suddenly his drooping eyes opened. He looked over his shoulder and beckoned them closer. 'Shush,' he whispered. 'Mhirr-cuin must not know.' He leaned forward. 'Mhirr-cuin does not approve of feasts. Mhirr-cuin does not like merriment. If she knew we had been happy she would punish us.' He put his finger to his nose.

'So they will not say anything about me to anybody. Not that there is much for them to tell. They know my name is Wheg-ling – they knew that already from the Marsh People's descriptions of me. And they know that I escaped from the village on the Mountain-In-The-Sea before the Great Fire. But I did not tell them how I escaped, nor how the fire started. Everybody up on the ridge and on the hills around the Great Marsh saw the blaze, but nobody knows what caused it. Nor has anybody mentioned the Dragon of the Marsh.' He grinned sardonically, grunting to himself. 'You see, O Witch of the Cave, there were no survivors. You used your power too well. Not one person lived to speak of your magick, to tell how you spirited away me and the boats, how you commanded the Great Horned Ruler of Fire to burn the village, nor how you brought the Dragon of the Marsh to eat those who were not drowned or consumed by flame. Nobody said "Oooh, look, the Witch of the Cave is more powerful than the Witch of All the Peoples." Instead they say "The Marsh People died because they did not perform Mhirr-cuin's dances and spells properly, because they did not make sufficiently painful sacrifice to the Four Great Horned Ones, because somehow they offended

169

The Witch of All the Peoples and she cursed the boatmen and their families and so they all died." And Mhirr-cuin herself says this and all people believe her. And nobody mentions the Witch of the Cave because they have not heard of you. Is that not funny? All those people died so that you could demonstrate the power of your name. And they took your name with them into death. Go on laugh. Ha – ha – ha.' And with each exclamation, Wheg-ling's finger hammered the humour of the jest into the witch's angry stare.

'You fool,' snarled Ochy. 'Why did you not tell them of me? All my work, all my preparation, all my spells, all my magick, all expended in that great display of *my* power – and they still have not heard of the Witch of the Cave. It need not have been wasted if you had opened your mouth and told them of me. But no, you think that because you know some nonsense about so-called Magick Stones that you do not need to remember me. I tell you that in future . . .' Ochy pointed her left hand at him, its forefinger trembling with anger. She started to raise her right foot.

'That is enough!' Wheg-ling sobered so suddenly that Ahtola wondered whether he really had been drunk at all. Something appeared in his hand, seeming to leap from one of the flaps in his apron. It might have been a knife, but it was like no knife Ahtola or Ochy had seen before. The handle was normal enough, but what was meant to be the blade was obviously not of flint or stone. In one dimension it was broad and flat, but in the other, was so thin that edge-on it was virtually invisible.

'I told you I had used the Magick Stones,' warned Wheg-ling. 'And this is my magick. And long before you have finished cursing me, my magick will have removed your nose from your face, your eyes from their sockets and your tongue from your mouth.'

Red fire ran up and down the blade as it danced in front of Ochy's gaze. It fascinated her; she could not look away. Long experience with magick had taught her when to exercise caution when confronted with something new. She forced herself to smile, her body to relax; her hands waved emptily and meaninglessly. 'I spoke hastily. We . . . share the same cave. We are . . . friends?'

'I have promised to use the Magick Stones for you,' said the old man. 'That means that you and I are "partners" not "friends". People who use the magick I make, in common cause, are no longer "friends", but "allies". You learn new words and new loyalties when you learn to use the magick I have.'

'Do not bandy words with him,' shouted Ahtola. 'He is an old man. Bind him to you with a death spell; curse him if he does not

170

do as you command. You are the Witch of the Cave. Why are you afraid of an elm leaf from last fall?'

'Catch!' snapped Wheg-ling, and tossed the implement at the little girl's head. Instinctively her hands flew up to knock it away and it clattered back at Wheg-ling's feet. He retrieved it and used it to gesticulate at the girl while addressing Ochy.' You ought to invoke *your* magick to heal her fingers.'

Ahtola was staring wide-eyed at the gashes on her hands where they had come into contact with the strange knife. She looked up at him. 'It *is* magick,' she declared. 'It is so sharp. What is its name? How is it made? Where do you find the Magick Stones it comes from?'

'It is called "metal",' replied Wheg-ling. 'As for your other questions . . . you witches have your little secrets, and I have my secrets; that is fair.' He turned his attention to Ochy. 'I noticed that when you were speaking just now, you complained of the work you had wasted. Not once did you speak with regret of the people who had died, whose lives *you* had wasted. That is proof that you are the sort of person to use the magick of metal to achieve power over other people. I will make you weapons and tools of metal to fulfil whatever plans you have in your mind. And you will feed me. For we are – partners.'

'And this is the first of the magick weapons you have made for me?' Ochy felt her fingers reaching out for it.

'No,' replied Wheg-ling. 'This one is mine. If my understanding of you is correct, I think you will want more than one knife or spear to seize what you want to achieve. And it will take me a long time to fashion all those weapons. Even this one knife –' He flourished it once more before returning it to his apron flap '– took me a long time to make.'

'I will wait,' declared Ochy. 'Fashion me a magick knife which I may hold in my hand when I confront Mhirr-cuin. Then all peoples will know that I am a greater witch than her.'

'I could do,' nodded the old man, 'but Ahmorc will be dead by then.'

'My father?' asked Ahtola.

'Yes, Mhirr-cuin is going to kill him,' replied Wheg-ling. 'Listen, this is what I was told by the people who feasted me – secretly, remember. They said that they had had a good harvest. Mhirr-ling said that the people ought to celebrate. Mhirr-cuin said that there would be no celebration. Instead sacrifice must be made to the Four Great Horned Ones. Mhirr-ling said that the Four Great Horned Ones had already feasted on one sacrifice each and that was enough. Mhirr-cuin said that those four sacrifices had persuaded the Four Great Horned Ones to send the rain in the growing season and the sunshine in the harvest season. Now sacrifice must be made to thank them. Mhirr-ling said that he was the Artzan of the People and he forbade it. Mhirr-cuin said that he was no Artzan. He did not wear the bear's-claw and that now he was going to die and that she was going to rule without an Artzan. So she sent her Ghost and Mhirr-ling is dying. Mhirr-cuin has ordered the sacrifice to be made within the summer encampment of the People of the Bear. The other Peoples must come and share in that ritual of thanksgiving. And who will Mhirr-cuin sacrifice?' The old man paused, then answered his own question. 'Ahmorc. Your father. Because Mhirr-cuin says that he has the greatest faith and so he is the most acceptable to the Four Great Horned Ones. And he will do what she says because she has spellbound him. And even if she had not, I think Ahmorc would will himself to death, because all his family have been sacrificed to the Four Great Horned Ones, and he alone remains. So . . .' his tone becoming decisive as he spoke directly to Ochy, 'if you want to save Ahmorc and if you want your friend Mhirr-ling to become Artzan and if you want to do something useful with your powers and prove that you can do it all, you had better take this Bear's Claw to the People of the Bear now.'

Wheg-ling reached round for the neck ornament hanging from one of the antlers behind him. He made to toss it across to Ochy, but checked himself in mid-throw, weighing it in his hand. He looked up at the witch from under his eyebrows. 'These things do not interest me, so I have not handled this before. It is strangely heavy. Tell me, Witch of the Cave, what is inside it?'

Ochy shrugged. 'A bracelet. Its mate lives in the land towards the sunrise. Whoever wears both is the true king of a great people. Htorr-mhirr, the last Artzan of the People of the Bear, made me promise to give it to Mhirr-ling.'

With a sudden movement, Wheg-ling whipped out his knife again and sliced through the thick leather stitches as if they had been made of rotten grass. Ahtola made some sound of objection to waste, but the old man said she could sew it up again just as speedily.

He inverted the open claw and tipped out the golden fire of the sun. It was a crescent of yellow light, throbbing and radiating in the fireglow.

'Whee-ooo-oooh,' whistled Wheg-ling. 'This is beautiful.'

He peered at it close to the fire, turning it delicately in his muscular hands so that he could examine every detail. Occasionally he rubbed it with his thumb.

'This is no bracelet,' he declared at length. 'You wear this on your chest –' he held it in position, vertically, '– like this. See these two holes . . .' He pointed out the perforations halfway up one of the horns of the crescent. The two heads, one mature and dark, the other childish and fair, bent over the object. 'The neck thong goes through them.'

'But what is it made of?' asked Ochy.

'This,' he held it upright between thumb and forefinger, jerking it slightly with each word, 'this comes from more Magick Stones of Power. This – this is gold – pure gold.'

Ahtola took it from him and sniffed. 'It does not look very powerful to me. Gold is not as sharp as the metal you make.'

'If you have enough gold,' declared Wheg-ling, 'you will have power over the whole world.'

'Can you make gold from your Magick Stones?' asked Ochy.

'No,' replied the old man, massaging his lame leg. 'I wish I could. But what I make with my Magick Stones gives the user the power to take all the gold he wants.' Wheg-ling smiled cynically. 'But sometimes what I make with my Magick Stones can be taken by the man who has the gold.'

'I do not think I understand,' puzzled Ochy.

'No, I do not think we will ever understand,' sighed Wheg-ling.

'What I do not understand,' said Ahtola, 'is why this ornament is worn like this,' she held it vertically. 'It seems proper to wear it like this.' The crescent embraced her throat.

'Yes, that is how most lunulae – little moons – are worn. But this one – see here –' Again the two faces focused on his tracing finger. 'Here is the outline of an axe.'

Sure enough they could pick out the shape of an axehead.

'Now, the one that I have seen was worn with the crescent facing the other way and with the axehead pointing the other way too, so that if you were to wear them together, you would get the effect of a double axe, just like this.' His fingers dug into Ahtola's shoulder twisting her round so that Ochy could see the dark blemish there. The child gave a little cry, and Wheg-ling released her. For a moment his fingerprints showed white on the sensitive skin and then darkened as bruises began forming immediately. The two adults ignored her.

'You say you have seen one like this before,' interrogated Ochy. 'Where?'

'Towards the sunrise, like your Htorr-mhirr said. It was worn by a big man with red hair and beard. It is still worn by him, I expect. He is king of that land, although I have heard it rumoured that he is not the rightful king. It is a rich land with many fields and cattle. If your Mhirr-ling is the true ruler of that land, he will certainly be king of a great people.'

'That is the land of which Mhirr-ling is the true Artzan,' declared Ochy. 'I have never heard of the place before now, and I do not know how I know that – but of that I am certain. Will you guide us there?' she urged. 'Will you make weapons of metal from your Magick Stones for me to use so that I can gain power over that land and give it to Mhirr-ling?'

The old man nodded, and then shook his head in silent amusement. 'Is it not as I said? The prospect excites you, does it not? Yes, I will make whatever weapons will be best suited to your purpose. But you will have to ask the trackmen among the Marsh People to guide you there?' He held up his hand at her protest. 'When they return they will learn what you did to their village and to their kinsfolk and they will hate you. But they will also fear you – and they will do what you say. But I will not go to the Land-of-Broad-Fields – to Aks-khai-bor. – with you.' Wheg-ling paused, scratching his head contemplatively. 'I do not know whether Mhirr-cuin has already sent her Acolytes along the footpaths to that land, or whether somehow she learned her ideas through acolytes *from* there. Or perhaps the Ghosts impart the same knowledge to different people in different places at the same time.' He shrugged. 'It happens to workers with the Magick Stones of Power. So it can happen to other people too. But what I do know is that like your People of the Bear here, the people of Aks-khai-bor worship the Four Great Horned Ones. And like your Mhirr-cuin, they sacrifice people to them. And like you, Ochy, King Ughter – that is the name of their priest-king – sacrifices whole families at a time to the Four Great Horned Ones. He once asked me to use the Magick Stones of Power for him, but I did not like his idea of partnership, so I left. I have not forgotten him. And he has not forgotten me. So I should prefer not to visit Aks-khai-bor again.' He grinned ironically. 'You ought to see King Ughter at work. He can burn down a village and all its inhabitants even better than you can.'

Ochy bristled at his implied rebuke, remembering the screams and the flames, red, yellow, orange, gold – the gold of power (like the lunula here) and green, even blue flames: all the colours, they were so beautiful, the beauty she had created with her magick – and the terror – that fear in the eyes of the woman who had come

174

to her raft – and the way the People of the Marsh had shrunk from her even before she had summoned the Dragon and burned their village. She felt her belly churn with excitement at the memory. And then she clamped her hands together in an even fiercer agony of frustration, that nobody knew that it was she who had done all that. Even after the total destruction of the Mountain-In-The-Sea, still nobody knew of the Witch of the Cave and her power. She raised her clenched fists aloft. 'Now! They must know now! Now is the time for me to give Mhirr-ling his inheritance, his inheritance as Artzan of the People of the Bear, his inheritance as King of Aks-khai-bor. Now is the time to deliver Ahmorc from the spellbinding of Mhirr-cuin. When I command, you, Ahtola, his undead daughter, will release him. When I command, you, Dhogh, my Ghost, will destroy the Ghost of Mhirr-cuin. And you, Wheg-ling – my partner – will begin making the weapons of metal for Mhirr-ling to use when he claims his inheritance as Priest-King of Aks-khai-bor. I shall confront Mhirr-cuin naked except for my necklaces of charms, so that all peoples shall know that it was *my* magick and my magick alone which defeated her, that it was my power over the Four Great Horned Ones which destroyed her and removed her head from her shoulders. No one else will die, so that all shall bear witness that I, Ochy, the Witch of the Cave, am greater than Mhirr-cuin. And it will be me that all peoples will acknowledge as Witch of All the Peoples.'

As the echoes of her furious speech shattered themselves against the rocks of the cave, Ahtola – for the first time – cowered away from the violence of the witch's emotion. The wolf, too, sheltered behind the little girl, whining softly. Only Wheg-ling remained unmoved, nodding to himself as he listened to the outburst which he had been expecting ever since his first encounter with this woman.

37

With the Bear's Claw and the lunula in a leather bag hanging from a waist-thong, Ochy scaled the steep path to the top of the ridge. She noticed that the clear blue sky of the past moon had gone. Now a yellowish overcast covered the heavens. The invisible sun seemed even hotter in the heavy atmosphere, and Ochy's sweat evaporated as soon as it poured from her with the exertion of her climb.

No birds sang, no creatures moved, as the witch jog-trotted across the landscape she had known so well as a child. The only sounds were the crackle of dry vegetation beneath her feet, the rattle of the necklaces bouncing on her breasts, and the chomping of her jaw as she chewed a mouthful of ivy leaves.

To Ochy's eyes, the summer encampment had hardly changed since that fatal morning so long ago: the hawthorn hedge still topped the encircling earth rampart. There were certainly more tents; even from a distance, she could see their pinnacles packed closely together. She had expected that this would be so – extra dwellings for the People of the Beaver and the People of the Wolf.

There was no sign of life outside and no sound came from within. Deliberately and openly, Ochy walked around the encampment until she had returned to her starting point. There was no challenge, no cry of interest, no enquiring head peeping over the top of the hedge. It was a camp of the dead under a dead yellow-grey sky.

The entrance was completely blocked by an impenetrable hawthorn bush. To one side the bear's head still grimaced from its pole, but now it was flanked by the masks of beaver and wolf. Ochy considered the thornbush. It was not the first time the witch had faced such obstructions. She spat out the mashed ivy leaves and a few moments later was inside the encampment.

Her first impression was of circles. Within the bank and hedge were tethered all the cattle, sheep, pigs and goats, all standing silently facing inwards. Then came the circular tents, pitched so closely together that there was hardly room to step between them. Beyond them were the people, all holding hands and all facing inwards. In spite of the heat – the sky was quite grey now – all of

176

them; men, women and children, incongruously were wearing all the clothes they possessed – cloaks, kilts, necklaces, leggings. Ochy smelt the sweat streaming from their pores, collecting and drying in the folds of their thick apparel. She also smelt the tension in the air.

As the witch moved around among the animals, she caught glimpses of the open space enclosed by the impassive circle of watchers. The hard trampled ground was thick with powdery dust, now being flicked by occasional puffs of dry wind. In the middle was a shallow pit filled with brushwood and logs. As befitted the centre of attraction, and in company with the layout of everything else this day, the low mound of firewood was circular. Four stout branches, gnarled, twisted, bifurcated, and vaguely recognisable as representing some facial feature or expression, had been rammed into the earth at equidistant positions on the rim of the firepit.

By now Ochy had noticed that three of the tents were slightly removed from the rest, and a fourth was even further separated. This one had a single staff stuck into the ground in front of it. Stones, twigs, and bits of jagged bone projected from its convoluted stem, which was surmounted by a horned human skull. The other three tents were fronted by Wolf, Beaver and Bear totems, and it was towards this last that Ochy made her way.

Sometimes one of the tethered animals looked at her; sometimes one of the men twitched as though he had heard her, or somebody on the far side of the circle moved his or her head slightly, puzzled by what they thought they saw amongst the cattle.

Outside the Bear Tent, Ochy waited for a moment, listening, and then squirmed under the bottom of a loose piece of hide. It was very dark and stuffy inside. A smoky fire thickened the atmosphere. Elsewhere the floor was covered with piles of cloaks, tools, baskets and pots, the usual things accumulated by any family of the People of the Bear. In one place an extra large bundle of skins moved slightly, emitting the faintest of rasps. Ochy moved closer as her eyes became accustomed to the gloom. It was a man, a big man, with thick black hair and beard, matted with spittle and dry vomit. It was Mhirr-ling. He could hardly breathe. Again he half-choked; then was so still that Ochy thought he had breathed his last, until another tiny rattle sounded in his throat.

Right beside his upturned face, was a furry mass of tawny grey, the biggest wildcat Ochy had ever seen. Its head turned towards Ochy. Its eyes glowed orange in the dark, and then it was gone.

Instantly the invalid's harsh rattle bubbled deeper and more often in his chest. He belched softly and tried to move his head.

Quickly the witch removed the constricting covers and rolled Mhirr-ling over onto his side. With one hand she found a wooden bowl and held it by his mouth as he hawked deep in his throat and spat out thick phlegm. He half relaxed, tensed again, and his body heaved as he fought to clear his lungs of the muck within them. At last he sank back on his side. Ochy squatted beside him.

'I do not know who you are,' he whispered, 'but you have saved my life. This time Mhirr-cuin's Ghost was staying with me until I died. And you have sent it away – but it will return.'

'If it returns, my Ghost will come also; not to drive it away, but to destroy it,' declared Ochy vehemently.

'Nooo,' moaned Mhirr-ling sadly. 'No one can undo what my sister has decreed. And she has decreed my death. Even if *she* were to die the Four Great Horned Ones and the Ghosts would still obey her commands.' The effort of speaking had exhausted him, and he lay back with his eyes closed.

Ochy did not let him rest; there would be time for that later. 'Mhirr-ling!' she shook him. 'I have done more than save your life. I am keeping the promises I made to your father Htorr-mhirr.' She untied her waist-band and opened the little bag.

Mhirr-ling was sitting up now, coughing and wiping his mouth with the back of his hand.

'I am the Witch of the Cave,' began Ochy. 'I was with your father when he breathed his last breath. He made me promise that I would take the Bear's Claw from around his neck and put it around yours. This is what I am doing now. Now you are the Artzan of the People of the Bear. I have kept my promise.' She put his hands together, enveloped them with her palms, and raised his fingers to her lips. 'Hail, Artzan of the People of the Bear.'

For a moment there was silence as Mhirr-ling released his hands and turned up the Bear's Claw so that he could look at it.

The witch was speaking again. 'Your father made me promise that I would take out the ornament sewn inside the claw and put it on you.' Again her fingers opened the bag. 'This is what I am doing now. Now you must find its mate in the land towards the sunrise and be Artzan of a great people. I have kept my promise.'

Once again Ochy took his hands between hers and kissed them. 'Hail, Artzan of Aks-khai-bor.'

Mhirr-ling stared down at the unfamiliar shape glowing on his chest. Ochy was addressing him again. 'Your father made me promise that I would bury him in the soil of his homeland as proof that you have become Artzan of Aks-khai-bor. I shall be with you on that journey, for I have yet to keep that promise.'

A third person had materialised within the tent, a cloaked figure whose face was hidden deep within a tall hood. Its arms were folded, cradling a bundle of tawny-grey fur: the wildcat.

Abruptly, Mhirr-ling's breath whistled within his throat, he tried to open his mouth, and his tortured lungs squealed.

'Not long now, Mhirr-ling.' The woman's voice was soft, and full of menace. 'My Ghost tells me that you would have been dead already if a strange woman had not entered your tent, a woman so strange that I have come to see her for myself.'

Ochy did not move from her squatting position, did not even raise her eyes.

Mhirr-cuin was still speaking to Mhirr-ling, to herself, to her Ghost, to the woman she did not recognise. 'This strange woman I see grovelling before me is of no consequence. She is of the common people: my Ghost tells me so. She has no power over the Ghosts as I have. She cannot drive away my Ghost, Mhirr-ling. *This time*, my Ghost will watch with you until you die – my brother.'

38

Mhirr-cuin's green-sleeved arms turned the big wildcat to face the helpless man on the floor. Mhirr-ling's eyes bulged in panic, his breath was stopped in his throat, his lungs heaved. The cat purred as a white finger emerged from the green folds and stroked the tabby head.

'What pretty toys you have about your neck, my brother. And they have come too late. The People would have accepted you as Artzan, but now you will die. They will have no choice but to accept my absolute rule. And soon I shall have power over all peoples.' Mhirr-cuin was purring.

Then she was shrieking, pulling the snarling, struggling wildcat away from her. Its claws caught in the nettle cloth, ripping the skin beneath. Mhirr-cuin dragged the cat free and held it in both hands at arm's length. Its legs stuck out, twisting; its body squirmed. A crescendo of yowling filled the dark tent, as white teeth appeared beneath a tent flap followed by a grey head and body. It was Dhogh.

With an eager howl, the wolf leapt up at the wildcat, but already the bundle of tawny fur had scrabbled clear of Mhirr-cuin's fingers, leaving blood oozing from lines of scratch-marks. The cat fell, turned, one paw raking Dhogh's muzzle.

The wolf's hair bristled; the cat looked twice its normal great size. The canine jaws snapped between each feline spit and claw. For another moment the cat stood, ears and whiskers back, paw upraised. Then, in the twinkling of an eye, the other claw boxed Dhogh's ear, and the wildcat fled.

Round the cluttered tent they raced, growling and snarling at each other. Up over the bundles of skin, across the recumbent form of Mhirr-ling, around Ochy squatting motionless. Each time they passed, Mhirr-cuin aimed a kick at the wolf or grabbed for his neck fur. Once she briefly gathered up her pet but it immediately clawed free of her protective embrace. Dhogh jumped up at her body, and she staggered back, shouting and beating at the animal.

The cat hurtled up one of the sloping tent-poles, until completely upside-down above the yapping wolf, it lost its grip and fell, twisting to land right way up on Dhogh's head. The wolf backed away and then pushed forward again, trying to dislodge the tawny bundle raking his eyes and ears. His head went down and he somersaulted over one of the obstacles in the gloomy tent. The wildcat fell clear, one claw taking an ear with it. Dhogh rammed his muzzle into the cat's belly fur, another claw ripped his eye. His head lifted momentarily, the cat swinging from his nose and a scraping back leg tearing his lower lip. The cat dropped free, the wolf jumped after it, knocking his quarry into the half-smouldering fire.

Now the stink of singeing fur was added to the tent's foetid smell of sickness. Agonised cries filled the gloom. The wolf was straddling the burning cat, blood spurting from every flick-flick of the feline's back claws.

Mhirr-cuin grasped Dhogh's tail. He turned on her and instantly she let go. The smouldering wildcat made a dash for safety and the wolf shot between Mhirr-cuin's legs after his prey. The Witch of All the Peoples went down in a flurry of green cloth and white thighs, her grabbing hand and the animals' frenzied exit tearing loose the leather flap covering the doorway. Fresh air flooded in and a shaft of daylight illuminated the gore marking floor and walls.

Outside they saw Dhogh overtake the cat, bowl it over, turn, and with one flash of pointed ivory snap its spine. Although still connected, the animal's front and rear quarters flapped without coordination. Standing straddle-legged, the wolf seized the wildcat in his jaws, shaking the furry prize so that its head and loins beat upon the earth so quickly that the eye could not register the movement. Then, half-blinded, an ear missing, blood matting his grey coat, Dhogh picked up the lifeless bundle and trotted out of Ochy's sight. A dark stain was left soaking into the powdery earth. From what she could see of the circle of watching humans, they had observed this slaughter without interest or emotion.

She looked up at Mhirr-cuin, who seemed to have recovered her composure. 'I am the Witch of the Cave, Mhirr-cuin. I am here to tell you that your time has come. Today, you will be shaken by the Four Great Horned Ones, as my Ghost shook your Ghost. Today, the Four Great Horned Ones will sever your head from your shoulders and all peoples will know that I and I alone have power over the Ghosts and over the Four Great Horned Ones.'

Mhirr-cuin had stepped back at the other woman's quiet vehemence, but then she recovered her composure. 'I know you. You are no witch. You are Ochy, daughter of Vhi-vhang, who also was no witch. She was simply an old crazy woman – of the common people.' Mhirr-cuin drew herself up, speaking with contempt in her voice. 'But I am the Daughter of Kings. I am the Witch of All Peoples. I do not know how you came here nor what you have done nor what mad ideas fill your little head. I will not have my plans thwarted by anybody or any thing.' The cowled head nodded in satisfaction. 'This day I shall sacrifice Ahmorc to the Four Great Horned Ones. You may try to interfere if you wish. Your presence – and the manner in which I shall deal with it – will provide me with yet another opportunity of demonstrating my total power over the Realm of Living Things and over the Realm of the Ghosts.'

Without warning, Mhirr-cuin bent down and with her left forefinger and thumb pulled out a single strand of Ochy's black hair. It was done so quickly that Ochy hardly felt the prick of pain. And then Mhirr-cuin was gone.

Mhirr-ling was already breathing more strongly now that Mhirr-cuin's Ghost had gone. Ochy too made for the doorway, then halted. She thought for a moment, separated the bluestone with the Secret of Time from the other necklaces around her throat and lifted it over her head. She knelt and placed it about Mhirr-ling's neck.

'One day I shall tell you the story of this stone,' she said. 'But until then, guard this well. I do not want Mhirr-cuin to harm the Stone with the Secret of Time.'

39

Outside, Ochy immediately noticed three things: the sky was now so dark grey, as to be almost black, with distant thunder in the air and little puffs of wind blowing now hot, now cold, now dry, now damp; the ring of watchers had not moved and were still standing as though carved from stone; and a man's body had been spreadeagled upon a couch of ferns topping the mount of firewood, his wrists and ankles tied to the four gnarled stakes.

It was Ahmorc, his mind now totally spellbound by Mhirr-cuin's magick. He was chanting:

'Thank you for the harvest
O Great Horned Ruler of the Air
Thank you for the harvest
O Great Horned Ruler of the Fire
Thank you for the harvest
O Great Horned Ruler of the Water
Thank you for the harvest
O Great Horned Ruler of the Earth
Thank you for the harvest
O Great Horned Ruler of the Air
Thank you for the . . .'

Ochy walked out and raised her arms wide, revolving slowly so that all eyes were focussed upon her. Even Ahmorc, who could not see her from his horizontal bondage, sensed that something was happening and fell silent.

'People of the Bear!' she cried. 'People of the Beaver! People of the Wolf! I am the Witch of the Cave!'

The watchers observed her without expression, as if in a trance. Ochy had no way of telling whether they understood her or even whether they were able to hear. All of them must have been spellbound by Mhirr-cuin, she decided. But she continued: 'I am Ochy whom Mhirr-cuin gave as sacrifice to the Great Horned Ruler of Water. But the Great Horned Ruler of Water rejected her sacrifice and gave me life so that I should stand before you today. I am Ochy, daughter of Vhi-vhang, whom Mhirr-cuin gave as sacrifice to the Great Horned Ruler of Earth. But the Great Horned Ruler of Earth rejected her sacrifice in its entirety, and the head of Vhi-vhang lives and talks with me in my cave today. I am the Witch of the Cave: I commune with the Ghosts and with the Four Great Horned Ones. They are all mine to command. At my bidding the Four Great Horned Ones burned the village of the Marsh People and sent the Dragon of the Marsh to eat the boatmen of the People of the Marsh. And why did I do these things? Because the People of the Marsh gave themselves to Mhirr-cuin, and I have vowed to destroy Mhirr-cuin and all that is hers and all that she intends. And why have I vowed this? Because she is a false witch, because her ways are the wrong ways, and because the Four Great Horned Ones are not with her as they are with me. As proof of their favour, the Four Great Horned Ones have given me power to withstand pain and cold, fire and fatigue; they have given me strength to rend wild animals asunder with my bare hands. Mhirr-cuin can do none of these things. She cannot even give her Ghost the strength to resist my Ghost. My magick too is greater than hers. She cursed Mhirr-ling to death, but I have restored him to health and made him Artzan of his people thus keeping the promise I made to his father Htorr-mhirr when he breathed his last breath *after* Mhirr-cuin killed him with her magick.'

'She lies!' Mhirr-cuin's voice cried out across the circle. The hem of her green cloak floated through the dust towards Ochy. In one hand she carried her Magick Staff with its jagged projections and horned skull. In the other was a little poppet. '*She* did not restore Mhirr-ling to health. It was *I* who chose to lift the spell which *I* had placed upon him. *She* may have torn animals to pieces and destroyed the village of the Marsh People, but *she* cannot make the rain fall in the growing season, nor the sun shine in the harvest season. The Four Great Horned Ones do this at *my* command because they are pleased with the sacrifices which *I* give them. *I* bring life – but *she* brings only death.' Mhirr-cuin pointed her staff at Ochy. '*She* says she is a witch, the Witch of the Cave. A witch should be able to bring life as well as death. Let us see if *she* can deliver Ahmorc from the death spell *I* place upon him.' She raised her voice, 'Come, O Great Horned Ruler of the Fire! Come and eat!'

Mhirr-cuin held her wand before her at arm's length; the horned skull waved to and fro. Tendrils of smoke writhed up from the heap of firewood. Ahmorc, his faith tested beyond endurance, proved, and promised life, cried out in alarm.

'Deliver him!' commanded Mhirr-cuin. 'If you can.'

As Ochy turned towards Ahmorc, the Witch of All the Peoples squatted down and wedged the poppet's feet into the ground. Instantly Ochy felt her legs stiffen, her feet lock. She was rooted to the spot.

Ochy looked at the effigy, viewing it in close-up although several paces away from it. It was a woman, naked except for a series of necklaces, a woman with tanned skin and glossy black hair. It was a perfect likeness of herself. And Mhirr-cuin had made it in a few moments. Even now, a part of Ochy's mind admired her rival's genius.

Mhirr-cuin was speaking again. 'You see, she cannot move.'

She laid down the staff and placed the fingers of one hand about the poppet's neck and shoulders, while her other hand tugged at the replica necklaces. Ochy felt her neck constricted, the thongs cutting into her flesh, until something broke and beads and pebbles cascaded to the ground.

'You see,' cried Mhirr-cuin. 'She is no witch. Even her charms are not proof against my magick. And see here . . .' She pointed at Ahmorc's funeral pyre. 'See how the smoke rolls upward. That is proof that my sacrifices are always acceptable to the Four Great Horned Ones.'

'They are not,' came a new voice.

For the first time there was a gasp from the watching circle and a general movement of heads.

It was Ahtola. 'Mhirr-cuin sacrificed me to the Four Great Horned Ones so that this year there would be rain in the growing season and sunshine in the harvest season,' she announced standing with her arms open in general wide embrace. 'You all saw that. But look at me. Now I am undead. The Four Great Horned Ones sent me back to tell you that Mhirr-cuin's sacrifices are no longer acceptable in their sight. What pleased them was the sacrifice of the Marsh People and their village by the Witch of the Cave. That was why they sent rain in the growing season and sunshine in the harvest season this year. The Four Great Horned Ones bless those whom the Witch of the Cave favours: they destroy those whom the Witch of the Cave does not favour. They sent me back from the dead to tell you that and to tell you that they reject the sacrifice of my father Ahmorc by the false witch, Mhirr-cuin. And now I shall deliver him, so that in future time he may become Artzan of this people.'

The little girl advanced across the open ground, passed between Ochy and Mhirr-cuin and disappeared into the thick smoke that

185

now obscured the body of Ahmorc. From time to time a glimpse of golden hair or a hand could be seen through the pall. Then both their bodies appeared, moving on invisible legs through an ascending cloud of smoke. As their feet touched the hard-packed earth, the timber flashed into flame, the smoke was swept away, and a whirlpool of fire snaked into the sky. It was now so black that the encampment would have been in total darkness were it not for that freshly kindled beacon.

'You have interfered too long.' Mhirr-cuin was quivering with rage. 'Ahmorc may have been delivered for the present but he is still within the circle. He cannot leave; no one can leave before the sacrifice has been made. Who will the Four Great Horned Ones choose?' Her green-clad finger swept away from Ochy, paused on Ahmorc, hesitated on each watcher – silent now again, each one feeling the power choosing, then passing him over – and coming back to rest on Ochy. 'You will die this day as a sacrifice to the Four Great Horned Ones. You will bleed, you will die. I scratch you above the breath.'

The green sleeve slid back, long fingernails reached out for Ochy's forehead.

'Stop, Mhirr-cuin!' commanded the black-haired woman. 'Stop. Think. Take care. Think of what will happen if you touch me while I am bewitched by you.'

Mhirr-cuin's hand paused, then boldly nearly brushed the skin, hesitated, recoiled. She turned on her heel, picked up her magick wand, looked at Ochy, and brought it down on the poppet. Ochy felt the blow like an axe through the top of her head. Again and again the blows fell. As the wand rose, lightning rippled across the sky. Thunder rolled each time the magick staff struck. Ochy felt her body being pulverised; her limbs ached, her spine was snapping, her bones turning to liquid. Her nose began to bleed; blood oozed from cuts where no cuts were. Her eyes were closing.

There was a cry from far off; somewhere very distant. A familiar cry: Ahtola's voice; something flying through the air, turning over and over.

Ochy got one hand to it, half bounced it, caught it and clasped it to her body. She tried to focus on it. It was something in a green covering. She pulled the material off and saw that it was the figure of a woman, a naked woman, with bright red hair and bone-white skin.

She looked across at Mhirr-cuin; her cloak gone; now a naked woman, with bright red hair and bone-white skin.

Mhirr-cuin laughed at her, smashing the horned wand onto the poppet of Ochy wedged into the ground. Ochy felt her arms go numb: she lost her grip on the little doll of Mhirr-cuin, tried to grab it in mid-drop and knocked it away so that it fell on the earth just out of reach. Mhirr-cuin ran over and raised her staff to smash it into the soil.

'Wait, Mhirr-cuin,' gasped Ochy, thankful for this respite. 'You will be striking your own poppet, striking your own self.'

Mhirr-cuin stared at her, then returned to her former position. Taking her wand in both hands she swung at Ochy's effigy, knocking it further and further over. The black-haired witch felt herself going over. Her feet were still immobile, but her body was being smashed horizontally so that she leaned over almost parallel with the ground. Soon she must touch the earth and then she knew that she would die.

But now, as she strove to keep her hands clear of the powdery soil, she brushed the poppet of Mhirr-cuin. It was within reach. With a backward flip of her wrist she sent the little doll flying into the air.

Mhirr-cuin saw its direction, dropped her magick wand and ran, hands wide apart, shouting, 'No, no, no!'

With a soft plop the poppet fell into the fire.

Mhirr-cuin was catapulted onto her back. She rolled over screaming, got to her feet, ran round the circle beating at her hair. She rolled on the ground again, shrieking and smothering herself with dirt, flapping at her body. She stood, face contorted with agony, staggered one step, two steps, dropped, kneeling, covering her face with her arms, and collapsed, moaning incoherently.

'Release me, Mhirr-cuin,' commanded Ochy. She was still leaning less than hand height above the ground, her arms spread wide like some low-flying bird. 'Release me from your spell, Mhirr-cuin.'

There was an answering groan.

'Release me from your spell, Mhirr-cuin, and then I shall release you, Mhirr-cuin,' persisted Ochy.

There was another inaudible croak, a faint finger movement, and Ochy collapsed on the ground.

40

Mhirr-cuin was the first to recover. She stood before Ochy while the latter was still struggling to her feet. 'I am the Witch of All the Peoples,' she began, swallowing hard after the torment she had just suffered.

Ochy faced her, mouth wide open as she gasped for breath, near-sobbing with relief from the unremitting pain she had undergone.

'You call yourself the Witch of the Cave. Very well; you will remain in your cave for ever. 'The red-haired witch was standing on her left leg, her right eye shut, and her left hand extended at her adversary.

'I call upon the Great Horned Ruler of the Air
To send chill winds upon you
Within your cave.
I call upon the Great Horned Ruler of the Earth
To turn you to stone
Within your cave
I call upon the Great Horned Ruler of the Water
To send icy floods upon you
Within your cave
I call upon the Great Horned Ruler of the Fire
To send fierce flames upon you
Within your – aaagh!'

Absorbed in her curse, Mhirr-cuin leaned forward until the tip of her finger was just inside Ochy's wide-open mouth. The nail touched a gum, and Ochy involuntarily snapped her jaws shut.

As Mhirr-cuin lost her balance, she swung her right palm round, slapping Ochy's cheek and clamping the opening teeth about her fingertip again. A blow to her midriff jolted Ochy's jaws apart and she tottered, grabbing at Mhirr-cuin for support. Half-tangling, they tripped and rolled and broke apart.

Mhirr-cuin came up first, holding her magick wand, swinging it. It caught Ochy across the neck as she got to her knees, flinging her to one side. Another blow slashed her breast, and then at her head. As it returned towards her face, Ochy ducked under Mhirr-cuin's swing, grabbed the staff with one hand and came up behind the unbalanced redhead. Ochy seized the other end of the wand and jerked its spiky stem back into Mhirr-cuin's throat. Choking, she forced her back into Ochy to get away from the throttling wood, but it only pressed the harder. She eased her bottom forward, and then thumped it rearwards into Ochy's belly, once, twice, three times, then bent forward and hurtled the Witch of the Cave over her head onto her back.

Both retained their hold on the wand, but now it was the black-haired witch whose eyes and tongue bulged as the unrelenting branch cut into her throat. She saw Mhirr-cuin's red-framed face upside down behind her head, forcing downwards with all her strength. Ochy pressed upwards, her chest and arm muscles, slowly, so slowly, forcing the restriction up towards the thunder-filled clouds. The Witch of All the Peoples bore down with all her weight, but inexorably the wand climbed upwards. Ochy could breathe again now, and then suddenly both were on their feet, facing each other, all four hands gripping the staff.

From now on the magick wand took on a life of its own, divorced from the struggles and efforts of the two witches. Both still retained their hold on it, but sometimes it was high in the air, their arms upstretched, breasts and bellies touching, their teeth lunging at each other's throats. Sometimes it was flat on the ground, held at arm's length by grovelling figures, whose toes sought leverage in the dirt. Sometimes the wand rolled end over end across the ground twisting them about its axis. Sometimes it lodged vertically between their bodies, raking their flesh, so that their skin slithered in the other's blood and the grinning skull rammed its horns towards eye and mouth and nostril.

Then, side by side, they held it, each with an arm about the other's neck while their outside hands gripped the bottom of the staff. They started to turn, revolve, gyrating faster and faster.

Which one let go first, they did not know, but suddenly the magick wand was gone, landing in the blazing embers on the far side of the fire. It erupted in a brilliant shower of sparks and flames, explosion following explosion as though its magick powers were being violently released.

With a cry, Mhirr-cuin jabbed her elbow into her opponent's breast. As Ochy oofed, the redhead dashed around the firepit to save what was left of her wand. Ochy hurdled the blaze – feeling the flames lick between her thighs – and landed astride Mhirr-cuin, bearing her to the ground, her fingers about her throat.

189

The redhead reached up, her thumbnails gouging into Ochy's eyes. Ochy squeezed harder, hoping to strangle the life out of her enemy before she was herself blinded. There was no time. She seized Mhirr-cuin's wrists, dragged them down, and was heaved over onto her back. Again Mhirr-cuin reached for Ochy's eyes, but her wrists were gripped tight. She could only get two handfuls of black hair before her body was forced away by Ochy's knees against her breasts.

The Witch of All the Peoples went back further and further, pulling the Witch of the Cave up with her. The redhaired woman's spine was pressed against one of the gnarled posts at the edge of the fire. It started to give, cracking and leaning over the pit.

By now the sacrificial blaze had died down to a low tangle of fiery timbers and white-hot ash, alive with running, curling flames of red and yellow, blue and white. Mhirr-cuin felt the fierce heat on her back, smelt her hair singeing. For a moment she forced Ochy away and then the stake snapped, her wrists were released, her hands were empty and her breasts free from pain, as she was projected to her feet and screaming, toppled, arms flailing, backwards into the fire.

At that very instant, a lightning-white cataract of solid water fell from the sky, dowsing the flames and turning a pool of fire into a grey quagmire. Mhirr-cuin fell into cool dampness.

Immediately, she was up, the imprints of her body and feet revealing glowing orange under the sodden ash, latent heat that was promptly extinguished by the waterfall from the heavens. By the time Mhirr-cuin had taken two paces and Ochy had reached her feet and stepped towards her, the whole firepit was awash with cindery water.

At last the circle of impassive watchers had broken, remaining within the perimeter of the animal lines, but sheltering in the doorways of tents, children peering between their elders' legs. They still observed the combat that would decide their destiny in silence. Speech would have been useless; the torrential rain drummed on the taut skin of the tents so deafeningly that even the thunder in the sky went unheeded.

The storm was directly overhead now, lightning flash and thunderclap instantaneous companions. The sky was so black, the rain so thick, nothing could be seen until each blue-white flash froze every movement, permanently etching each detail of the sudden scene on the viewer's eyeballs — until the everlasting imprint of the next illuminating stroke.

Flash! The rain hitting what had been hard ground so violently that the splashes bounced into the air, to be smashed by more raindrops until a knee-high veil of mist hid the two women writhing in the watery mud.

Flash! Two women, standing legs apart, waists bent, their hands locked in each other's hair, so dark-sodden and heavy with water, it was impossible to tell which was red and which was black.

Flash! Two women; one her back arched in triumph as her fingers bore down on the other's throat.

Flash! Two women; one her back hollowed in agony as two handfuls of nails tore crimson furrows from shoulder to buttock.

Flash! Two women; trying to drown each other in the flooded firepit.

Flash! Two women; one whirling two-handed one of the stakes from the edge of the pit, connecting with the other's shoulder and side.

Flash! Two women; one her teeth bared in effort as she smashed gnarled, knotted wood into the other's face, penetrating, splintering bone.

Flash! Two women; one her legs scythed from under her by the spiked timber in the hands of the other.

Flash! Two women; one lying face downwards in the misty mire at the feet of the other, standing victorious, legs apart, as two-handed she raised the forked and twisted branch above her head.

Flash! A pillar of blue-white fire mounting upwards from feet, legs, torso, head, arms and stake, climbing to the clouds and beyond, serpents of flame running in and around the great column. And then darkness, complete, utter, impenetrable darkness; and silence, stunning, ear-fizzling silence.

No, not quite darkness; odd shapes, sparkling lights; inside the mind – or outside the eye?

No, not quite silence; little sounds, crackles; inside the mind – or outside the ear?

Now there were tiny voices, the sound of water, water cascading down tents, running off leaves, trickles, streams, rivers, searching for the sea.

The rain had stopped, the clouds were opening – and there was a figure, a blackened, gnarled figure, legs apart, arms raised, holding a twisted branch; but which was wood and which was flesh, which was broken bark and which was charred skin, it was impossible to tell.

Slowly the tree-figure toppled over. The rounded shape that had once been its head broke off, fell separately, and rolled across to rest against the face of that other woman, still lying motionless on the sodden ground.

41

'The Four Great Horned Ones have chosen!' Ahtola's voice rang out, clear as the patches of blue sky appearing through the grey murk above. 'The Great Horned Ruler of Fire has been their messenger. Mhirr-cuin is no longer the Witch of the People of the Bear, the Beaver, the Wolf and the Marsh, and of All Peoples. Mhirr-cuin is no more. The Four Great Horned Ones have chosen Ochy, the Witch of the Cave as the Witch of the Peoples of the Bear, the Beaver, the Wolf and the Marsh. Hail, Ochy, Witch of All The Peoples!'

Then the little blonde girl turned to greet the man emerging from the tent with the Bear Totem: 'Hail, Mhirr-ling, Artzan of the Peoples of the Bear, the Beaver and the Wolf! Hail, Mhirr-ling, King-to-be of the Land of Aks-khai-bor!'

Mhirr-ling blinked in the growing light, brilliant compared with the gloom of the tent he had left behind him. He opened his mouth to speak, but a final spasm of coughing shook his body and he turned away to spit out the phlegm. But already Ahtola was addressing someone else, her own father: 'Hail, Ahmorc, Artzan-to-be of the Peoples of the Bear, the Beaver and the Wolf!'

Ahmorc stared at her for a moment, then looked around the encampment. The only movement was in the middle where Ochy was struggling to her knees. Ahmorc strode decisively through the mud. As he went, he picked up a stout stick, its gnarled outline showing that it had once been Mhirr-cuin's vicious magick wand. He put the staff under Ochy's hand and for a moment he supported her. Then – with angry independence – she shook him off and stood leaning on the stick unaided, trying to take the weight off the agonising pain in her right leg.

Beside her was Dhogh. From his teeth, dangling on a length of unburnt red hair, was a near-round shape – the charred head of Mhirr-cuin. Its – her – eyes were undamaged. Wide-open, they glared malevolently around the encampment, as the grisly trophy swung gently from the wolf's jaws.

Ochy took a step forward – and screamed with pain – but inside her mind. All that emerged from her broken mouth, was a bloodied grunt. She would not let the Peoples know her agony.

She was Ochy, the Witch of the Cave, the Witch of All The Peoples. Had she not trained her body to withstand pain and cold, heat and fatigue? Had she not forced herself to think on other matters while her self-tortured body suffered? She would not die of these hurts: of that she was determined. But she yearned for the familiar security of her home cave where no one could see her suffering, where she could be alone until the pain eased.

'O Great Horned Ruler of Earth,' she prayed to herself. 'Give my body strength. O Great Horned Ruler of Fire – give my body energy. O Great Horned . . .'

At each imprecation, she took a step forward. Then when she had exhausted her prayers, she concentrated on what she had achieved that day. She had defeated Mhirr-cuin and was bearing her head away – in triumph? No, not in triumph. She felt no elation at the victory she had won after all those winters of dark and bitter plotting. Nor did she feel saddened, empty of purpose now that she now longer had Mhirr-cuin to hunt through the World of Ghosts. No, the deed was done. And now there were other things to do, with her power.

Everyone now knew that the Four Great Horned Ones obeyed the command of the Witch of the Cave. The People would be expecting her to cast spells, perform sacrifices, bless their crops and their hunting, curse their enemies – and her enemies. What form should these ceremonies take? Should she conduct them here – or in the secret recesses of her cave, sending her Acolyte Ahtola to announce her requirements and their fulfilment? Should she take more Acolytes and train them in the ways of the Four Great Horned Ones? Or should she work through Mhirr-ling as Artzan? Did she want to control him as Mhirr-cuin had done? And what had Ahtola foreseen with her prophecy of Ahmorc as Artzan-to-be? Perhaps that would happen when Mhirr-ling went away to become King of Aks-khai-bor? For Ochy still had to keep that promise and her promise to bury Htorr-mhirr in the soil of his native land. Perhaps there Ochy would learn the meaning of the Secret of Time? She was glad she had entrusted her Stone with the Secret of Time to Mhirr-ling's safekeeping. It could so easily have been harmed during her duel of magick and violence with Mhirr-cuin. And it would be safe with Mhirr-ling for the time being until his journey began. But perhaps he ought to take the Stone with him on that adventure. Suppose he did not want to give it up? Ochy suddenly felt cold at the prospect of never seeing her favourite stone again. If necessary, she would employ all her magick power to force him to return it to her. That would be using her skills properly – or would it? Then she thought, I will ask my friend, the Ghost of Darkness. She remembered how Mhirr-cuin's final curse had been to turn her – Ochy – to stone within her cave. Perhaps the stone Ghost of Darkness was her own self returned from times-to-come, to tell her of what was to come. Perhaps that was why she loved the Ghost of Darkness . . .

Her thoughts were wandering; pain crowded her. She must concentrate her mind, keep the hurt at bay, reach her cave. 'O Four Great Horned Ones,' she prayed. 'Give me strength to set one foot in front of the other.'

Slowly – not only her body, but also her vision seemed lopsided – Ochy made her way out of the silent camp.

By now the people had left their tents and had gathered in a concourse on the drying earth. They opened to let her through, coalescing again behind her. And then somebody was laughing. And then they were all cheering and waving, capering and running towards –

'Stop!'

Ochy had turned round at the gateway. The people too, paused in their celebration, turned and looked back at her as if she herself had shouted.

Ochy pointed. The crowd opened again, as if each man, woman and child feared the power emanating from that deadly limb and the magick stick it held.

In the distance, far down that channel of human faces, was the body of Mhirr-cuin.

'Stop! Do not defile her body.' Balancing painfully on her left leg, Ochy was certain she had not uttered those words. She had meant to say them, but her mouth seemed incapable of forming speech. Yet it was as if the thoughts of her mind were being echoed aloud.

No, it was not she who was speaking – but Mhirr-ling. All the people were looking at him now, as he voiced the words Ochy could not frame. 'Stop! Mhirr-cuin was your Witch. She cared for you in many ways. She taught you many things. She taught you how to act as one. She did what she thought was best. Her head belongs to the Witch of the Cave, but her body must be buried with the reverence due the Witch of the Tribe, the daughter of an Artzan, the grand-daughter of a great king, and an acceptable sacrifice to the Four Great Horned Ones.'

Yes, Mhirr-ling had said the very words Ochy had intended him to utter – or had he? For a moment, she believed she had control over his tongue – his thoughts? But then she sensed her

195

concentration wavering again, felt the pain wash over her.

'O Four Great Horned Ones,' she grunted, forcing her mind to ignore the agony.

While the people responded to Mhirr-ling's commands, witch and wolf turned again and limped out of the opened gateway.

Each leaf and blade twinkled with raindrops. The trees were turning russet.

It had all begun at the fall of the leaf, Ochy remembered. And now it was ending at the time of leaf-fall. Then she had raced across these hills with childish energy; now she staggered, a broken, aged woman.

But still before her – as on that first occasion – there floated the conical peak of Htorr-mhirr – the Mountain-in-the-Sea. Soon those Marsh People who roamed the summer tracks would be returning to find their village destroyed, the boatmen and their families dead, the dragon marauding through the swamps, unless he was sleeping in his lair by now.

But not Wheg-ling, the old man who knew about the Stones with the Secret of Power over other people, the magick stones with which he made – what was it called? – metal. Now, suppose he and Mhirr-ling . . . ?

And the plan began to take shape in Ochy's mind. She would need the help of the Marsh People. To win their trust, she would kill the dragon for them. And to do that . . .

Gradually her concentration on the details of her schemes-to-come numbed her sense of pain. A line of rooks flapped happily against the pale blue. The sun was going down amid the last clouds in the sky, tinting their edges, radiating beams supporting the vault of heaven.

Golden light flooded the countryside.

It was a fine, clear evening.